Together th
they fall.

"The question is," Rob said, "can we work together? Can you refrain from verbally gut-punching me at every opportunity?"

Judy checked out his impressive chest and shoulders. "You're built to take it."

"Oh, I can take it. It's just that I may be a low-life reporter, but *I* didn't ruin your life." He paused, his gaze drifting down over her face, feature by feature, lingering on her lips, moving down to her breasts. "In fact, given different circumstances…"

She expected him to say something like "Given different circumstances, a good reporter could even *save* your life."

But he said, "Given different circumstances, I think I could add a lot to your life."

She reacted to the jolt that went through her at the look in his soft dark eyes by responding, "Then it's fortunate things are as they are, because one of us would have been in for a rude awakening."

He smiled at her in that old arrogantly suggestive way. "Trust me, Lowery," he drawled. "It would have been you."

Muriel Jensen is acknowledged as the author of this work.

ISBN 0-373-82559-5

HOT PURSUIT

MURIEL JENSEN
Hot Pursuit

Love was just one life-threatening
episode after another.

Harlequin Books

TORONTO • NEW YORK • LONDON
AMSTERDAM • PARIS • SYDNEY • HAMBURG
STOCKHOLM • ATHENS • TOKYO • MILAN
MADRID • WARSAW • BUDAPEST • AUCKLAND

WELCOME TO A
HOMETOWN REUNION

Twelve books set in Tyler.
Twelve unique stories. Together they form a
colorful patchwork of triumphs and trials—
the fabric of America's favorite hometown.

Around the quilting circle...

Emma, Bea and Tillie, taking a well-deserved break, pushed their chairs back from the quilting frame, while Martha Bauer distributed slices of apple cake on paper plates decorated with festive cornucopiae. "Has anyone read Judy Lowery's book yet?" she asked. Then, without waiting for a reply, she added, "Now, there's one woman who needs a husband."

"Why?" Emma shook out a napkin that matched her plate. "She's going to be rich and famous. She doesn't need a husband."

Bea smiled. "I don't think success in publishing is quite that simple, Emma."

"If there was a man in her life," Martha explained importantly, "maybe she'd write about romance instead of murder."

Tillie frowned doubtfully as she accepted a cup of tea. "I don't know. I've seen her with the Friedman boy at the newspaper, but as I recall, they were shouting at one another."

Martha grinned, her bright eyes filled with interest as she looked at her companions over the rims of her glasses. "Life's funny, isn't it? When a man inspires passion in a woman, she wants to murder him as often as she wants to love him. But who'd have it any other way?"

PROLOGUE

BRITT MARSHACK WAS the first person in the Tyler area to spot the limousine. She had bundled up her two-year-old son against the early November chill and tugged him along beside her as she walked to the mailbox where their private lane met the road.

"Bus!" Jacob exclaimed excitedly, pointing a mittened hand as the boat-long silver limo sped past, headed for town. "Biiiig bus!"

The tinted windows protected the passengers from view, but Britt knew who'd hired the limousine with the Airport Rental plates as surely as she knew her own name.

She reached into her jacket pocket for the cellular phone that went everywhere with her, and locked her escape artist son between her knees as she hurriedly dialed Judy Lowery's number. Britt cried out in frustration when she heard a busy signal.

She pocketed the phone, caught her son's hand and began to run with him toward the house. "Come on, Jakie," she encouraged. "Let's have a race to the car!"

ROB FRIEDMAN TURNED onto the highway from the lake shore road and patted the camera on the seat beside him. It had been a slow news week, and he'd been wondering what to do about a front-page picture for the *Tyler Citizen* when Sheila Wagner, the manager of

Timberlake Lodge, called to tell him there were snow geese on the lake.

He'd taken a couple of shots of their pristine whiteness against the brooding fog and an arty one of a paler gray young goose in the reeds. It was hardly grit-quality reporting, but that was hard to find in Tyler, Wisconsin, in the middle of fall. The high-school football team had lost its last game, and Rob knew everyone would be happier if he buried that on a back page somewhere.

So he'd made a few atmospheric notes on the tape recorder he kept in his pocket, and was already mentally working on the caption.

His thoughts were interrupted, however, when he hit fifty-five and the old red Ford Escort began to shudder. He groaned and slowed to fifty.

God, he'd be glad when Daphne and Vic could come home and he could reclaim his Cherokee. Daphne's old car wasn't built to chase ambulances or follow back trails in search of a story. It was happiest on smooth highway—preferably in a hospital zone.

And when Daphne did come home, he would be relieved of all responsibility toward her sister, Judy. Frankly, he couldn't wait. The woman was arbitrary, argumentative and downright cranky. His attraction to her was probably the result of some karmic predisposition to self-destruction on his part. Hadn't he sabotaged his own career at the *Chicago Sun-Voice?* He was a danger to himself, plain and simple.

But he couldn't do anything about getting Vic and Daphne home until David Heath, a private-detective friend of Vic's in L.A., located the car in which Daphne's husband had been killed. Without it, there was no hope of building a case against the murderer, whom they all suspected to be the victim's mother. And checking every auto-wrecking yard in southern California in the thin hope that the Mercedes hadn't been destroyed in the interim had to take time.

Rob pulled up at the light at the intersection of Main Street and the highway, telling himself that he should call Dave and see how the search was going. Then he noticed the vehicle on the opposite side of the intersection.

The Rolls hood ornament caught his eye first. Then he saw the silver-gray body, so highly polished that it reflected the trees at the side of the road when the driver turned onto Main Street. The lines were long and sleek. The limo bore Illinois plates in the Airport Rental frame.

Rob's heart thumped against his ribs. It was her! Celeste Huntington, Daphne's mother-in-law. He'd known it was just a matter of time before she grew tired of waiting and came to Tyler herself, since her "spy"—the man she hired to observe Judy in the hope of learning Daphne's whereabouts—hadn't turned up a single clue.

Rob followed the limo into the turn, keeping the prescribed car-length behind as he dialed Judy's number. He had to warn her. She could be trusted to be cool and competent, but he imagined Celeste Huntington was feeling pretty desperate by now. It had been a month since her daughter-in-law and granddaughter had gone into hiding, and she had to be convinced that Judy knew where they were. He and Brick and Judy had prepared for just this eventuality, but he wanted Judy to have the advantage of forewarning.

A busy signal pulsed irritatingly in his ear. He swore and stabbed out another number. And as he did, the Escort coughed, sputtered, then simply stopped.

Rob punched the steering wheel, swore abusively and watched with disbelieving helplessness as the limo continued down the tree-lined street toward downtown Tyler.

"Sheriff's Dispatch," a courteous voice announced from the cell phone still cradled on Rob's shoulder.

"Give me Brick," he demanded, dealing the steering wheel another blow and taking hold of the phone.

"I'm sorry, he's out of the office at the moment. What's the nature of your—"

"It's an emergency!" he interrupted. "Patch me through, wherever he is!"

K. J. EBER WALKED AWAY from the Hair Affair, his camera slung over his shoulder, his notes on the new manicurist tucked away in one of the many pockets of his photo vest.

Rob teased him about the vest being an affectation, but K.J. had always seen himself in one. Of course, in his dreams he'd been in New York City, photographing scenes he would highlight in his internationally syndicated cartoon strip, not stuck in Tyler, Wisconsin, living with his family, and making diddly as a reporter and sometime cartoonist for the local weekly.

He stepped off the curb at the corner, then jumped back up again when a silver limousine that appeared to be half the length of a football field sped around the corner, heading west on Gunther.

K.J. blinked. A limo in Tyler? Whoa!

Then the truth came to him in a flash of understanding: it was her. It had to be. Rob had said to be on the lookout for any sign of the rich broad he was sure would be coming to see Judy Lowery. He needed an extra pair of eyes to help watch for signs of trouble, he explained, so he'd shared with K.J. information that only the Marshacks, Brick Bauer and Judy knew about Daphne Sullivan and her daughter, and about Vic Estevez's disappearance.

K.J. didn't know all the details, but the old broad was after her granddaughter, who was hiding out with the woman's daughter-in-law and some guy she'd hired to find them. But the detective had turned on his employer and taken the pair away instead. Rob and Brick had helped them get away.

To cover for Daphne and Vic, Judy was telling anyone who asked that Vic had proposed marriage and taken Daphne and her daughter Jenny to Santa Barbara to meet his family.

The limo was heading for Judy's.

K.J.'s heart began to thump. He ran the half block back to Hair Affair and asked breathlessly to use their phone. But Rob's cell-phone number was busy.

All right, K.J. told himself. *Stay calm.* Rob, who was half ice, was always telling him to stay calm; that panic stalled your brain.

If this was indeed Celeste Huntington, she'd want to know what Judy knew. And Rob had made it pretty clear that the woman was ruthless. K.J. had to get help for Judy, but he didn't have time to call the sheriff.

He started running toward Judy's house, his plan of action not clearly formed in his mind. Physical confrontation wasn't his best thing.

But Rob would hate it if he missed this story. And if somebody didn't help Judy, the story might turn out to be her obit.

CHAPTER ONE

"I KNOW, I KNOW. Men are great as long as you don't trust them." Judy sat in her office chair, her Mylar aerobic shoes propped up on her computer desk in a corner of her living room.

Gina Santori, a bright, imaginative nineteen-year-old who was taking Judy's night class in fiction writing at the high school, had called for characterization advice, and the conversation had gotten around to real men rather than fictional ones.

"I love K.J.," Gina said with a sigh, "but with that cartoonist's turn of mind, he sees everything as a joke. I think our relationship is just one prolonged comic strip. I can't get him to discuss anything seriously."

"Then don't push it. You're too young to be thinking seriously about anything, anyway."

"That's what my father keeps telling me, but I think it's because he likes having me work with him." Her voice took on a wry note. "I think you lose your appeal with prospective dates, though, when they ask you what you do and you have to reply, 'I'm in construction with my father.' At least Dad's a man I can trust. Thanks, Judy. Got to get to work."

"Call me anytime." Judy dropped her feet to the carpet and booted up the computer. "What are you guys working on today?"

"We're doing some renovations to the Yes! Yogurt offices."

"Mmm. Have a cone of Caramel Chocolate Cookie for me."

"Right. Bye."

Judy propped her feet up again, moved the keyboard to her lap and clicked her way through the options offered on her monitor until she found the *Murder by Marriage* file.

She settled down to it with a sense of satisfaction. Her latest book was developing a pulse of its own and had a power she thought her first book lacked.

In the ten pages she'd finished yesterday, her heroine, a pediatrician, was beginning to suspect that her husband of six weeks, an attorney who'd defended her in a wrongful death suit, had murdered her first husband.

Today the heroine would deal with the suspicion and try to decide what to do while her husband wandered in and out of their bedroom and sauna, trying to convince her that they should take the honeymoon they'd delayed and go to Cozumel. She would vacillate between thinking she was crazy to suspect him, and remembering the many details that pointed to his guilt.

Judy saw the setting in her mind: a lush condo with every amenity, a white bedroom filled with pillows and billowing sheer curtains.

Then suddenly the mental image was superimposed with that of a rough cabin in a snowy wilderness. She could see her sister, Daphne, at the window, watching the landscape in concern, her toddler in her arms.

Judy closed her eyes and let the frustrated worry course through her. There was nothing else she could do. Her sister and her niece were in hiding somewhere under the protection of her sister's lover, Vic Estevez, the former DEA agent turned private investigator who'd rushed them out of town at the first sign of danger.

That had been a month ago. Vic hadn't told anyone where he was taking them. Anyone except Rob Friedman, who'd helped them make their escape. The only clue Judy had to their location was that Vic had had them pack warm clothes.

Next to the anguish of not knowing where her sister was, Judy considered the fact that Rob knew a festering annoyance she could hardly tolerate.

She disliked the newspaper publisher with a sincerity that was heartfelt and complete. He represented everything she'd come to distrust and despise at an early age. And to top that off, he'd critiqued her first book in the *Tyler Citizen* and called it "predictable and verbose."

She would not forgive him in this lifetime for either offense.

But she had to get some work done. Daphne and Jennifer were safe with Vic, even if Judy didn't know where they were, and she could do nothing about their situation until Rob got things rolling. And *he* could do nothing until he heard from Dave Heath.

Rob had explained the auto-salvage-shop search to her, and though she understood the tedious nature of it, she was growing impatient with the wait. She wanted to take action. She wanted to bring Daphne and Jenny home.

But all she could do at the moment was keep writing and trust that Vic's P.I. friend would finally come through for them. For someone who seldom trusted anyone, that was a tall order.

Closing her eyes, Judy tried to clear her mind and put herself back in the fictional white bedroom and the domestic discussion with its simmering undercurrents. She was almost there when the doorbell rang. The melodic ring was followed by several sharp raps on the door.

"This is going to be one of those days," she grumbled to herself as she lowered her feet, put the keyboard on the desk, went to the door and pulled it open.

She knew instantly that it was not going to be "one of those days." It was *the* day. Rob had insisted it would come, but she hadn't been so sure. It was going to be hard to admit to him that he'd been right.

"Judith Woodruff Lowery?"

The question was asked by a gray-haired woman Judy guessed to be in her early sixties. She was swathed in a fox fur coat, and there was a giant diamond on the veiny hand that held the coat closed at her throat.

She had perfect symmetry of features—lightly but expertly made-up aquamarine eyes, an aquiline nose, a thin-lipped mouth colored in a very contemporary shade of red. But the overall effect did not produce beauty. It was too cold for that, too... empty.

Judy knew she was face-to-face with Celeste Huntington, the woman she hoped to prove had murdered her sister's husband and was trying to steal away Daphne's child.

But Judy had to pretend she didn't know. She had to make Celeste believe Daphne had never been to Tyler, that Judy hadn't seen her sister since she'd run away from home at age fifteen.

Beside Celeste was a giant man in the uniform of a chauffeur. She guessed him to be middle-aged, though he had the muscular physique of a much younger man. Waiting at the limo were two other men in suits who looked as though they worked out at the same gym. Half the neighborhood, Judy noted, had come out to gawk at the limo.

She forced a cordial smile. "Yes. I'm Judy Lowery. But I already have an Avon representative." She tried to close the door.

It came to an abrupt halt when the woman slapped a hand out to stop it, and the chauffeur backed up the action with a beefy arm.

"I am...Celeste Huntington." There was a dramatic pause before the woman said her name. She obviously expected to cause fear, or at least concern.

Judy took special pleasure in looking blank. "I am..." she said, pausing with the same emphasis, "pleased to meet you. But what are you selling?"

The fox fur rose and fell as Celeste Huntington drew a breath. "I'm your sister's mother-in-law. May we come in?"

Judy considered a moment. Rob's instruction if the woman did show up on her doorstep was that Judy should not let her inside under any circumstances until she'd called him.

But her life had become geared to thwarting Rob, so she opened the door widely. With a pretense of great surprise at Celeste's announcement, she invited her in.

She wasn't afraid of the woman. If she made one wrong move, Judy had no compunction about taking her on. She'd held Celeste's men off with a knife the night Daphne left.

Judy even pretended not to mind when the chauffeur followed Celeste inside, though the thought of taking him on was less appealing. He was built like Hulk Hogan, complete with bulging biceps, lantern jaw and straight, longish blond hair under his cap.

She gestured toward the sofa and sat on the arm of the matching chair. "You know Diane?" she asked with appropriate astonishment. "You've seen her?"

Celeste shrugged off the fox coat, revealing a red wool suit that had to have a designer label. Its fit was exquisite.

"Come now, Judy," Celeste said, resting her elbows on her knees and leaning forward. "Let's not play this game. I know Diane's been here using the name Daphne Sullivan, and that she's now run off with the man I hired to find her."

Judy blinked at her. It paid, she thought, to write fiction. She knew just how indignant surprise should look and schooled her features to reflect it.

"I have no idea what you're talking about, Mrs. Huntington," she said. "I haven't seen Diane since she ran away as a teenager. You're telling me she married your son?"

Judy watched for a flash in the woman's eyes, a betrayal of feeling for the son she'd inadvertently murdered when he'd taken the car she'd rigged to kill Daphne.

But there was nothing. Either the woman had all feelings—even grief—under complete control, or she had no feelings at all. She simply met Judy's eyes and held them.

"I know she was here for nine or ten months and ran off at the end of September. Now, I have a court order to assume custody of Jennifer. Where is she?"

Judy shook her head in puzzlement. "Who is Jennifer?"

Celeste gave the chauffeur an exasperated glance. He shook his head and rolled his eyes.

Judy pretended not to notice.

"Jennifer," Celeste replied with a great show of patience, "is Diane's daughter."

Judy gasped. "I have a niece?"

"You know you have a niece, dear," Celeste said calmly. "You put her and her mother up here at your farmhouse in the country. Where is she?"

"How old is she?" Judy asked, as though she hadn't even heard Celeste's reply.

Celeste was quiet a moment. Then she said, without a thread of sharpness in her tone, "Judy, stop this. You know Jennifer is two and a half, that she spent almost a year here with her mother and that they're now hiding from me somewhere with Vic Estevez, my private detective."

"Hiding from you?" Judy asked. "Why? And if my sister married your son and they had a child, where is he? Why isn't *he* here looking for her?"

That did it; a flash of something appeared in the woman's eyes. There for only an instant, it made Judy's blood run cold. It was a kind of evil hatred, a malevolence so intense she almost was afraid. Then she remembered how important it was to Daphne's and Jennifer's safety that Celeste not suspect it.

"They aren't divorced already, are they?" she asked guilelessly.

"He's dead!" Celeste shouted abruptly. Then she drew a breath, shrugged her shoulders to adjust the line of her suit and said again more quietly, "My son is dead."

Judy was able to express genuine regret, because she knew Daphne had loved him. "I'm sorry. Would you like a cup of coffee?"

Now Celeste looked at her as though Judy had just emerged from a saucer-shaped spacecraft. "No," she replied evenly. "I do not want coffee. I want Diane."

"Well..." Judy made a show of thinking back. "The last I heard of her, about ten years ago, was that she'd gone to Las Vegas. You might try..."

Celeste apparently decided it was time to play her ace. She took the long snakeskin clutch bag that she'd deposited beside her on the sofa and turned it upside down on the coffee table. Bundles of bills fell onto the marred oak surface.

Judy saw Presidents Jefferson, McKinley and Cleveland on the one-hundred, five-hundred and thousand-dollar bills.

"That's one hundred thousand dollars," Celeste said. She looked around the modest living room in disdain, then focused on Judy's eyes. "I imagine you can use it. *Murder by Moonlight* hasn't exactly put you on the *New York Times* Bestseller List, has it?"

The display of cash had little effect on Judy's performance, but the fact that Celeste had looked into her life far enough to assess her royalties was a little unsettling. Rob had warned that the woman would use all the resources at her disposal as she investigated her, and as Angus Watson, her spy in Tyler, observed her, but it was disturbing to be faced with the evidence.

"No, it hasn't," Judy admitted with what she hoped was modest acceptance, "and I'd love to be able to claim that money, but I'm afraid you're mistaken about Diane's having been here. I haven't seen her for the last decade."

Celeste stood and walked around the room, her designer suit looking out of place among Judy's eclectic collection of old furniture and memorabilia.

Judy watched her move among her things with a twinge of anger she worked very hard to suppress.

The woman touched a photo of Britt and her children on the mantel. "Brittany Marshack," she said, turning to smile at Judy. The gesture was cold and somehow threatening. "And Matt, Christy, David, Renee and Jacob."

Judy smiled back, folding her arms to hide knotted fists. "You know Britt? Then you probably know her husband, Jake. Big guy. Possessive. Protective."

Celeste put the photo back and went to a low table that held a motley collection of angel figurines. "Did I mention that I have connections at Bookcase Distributing?"

A cash bribe, followed by a vague threat, followed by another bribe? Judy could hardly keep up.

"I'd rather hear what else you know about my sister," Judy said. "When did *you* last see her?"

Celeste leaned over the table, hands clasped behind her, as she studied the collection of berobed and winged figures. "Your novel is a midlist title," she said absently, "with nothing much to make it stand out from all the other books sandwiched between the hot lead titles and the standard, steadily selling backlist of well-known names. Let's face it—if your sales don't improve, Minuteman Publishing isn't going to buy another title from you, even though you once worked for them."

Judy knew that was true, and the prospect was always on her mind. "How is it that you know so much about publishing?" she asked innocently.

Celeste straightened from the table and shrugged, as though that was of no consequence. "What matters is that I know important people in distribution. I can get your book talked up as a sleeper hit, get you mentioned on a few talk shows, perhaps—give you a second chance at the market. What do you say?''

Judy grinned. ''Sure. I'd love that.''

Celeste smiled, picked up a tall angel dressed in dark blue brocade and examined it with a well-manicured fingertip. ''Good. Consider it done. Now, where's Diane?''

Judy blinked in a show of thickheaded confusion. ''I don't know. I just told you. The last I heard she went to Las—''

Celeste's eyes blazed cold fire for an instant before she slapped the angel viciously against a corner of the table. The delicate head and part of one wing flew off, and everything on the table toppled.

Judy didn't flinch, but felt the blow as though it had been dealt to her, which she was certain was Celeste's intention. The gloves were off. Rob had been right—again.

Celeste came toward her, the headless angel held up in the hand adorned with the large diamond. Her eyes were as clear as the stone, the hatred in them just as sparkling and cold. Her small mouth was set in a vicious sneer, her bottom lip twitching slightly.

''I will ask you one more time,'' she said, her voice a tremulous whisper, ''and if you don't answer me, Gunnar will ask you. I think you'll find his questions less comfortably phrased than mine. So, try to think, dear. Where is—''

A knock on the back door cut off Celeste's question and was followed immediately by a wolf whistle and a young male voice calling, ''Judy! Where are you, light of my life?''

Celeste backed away and Judy stood as a tall young man materialized in the doorway to the kitchen, a camera over his shoulder.

Celeste glowered at the chauffeur. "You didn't post a man at the back door?" she whispered harshly.

The big man looked distressed and embarrassed.

Judy smiled in mild confusion at K. J. Eber, wondering what he was doing here. She knew he was Rob Friedman's man Friday at the paper, but she was only casually acquainted with him.

Still, he was a tall, able-bodied man in his midtwenties, and she was very glad to see him.

He smiled with polite interest at Celeste and the chauffeur. "Good morning," he said cheerfully, then he turned to Judy, took her arm and tried to tug her toward the door. "Come on, we're late," he said urgently. "Did you forget you're talking to the journalism class at the high school?" He shook his head apologetically at the man and woman standing near the sofa. "I'm sorry to interrupt, but she..." He stopped when his eyes fell on the coffee table covered with bundles of currency.

The chauffeur caught the front of his shirt and lifted him onto his toes. "Shut up," he said.

K.J., hanging from the big fist like a loose-limbed puppet, grinned. "You could stuff a bundle of bills into my mouth. That'd work."

And while the chauffeur was distracted by his audacity, K.J. struck him on the ears with the sides of both hands. Gunnar flung him to the floor like a rag doll, then put his hands to his ears with a bellow of rage.

Judy ran to K.J., who was sprawled on the carpet.

Celeste rolled her eyes as Gunnar shook his head to try to clear it. He winced and rubbed his left ear, then bent to retrieve his cap.

"This is so tedious," she said in a bored tone. "Tell me where Diane is, Judy, or I'm afraid your friend is Gunnar food."

Judy was beginning to wish she'd followed Rob's instructions and refused to let Celeste inside. Nothing would make her reveal her sister's whereabouts, even if she knew where she was. But having someone else's safety thrust into the equation made bravado a little more difficult to fake.

She looked at K.J. apologetically, then straightened to face Celeste. "If I'd seen my sister in the last ten years, and if I *knew* where she was," she said, her anger and her hatred carefully controlled, "I wouldn't tell you, because you make Lizzy Borden look like Cinderella. Now get out of my house before I throw you out!"

She knew it was an empty threat, but she rather enjoyed making it. Her rule in life had always been No Surrender. She'd made it the day her father died, and she'd never broken it.

Celeste sighed wearily. "Do you really want this young man to pay for your stubbornness?"

"He has nothing to do with this," Judy said.

Celeste shrugged. "He does now. Gunnar?"

Gunnar slipped his hands under Judy's armpits and bodily moved her aside. Then he reached down for K.J.

Praying for divine intervention, Judy leapt onto Gunnar's back and dug her teeth into his already smarting ear.

His scream combined with a sudden, loud commotion that invaded her living room. She was yanked off of her prey and flung onto the sofa.

Rob Friedman turned Gunnar around and gut punched him. When the chauffeur merely blinked, he punched him again. Gunnar coughed and grabbed him by the throat with one hand.

Judy ignored her own surprise at Rob's sudden appearance and her secret delight that he wasn't able to take immediate control of the situation, and reached for the plaster-of-paris bust of Hemingway on the end table. She scrambled to her feet on the sofa and brought it down with all her might on the back of Gunnar's head. He sank to the carpet like a stone.

Brick Bauer, captain of the sheriff's substation in Tyler, ran into the room, followed by Jake Marshack. Both were tousled, and Jake had a bruise on his right cheek. Judy guessed that they'd fought their way in through the two men Celeste had left outside.

"Whoa," K.J. said, pulling himself off the floor, then sinking onto the coffee table and rubbing the back of his head. "Talk about perfect timing. We were about to become puppy chow."

"I'd like someone," Celeste said imperiously, "to explain to me what is going on. I come to pay a simple visit to my daughter-in-law's sister, and I find my chauffeur and my associates brutalized, my—"

Brick cut her off with a wave of his hand toward the pile of bills beside K.J. "What's this?"

"Bribery," Judy said, stepping off the sofa. "She offered me $100,000 to tell her where my sister is. When I told her I hadn't seen her in ten years, she refused to believe me and began breaking up my things. Then she sicked Gunnar on K.J."

"He had him by the throat when I came in," Rob corroborated.

"Just before he got *you* by the throat," Judy added.

He gave her a quick, diagnostic glance, then ignored her.

"Really." Brick picked up a bundle of bills still in its paper wrapper. "Where did this cash come from, Mrs. Huntington?"

"It's mine," she replied.

Brick's eyes went to Rob's then to Judy's, then back to the bills he held. Judy had seen a flash of humor in them.

"Don't usually see cash still bound like this unless it's taken from a bank or a cashier's office. And there was a bank robbery in Sugar Creek just two days ago. I think you'd better come with me, Mrs. Huntington, while I check it out."

"Don't be ridiculous, young man," she said, folding her arms. "The cash is mine. I'm CEO of Huntington Industries. I have more money than most banks. I'd have no need to rob one. Now, if you'll excuse me..."

She tried to march past him. Brick caught her wrist and slapped a cuff on it.

She stared at him in disbelief. "If you put that other cuff on me, Officer," she said, her voice breathless with disbelieving anger, "you are ruined, believe me."

"It's Captain, Ma'am," Brick replied, obviously taking a certain pleasure in bringing her other arm behind her back and doing precisely what she'd warned him against. "Please don't threaten me. You're already up on disturbing the peace, and that's just about a felony in Tyler. Even if you didn't rob the bank, you could still be looking at hard time. Now come along...."

She resisted at the doorway. A crowd of Judy's neighbors had gathered under the tall oak tree with its rich reddening leaves. They oohed and whispered.

A second police car had apparently arrived with Brick, and held the two men Celeste had left outside.

"I'm telling you, *Captain*," Celeste said, her emphasis on his title more derogatory than deferential, "the money is mine. And we did not threaten anyone."

"We'll trace the numbers on the bills," he said amiably. "If they don't match the Sugar Creek robbery, you're clear on that charge. But the big guy had a hold of K.J. when Mr. Friedman walked into the room. And your two men outside assaulted me and my friends."

"Mr. Friedman," she said with a venomous glance at him, "misunderstood what he saw."

Rob and Jake lifted Gunnar to his feet. He was just coming to.

"It's hard to misunderstand a fist in someone's face." Rob moved sideways through the door, pulling his burden. Jake followed, pushing.

Judy stood in the doorway while Celeste and Gunnar were placed in the back of Brick's car. K.J. came up behind her, still rubbing his head.

"I'll get you some ice for that," she said, drawing him back inside. "I don't know what made you come by this morning, but I'm grateful."

He wandered after her into the kitchen. "I saw the limo, and Rob's been saying for weeks that he expected her to show up. I tried to call him on his cell phone, but his line was busy."

"I'd seen the limo, too." Rob appeared in the kitchen doorway and leaned a shoulder against the molding. "But my car—I mean, Daphne's car—died a couple of blocks from town. I tried to warn you, but your line was busy, so I called Brick."

Judy packed a handful of ice cubes into a plastic bag, sat K.J. in a kitchen chair and put the cold compress to the knot at the base of his skull. "You should go and have that looked at," she cautioned. "Bumps on the head are nothing to fool around with." She avoided Rob's eyes. She'd glimpsed condemnation in them, and she didn't want to have to deal with that now. She was feeling uncharacteristically shaken. Now that a host of Tyler's men had come to her rescue, she could admit to herself that she'd been scared.

That was silly, she realized. The crisis had passed. But her body didn't seem to understand that. She had to reach a little deeper for her breath, had to concentrate to keep her hands and her voice steady.

"How did Jake get involved?" she asked, paying close attention to flattening out the ice cubes against K.J.'s dark hair. Jake was married to Britt Marshack, Judy's best friend.

"He was on his way to the Yes! Yogurt store," Rob replied, "and saw me stuck on the side of the road and stopped to pick me up. When I explained my mission, he insisted on coming along."

"You may praise me, if you like." Jake came up beside Rob. He was tall, with dark blond hair, brown eyes and an aura of competence. "Or pay me off with a cup of coffee."

Judy took one look at him, filled another bag and put it to his bruise. "You're wonderful," she said, kissing his sound cheek. "Sit down and I'll get you that coffee."

She bounced a glance off Rob. "You, too," she said. Then she added, lest he misunderstand, "Not the wonderful part, just the coffee."

He ignored her jibe with the ease of long experience and went to sit at a right angle to K.J. while Judy poured. Rob studied his assistant in concern. "You okay? You feel dizzy? Nauseous?"

K.J. shook his head, then winced. "No. I just bumped off the coffee table as I went down. I'm sure I'm okay."

"We'll have you looked at to be sure. What were you doing here, anyway?"

K.J. told him about seeing the limo. "Apparently everybody was calling everybody else, and I couldn't get through to you, so I just hurried over to see if I could help. I saw those hoods at the front door, so I went around the back and heard the old lady threaten Judy. I tried to make it look like we had an important appointment, but the big guy wasn't buying it. You think his mother put steroids in his baby food?"

Judy brought steaming mugs to the table, then patted K.J.'s shoulder. "This guy was pretty fearless," she said. "I think he deserves a raise."

K.J. smiled modestly at Rob. "That's not necessary. But a company car would be nice. A modest Ferrari, maybe."

"Maybe after your first Pulitzer." Rob hooked the toe of his boot around the leg of the fourth chair and pulled it away from the table. "Sit down," he said to Judy. "You look a little shaky."

She bristled instantly, as he knew she would. "I'm fine," she insisted, but she sat.

He saw the barely perceptible tremor in her fingers as she reached for the handle of her cup, and remembered the boom of his own heartbeat when he'd pushed through the door and seen her riding the hulking chauffeur's back.

The reaction was just the result of fearing he'd blown his promise to Daphne to keep an eye on her sister, but it had unnerved him all the same.

"So this is it, isn't it?" Jake asked Rob. "This is what we've been waiting for. It's starting."

Jake and Britt, close friends to Judy and Daphne, knew most of the story. And they'd been keeping a close eye on Angus Watson, one of Celeste's men who'd been involved in the attempt to kidnap Daphne just before Vic took her into hiding. Angus had escaped in the struggle, then tried to pass himself off as a wealthy businessman who finally had time to improve his golf game in quiet Tyler. After a stay at the lodge, he'd even rented Judy's farmhouse, where Daphne and Jennifer had lived.

The Tyler conspirators had never been certain if he'd done so under Celeste's orders, or if this had been a decision he'd made on his own, hoping that his display of resourcefulness would somehow endear him to his employer and spur her gratitude. But they'd known his real identity all along, because Rob had recognized him from that night.

It had been Brick's suggestion that they simply let him do what he'd been sent to do. "We'll just watch him watch Judy," he'd said. "He'll know what we're doing, but we'll know what Celeste's doing, too." To that end, he'd arranged to have the man's phone lines tapped.

The Marshacks had been watching him from their property, which abutted Judy's. Matt's telescope had afforded an excellent view of his comings and goings.

They'd also intercepted many of his messages to and from Celeste, and suspected that some kind of action was imminent.

Short and thick and squarely built, Angus Watson had become known about Tyler as he snooped around. He'd made a number of friends. Judy and her fellow conspirators had given him the code name "Stumpy," after he'd once confessed his nickname to Britt's daughter Renee.

In answer to Jake's comment, Rob nodded. "Yeah, I think so. If Vic's friend Heath isn't able to come through for us by finding the car, our only alternative may be letting Celeste get desperate enough that she shows her hand."

Jake nodded grimly. "I don't think finding the car's all that likely. I mean, if it was totaled in the wreck, the salvage shop would cannibalize it for parts and crush the body."

Rob looked just as grim. "I know. But Brick's going to haul Celeste in, make her cool her heels. We'll bring assault charges against her men, and that should convince her that Tyler isn't the pushover little burg she thought it was. That should make her pull back to try to find another way around Judy—which should buy us some time to find the car."

K.J. turned the icepack over in his hand and reapplied it to the back of his head. "What if that doesn't work?"

"Then we'll go to plan B."

"And that is?"

"That is . . ." Rob grinned and shrugged ". . . under development."

Jake patted Judy's hand. "Brick would like you to go down to the station and fill out a report. Want me to take you down?"

She smiled. "No, I'll be fine. I'm so glad something's finally happening."

What was finally happening, Rob thought, was that Celeste was getting desperate to find Daphne, to finally have things the way she wanted them. He liked to think that might result in the woman doing something overtly foolish—like trying to get Judy openly, this time.

But that was a danger to Judy he wasn't anxious to allow. The ideal solution would be to find the car Celeste had sabotaged and use it as the basis of a case against her.

His hope was that Brick's harassment of her would make her back off sufficiently so that he could employ his preferred solution.

Otherwise, Judy was in great danger. And if she was, so were Daphne, Jennifer and Vic. And so was he.

CHAPTER TWO

THE FRONT DOOR BURST OPEN, and Britt Marshack ran into Judy's kitchen, Jacob riding her hip. Her red-blond hair was windblown, her cheeks bright pink.

She looked at the quiet scene around the kitchen table and breathed a sigh of relief. "God!" she gasped, as Jake rose to give her his chair. Judy pulled up the step stool for him. "Was she here? Did she hurt anybody? I saw the limo go by when Jakie and I went to the mailbox, so we ran back to the car, but Jacob thinks it's great fun to hide on me and I couldn't get him out from under it! Then I tried to call Judy, but her line was busy, so I called Rob, but *his* line was busy. I finally called Brick, but he was out!" Britt fell breathlessly into the chair.

Judy related the morning's events while she went to pour another cup of coffee. Everyone involved filled in the details.

Britt frowned down at her son. "Thanks to you," she said, "we missed all the excitement."

Then, as Jacob reached for his father, she noticed the bruise on Jake's face and insisted on holding the ice pack to it herself while she interrogated him about his involvement.

Judy went to make another pot of coffee. Rob followed her.

"I thought we'd agreed," he said quietly, "that you weren't going to let Celeste in."

She gave him a scolding glance for being so predictable. "I wondered when you'd get around to 'I told you so.'" She measured out ground coffee and spooned it into a paper filter. "I wanted to assess her up close, to look into her eyes and see what she knew."

"Well, that was stupid," he said mercilessly, taking the carafe from her when she would have run it under the water to cover the sound of his voice. "If we'd been a few seconds later, you'd have been creamed."

"You're trying to tell me you wouldn't have liked that?"

He met her challenging gaze. "I might have enjoyed it a little, but I promised Daphne I'd keep you safe. For reasons I don't understand, she seems to have a fondness for you. I wouldn't like to finally bring her back to Tyler only to have to tell her you'd gone to your reward."

Impatient with him, mostly because she knew he was right, Judy wrestled the carafe from him. "Oh, go to hell, Friedman," she said.

"No thanks," he replied. "This month has been hard enough. I'd rather we didn't spend eternity together as well. Soon as you feel up to it, I'll drive you to the police station."

She filled the carafe, then pushed him out of her way to pour the water into the coffeemaker's trough. "Your car's broken down on Main Street, remember?"

"I'll drive you in your truck."

"I'm perfectly capable of driving my truck."

Across the room, K.J. and the Marshacks were engaged in an animated discussion of the situation. Rob leaned against the counter and watched Judy work.

She was a beautiful woman. No, that wasn't entirely accurate. As a writer, he'd always taken pride in finding just the right word to express what he wanted to say—to be sure it shaped the thought with all its subtleties and nuances.

Beauty suggested a sort of vulnerability, he thought. A sort of softness that had nothing whatsoever to do with Judy Lowery.

Handsome was a better word. She was a handsome woman. He let his eyes rove her features and decided that wasn't quite right, either. That was something one usually said about a fifty-year-old matron, and Judy exuded a youthful vitality and quickness.

Stunning? He supposed he could settle for that, though it didn't encompass the fulness of her physical appeal.

A wedge of crisp morning sunlight coming through the kitchen window highlighted chin-length, honey-blond hair and a strong profile as she reached to the sink for a sponge and wiped a small spill of coffee grounds off the counter.

She had well-defined cheekbones, a rounded chin and nicely shaped lips that he watched futilely for a smile. She distributed them to everyone else, but never to him. Her eyes were storm cloud blue. He'd always thought that appropriate.

She was taller than average. He was just over six feet tall, and the top of her head skimmed his nose.

His eyes ran over her simple sweater and jeans, and he amended his earlier description of her. If there was softness anywhere in her appearance, it was there in the curve of breast and hip. She was neither slender nor plump, but something in between—a kind of shapely perfection that fashion had starved out of most women long ago.

If anything about her made him wish things could be different between them, it was that body.

He sighed and shifted his weight. Even with things as they were, he'd promised Daphne he'd protect that body.

"I'll drive," he said, mentally dismissing all his careful observations. "Celeste frightened you."

She bristled again. He liked to make her do that and didn't bother to analyze why.

Judy knew there was no point in denying his accusation. A woman would have to be stupid not to have been frightened by Celeste's imbalanced ruthlessness and burly Gunnar's mindless obedience to her. And then, of course, there was the undeniable fact that their presence in Tyler meant something was finally about to happen.

But Judy had made her rule long ago and she would stick by it. She couldn't deny fear, but she didn't have to admit it, either.

"I'll give you a lift to your office on my way to the police station," she said as she went to the refrigerator for a bottle of apple juice. She poured it into a two-handled cup he guessed she kept on hand for her niece.

"I'll go with you to the police station," he corrected, grateful for all his dogged reporter instincts. Dealing with the woman was like dealing with a rock. "I want to talk to Brick, and then I want to talk to you."

She looked at him suspiciously, carried the cup to the table and handed it to Jacob, then returned to lean on the counter and look into Rob's eyes. Her tone was quietly quarrelsome. "Why?" she asked.

"Because," he replied intrepidly, "if we're going to put Celeste away and get Daphne, Jenny and Vic back, we're going to have to improve our style of working together."

She gave him an amusedly cynical look. "You mean I'm going to have to do what you tell me."

"Precisely."

"You're dreaming."

"I'm telling you," he said, "how it has to be."

She'd have argued, but Jacob dropped the cup of apple juice, Britt sprang up in apology to wipe up the mess, and Jake glanced at his watch and decided he'd better get to work. He offered to drop K.J. at the emergency room on the way.

"But I'm all right," K.J. insisted, dropping the now liquid-filled bag into the sink.

"Go with Jake," Rob insisted. "And let me know the results. If you feel like you need the afternoon off, take it."

K.J. studied him worriedly. "Afternoon off? Are you okay? You sure someone didn't hit *you?*"

"Funny. Go."

"THAT WAS A STUPID THING to do, Judy," Brick said, leaning toward her across the cluttered surface of his desk.

Judy turned to Rob, prepared to accuse him of urging Brick to fortify his own position on the matter, but he spread both arms in a denial of responsibility. "Don't look at me. Brick says that because it's true, not because I prompted him."

"If I hadn't let her in," Judy said, pleading her case, "she'd have known I suspected her of wanting to hurt my sister, so she'd have known I've seen my sister recently, right?''

Brick shook his head at her. "We don't want to save Daphne by getting you hurt or killed. We made a plan. If she came to your home, you weren't to let her in—you were to call Rob or me.''

Judy sighed. "A lot of good that would have done me. It seems you were all on the phone to one another. I did what I thought was the right thing at the time.''

"Curious," Rob observed, "that what I ask you to do never seems like the right thing to you.''

"That's because you're the wrong man," she said sharply.

For an instant, as Judy's eyes met Rob's, the room rang with silence. *The wrong man.* There was an implication that it mattered to her, somehow.

Judy felt Brick's glance touch her, then Rob as they stared at each other in confused awareness.

If Rob had any redeeming qualities, she thought, she might consider him passably attractive. He had a nice angular face, a strong nose, square white teeth in a romantically shaped mouth. His dark eyes were framed in darker lashes under nicely arched brows. And he had thick, dark hair that waved loosely away from a side part with a gloss and body she envied.

Her own stick-straight hair was thick, but defied all efforts to set it with a permanent, hot rollers or a curling iron.

He was tall, thick in the shoulders, lean hipped and graceful.

But he was a reporter, damn him.

"Guys?" Brick asked.

Judy pulled back into herself, instantly regretting the slip and the self-indulgent study, wondering how she would explain herself. Because Rob would insist that she did.

"Celeste's lawyer is on his way by private jet." Brick rolled his eyes over the vagaries of the rich. "I'm going to have to set her free. Of course, the money's hers, though it was fun to play with her dignity for a few hours. And I'm pretty sure the judge'll kick her men loose, despite their priors. Judy let Celeste and Gunnar in, so it'd be hard to convince a jury she didn't want them there." He frowned at Rob. "I hope Vic's detective friend in L.A. comes through on this. Otherwise, we'll have to hide Judy."

"What?" Judy sat up, looking from one man to the other. "Hide me where? No. Un-huh. No way. I have a book due in four weeks and I can't . . ."

Rob silenced her with a look. "Don't you get it? Celeste is going to pull back to rearm. If I don't find the car to open a case against her in that space of time, she's coming back after you with a vengeance."

That was a sobering thought. "Maybe—maybe they'll try another approach," Judy suggested in a thin voice.

"There is no other approach." Rob straightened in his chair and pinned her with the same look. "Vic knew what he was doing when he covered their tracks. He built a wall around their escape that has not one chink in it—except you. You're the only vulnerable spot."

She sighed impatiently. "No, I'm not. You and Vic wouldn't tell me where he took her, remember? I don't know where she is!"

"But Celeste doesn't know that. She's probably sure you know. So, if push comes to shove, we'll have to get you out of here."

"I have a better idea." Judy looked from Brick to Rob, certain she entertained pure inspiration. "If she's sure I know where Daphne is, wouldn't I be good bait?"

Brick exchanged a look with Rob, who slid down in his chair with a hand over his eyes.

"No, listen!" she continued, enthusiasm growing as she gave it more thought. "I could set up a phoney location! I could take them there, wear a wire and get Celeste to tell us everything. That would work. Why wouldn't that work?"

"No," Brick said calmly.

"Why not?" she demanded.

"Because it's poorly thought out and ridiculous," Rob replied. "That's why not. Not to mention predictable. It might work in cheap detective fiction, but not if you want to keep your sister and niece away from Celeste."

Judy huffed. "You mean, like I write."

"I didn't say that. When you write, you do at least try to conceal your moves."

"Why would it not work?"

Brick stood to pace across the office. Rob gestured widely, impatiently. "Do you think she'd trust your sudden capitulation? Do you think she wouldn't wonder why you suddenly changed your mind? That she wouldn't suspect a wire? Hell, after all the television cop shows, it would occur to an eight-year-old."

Brick sat on the corner of his desk and frowned at Rob. "There's no need to shout." He turned his attention on Judy. "There'd be no way to keep you safe," he said reasonably. "She always travels with three or four men. You'd end up in that limo with them, and even if we could follow you, you'd be too vulnerable every moment. I swear to God the woman's psychotic. I'd never approve the plan, and if you try to do something like that on your own, you'll just botch all we've done so far to keep Daphne safe. No. You have to do this our way."

Judy wasn't convinced he was right, but she knew the plan couldn't be executed without outside support. So she abandoned it.

"Fine," she said. "But you'd better know, if you end up having to hide me, that I'll need a laptop to continue my work and a supply of Patrick Swayze movies."

"And a carton of Pop-Tarts," Rob added. "Chocolate-peanut-butter."

At her look of surprise, he smiled with satisfaction. "I'm a reporter. I saw the box of twenty-four in your cupboard when you got the cup for Jacob. You start buying them in bigger quantities and we're going have to do an intervention and take you to Pop-Tart detox."

She wanted to laugh. The notion of a Pop-Tart detox was funny, but he wasn't. So she didn't. She dismissed him with a look and turned to Brick.

"Why do you think Celeste is going to back off for a while? Has she been in touch with Stumpy?"

Brick nodded. "Her attorney has. He called him with instructions to keep his eye on you, because she and the boys were going back to Palm Beach to regroup."

Judy smiled. "He's so easily handled, I almost feel guilty. He's like Inspector Clouseau, only on the wrong side of the law. I think he's even getting to like Tyler. I saw him at a potluck at Sarah Kenton's church the other night. I'd have thought he was there to keep an eye on me, but he spent most of the evening tête-à-tête with Marion Clark, the real-estate agent. He seemed to really like her seven-layer salad."

Rob pushed himself to his feet and offered Judy his hand. "Another brave warrior felled by domesticity."

She would have ignored it, but she felt weighted down by worry and the urgent wish that life could be normal again—whatever that was. She accepted it, surprising him as well as herself.

"Don't get complacent over Stumpy," Brick warned. "That could be an act for our benefit. So keep your eyes open."

"Right."

"And you find out *anything,* you let me know."

"Right again."

In the bright sunlight of the quiet side street, Judy headed for the driver's side of her truck, parked at the curb. "I'll take you back to the office," she said, putting her hand out for her keys.

"I'll take you to lunch," he said, ignoring her and using the keys to open the passenger side door.

She remained stubbornly near the driver's door. "It's my truck," she said.

He leaned an elbow on the other door. "But I've got the keys. Come on. I want to show you something."

"What?"

"It's a surprise."

She gave him a disparaging look over the top of the truck. "Aren't we a little old for surprises?"

"God, I hope not. I don't ever want to get that old. You coming?"

She thought a moment. She wanted to, but she'd made this rule long ago.... "No," she said.

"Okay." He climbed into the truck from the passenger side, closed that door, maneuvered around the gearshift and slipped in behind the wheel.

She frowned at him through the window. He rolled it down to grin at her. "Sure you don't want to come?"

She looked at him, then she looked at the sky, then she studied her feet. Then she looked at him again. In that time she'd counted to ten, but it wasn't nearly high enough. She still wanted to hit him.

"I'll put up with you," she said, her voice raspy with annoyance and the suppressed urge to scream, "to get my sister safely home. But the minute that's accomplished, I'm coming after you. You got that?"

The cool blonde with the soft curves was coming after him. Well. That thought could see him through some tough times.

"I got it," he said.

"Good," she replied, and walked around to get in the truck.

He drove through the Dairy King and, stopping at the order window, asked for a bacon burger, fries and a coffee. "What do you want?" he asked Judy.

"A Cheery Meal," she replied, straight-faced.

"A Cheery...?" he began, afraid he'd misunderstood. It was a child's meal delivered in a colorful bag and containing a prize that changed weekly. But in the face of her unwavering gaze, he turned to smile at the patient young woman at the window.

"A Cheery Meal, please," he said, then consulted Judy again. "Burger?"

"Chicken strips," she corrected. "A coffee, and the cookies, not the ice cream."

He passed on her order, then pulled up to the next window to wait for it. "So," he said, dropping his hands from the steering wheel to his lap. "If you can order a Cheery Meal, you can't be too old for surprises."

"Jenny collects the toys in them," she said, her throat suddenly constricting at the thought. She swallowed with difficulty and drew a breath. "I've kept up her collection while she's gone."

Judy sat quietly, looking composed, but he heard the anguish in her voice. He knew how close she was to her sister and her niece, how they'd finally found each other a year ago after a decade of separation. They'd pretended to simply be friends so that Diane, on the run from Celeste and her manipulations to gain custody of Jenny, wouldn't be found when Celeste looked into her background and discovered she had a half sister. Diane had hidden under the name Daphne Sullivan, had colored her hair and started a new life. She had lived in Judy's rental house where "Stumpy" now lived.

Rob hadn't known the story then. It wasn't until Vic Estevez came to town, hired by Celeste to find Daphne and Jenny, that the truth finally came out.

Vic had seen immediately that Celeste's claim of a greedy and neglectful daughter-in-law unfit to raise a child was false. But he'd stuck with his pretence of visiting Tyler with an eye toward relocating in order to get at the truth.

In the meantime, he'd fallen in love with Daphne and Jenny and had taken them to safety when Celeste got too close.

Rob remembered their departure that September night, Judy holding Jenny to her, then relinquishing her grudgingly to Vic so that he could put her into the car seat in the back of Rob's Cherokee.

He remembered the way the sisters had clung to each other. Vic had had to pull Daphne away, and Rob had had to hold Judy back when the car headed out of the driveway.

Then he'd taken her to the emergency room for stitches on a knife wound she'd sustained while defending Daphne. After that, he'd brought her home, and she'd gone into the house, leaving him standing on the porch, and had locked the door behind her. And there'd been a locked door between them ever since. Rob suspected he had to find the key to it if they were to work together to bring Daphne, Jenny and Vic home.

The clerk passed the aromatic bag, then a cardboard tray with the coffee, through the open window. Rob gave them to Judy, handed over the money and drove off, heading for Timber Lake.

"I know it's been a long siege," he said, glancing at her as he guided the truck along the road lined with trees. The oak and hickory leaves were rust and gold against the blue sky, and some of them drifted onto the road as they passed. A bank of sumac was still bright red. If Celeste Huntington had never entered their lives, it would have been a perfect day. "But don't worry. Vic's due to check in tomorrow. I'm sure they're fine, and I promise you Celeste is not going to get past us."

Judy wanted to believe that. It was all she had to cling to.

"The surprise is at the lodge?" she asked, dipping into her Cheery Meal and extricating a french fry.

"At the lake," he said, then put a hand out toward her. "Can I have one of those?"

"Nope, they're mine."

"*I* bought them," he protested.

"So you should." She munched on another one. "You stole my truck. You're the one responsible for this mystery ride."

He shook his head, looking back at the road. "You're going to like the surprise, and then you're going to feel guilty for being petty about the fries."

"Then we'll wait till after the surprise. If I feel like it's worth it, you can have a french fry."

He groaned. "Then could you hand me one of *my* french fries?"

She checked inside the bag. "You don't seem to have any."

"What? I ordered them. You heard me order them."

"Apparently the clerk didn't. You want a pickle? A napkin?"

"I want a french fry."

Judy set his bag aside and reached for her own again. "You're hardheaded, Friedman," she said.

He took the turnoff to the lake. "That's what makes me a good reporter and able to deal with you."

She held a french fry to his lips as he drove on. Rob caught the end of it in his teeth and drew it into his mouth. Being fed by her brought to mind a charming scenario that involved her and him, a Roman bath and peeled grapes. But he put it out of his mind with a simple, "Thank you."

"You don't have to, you know." She fed herself another. "Deal with me, I mean. I free you from Daphne's request to keep an eye on me. I can handle Celeste myself."

He gave her a disbelieving glance. "Like you did this morning? Like your plan to wear a wire and take her and her goons to some wilderness outpost where Daphne *isn't?* Give me a break, Lowery. You need me. And you can't release me from a promise I made to your sister."

"Why not? I'm the object of the promise. And now that I've come face-to-face with Celeste, I'm better able to deal with her. You can have all my fries if you'll get out of my life."

"Not a chance. Keep your fries."

"Bonehead."

"Brat."

At the sight of Timber Lake covered with snow geese, Judy momentarily forgot her irritating companion and drew in her breath with a little cry of wonder.

The birds were everywhere, bobbing on the water, circling in flight, drifting through the reeds, waddling on the bank. They were like undulating snow, blowing up to the sky and drifting down again to some music Judy felt rather than heard.

She was out of the truck before Rob stopped it, walking cautiously toward the bank, arms slightly outstretched as though to embrace the view before her.

Something stabbed at Rob, pleasing and hurting him at the same time.

He'd known she'd be as touched by the sight as he had been. What did it mean that he'd second-guessed her need to be comforted by nature because she wouldn't let any person close enough? And why did it hurt that he'd been right? Because he'd wanted to offer comfort himself, maybe, and knew he would be rejected?

What had she meant earlier when she'd said he was the "wrong man"?

He followed her to within several yards of the lakeshore, where she stopped, obviously unwilling to disturb the visitors. She pulled her light jacket around her as a cold November wind blew off the lake.

"Wow," she whispered. "Did you ever see anything more beautiful?"

"When I was here this morning," he said, "fog was lying over the water and there was a mystical quality to everything. It was pretty spectacular. Now it's..."

He stopped as a pair of snow geese took to the air, the purity of their color and the stark black of their wing tips breathtaking against the bright blue sky and the riot of autumn color in the trees across the lake. He couldn't think of a word to describe the scene.

She folded her arms, her head tipping back as she watched the pair of birds. "Glorious," she said, her breath a visible puff on the cold air.

Then she turned to him abruptly, her dark blue eyes shaded with a curiosity that bordered on suspicion. "Why did you bring me here?"

He shrugged a shoulder, trying to look innocent of any ulterior motive. "Because I thought you'd like to see them before the crowds hit. They're going to be on my front page tomorrow, and everyone in Tyler will be out here for a look."

She held his gaze, as though measuring the truth of his reply.

He'd been a hardcore interviewer in his old *Chicago Sun-Voice* days. He didn't flinch.

She finally lowered her eyes and turned her attention to the lake. Had he seen the barest flicker of disappointment in the smoky depths?

"Good," she said. "I was afraid you were trying to soften me up."

The pair of snow geese, completing a lazy circle of the lake, came in for a graceful landing.

Rob noticed that Judy was shivering, and knew she wouldn't take kindly to the offer of his jacket or the warmth of his arm around her. He took her elbow and turned back to the truck. "Soften you up for what?" he asked. "Seduction?"

She gave him a condemning look as they separated at the hood of the truck to walk around to their own sides.

"No," she said, climbing into the truck as he slipped in behind the wheel. "Seduction's not a danger for me because I have this rule."

"What's that?"

"No Surrender," she replied, bracing herself for the flack she was sure would follow.

He simply raised an eyebrow. "Never? To anyone or anything?"

"No. That's right."

He gave her a challenging smile as he reached for the coffee. "Is that why you hate me? Because I suggested improving our working relationship and you presumed I meant something sexual? That's sexist, Judy."

She hated the way he turned all her arguments on her. With everyone else she could speak calmly, intelligently. But Rob made her feel inept the moment he came within earshot. "I didn't mean—"

"You aren't required to be chummy with me," he interrupted amiably, handing her one of the cups. "I just thought that if I at least knew why you hated me, I'd understand this dark dynamic between us and be able to work around it."

Dark dynamic. She thought that an interesting label for it. He was good with pithy headlines and informative captions. She'd noticed that in the *Citizen*.

"I don't hate you," she said with a quick, cool smile as she put her cup on the dash and handed him his sandwich. "I just dislike you intensely."

He unwrapped his sandwich and considered her reply, then challenged her with his own cool smile. "Intense dislike is the same as hatred."

"No, it's not."

"Why not?"

"Because I said so. The way I mean it, it's not the same. And it isn't for you specifically..." Her expression turned vaguely sheepish at that and she glanced at him to see if he'd noticed.

He had.

He expected her to bristle with hauteur, but she laughed instead. That surprised him. And caused a weird warmth in the pit of his stomach.

"Okay, so I have said some nasty things to you, specifically. But you've said some about me, too."

He denied that with a shake of his head. "I said them about your book. And they weren't nasty, they were just critical."

"They were nasty."

He caught her glance again and mimicked her with a grin. "No, they weren't. Not the way I meant them, they weren't."

"Ha, ha." She bit off the end of a chicken strip.

The cab of the truck was quiet for a few moments while they ate. Then he put the second half of his sandwich on the dash and sipped at his coffee.

"So," he said. "You hate reporters in general. I got that. And I know it has something to do with your family, but I don't know what. Why don't you tell me, and get it out where we can deal with it."

"Thank you, but I've already dealt with it."

"Maybe, but now I also have to deal with it since it seems to be standing between us like an electrified fence." He took another sip of coffee, then leaned his

head back against the side window. "Did some reporter embarrass your family by making Daphne's...
work...public?"

"No." She took another bite of chicken, trying to
pretend that it didn't matter, that she truly had dealt
with her family skeletons and locked the closet. And in
a way, she had. But she wasn't one to forgive easily or
to accept injustice, so the past remained with her like a
subtle ache—unacceptable, unresolved.

Yet she had to talk about it. Rob was waiting, and
she'd learned over the past month that he was as stubborn as she was.

"My father..." she said, refusing to let the picture of
him form in her mind. She had loved him, though he'd
spent so much time away from home, and her memories of him were comprised of the lonely longing that
had accompanied her love. "He was a state senator.
Jarvis Lowery."

She saw Rob's eyes narrow, as though he were wondering why the name was familiar. "He had an affair
with another senator's wife, and there was a big scandal. Dad and Senator Dolan were on opposite sides of
a land development-conservation issue, and a young
reporter on the capital beat caught a stolen kiss behind
a committee-room door, suspected he was on to something and followed them to Mrs. Dolan's home. The
photos of their front-porch clinch were on the front
page the next morning."

Rob waited while Judy paused. She looked up defensively. "I know what you're thinking," she accused.

"Really?" He rested his elbow on the back of the seat
and studied her tolerantly. "What am I thinking?"

"That someone who fools around with another man's wife—particularly someone who's supposed to have the public's trust—deserves what he gets."

He shrugged apologetically. "That's pretty close. Not as much for what he owed the public, but for what he owed his family."

She dropped the piece of chicken she held into the bag, which she tossed to the floor. "You might revise your opinion if you knew my mother."

"Cold and hard?" he guessed.

She shook her head. "Helpless and simpering. She wanted a daddy, not a husband, and she competed with me for his attention. When he died, she had nothing to offer me—no love, no comfort, no reassurance that somehow we'd survive together. She locked herself in her room and the housekeeper took care of me."

"How did he die?" Rob asked quietly.

She met his eyes, her own darkening and losing focus. "He committed suicide in his study. The news media hounded him and us until there wasn't a moment's peace. An investigation turned up other indiscretions, and the details were all over the newspapers, all over the evening report." She shook her head. "My mother cried continually. I think he just couldn't take it anymore."

Rob had a little difficulty mustering sympathy for men in power who thought that power exempted them from rules of civilized behavior. Even if the senator had had a miserable life with his wife, what kind of man was he to blow himself away in his own study with a young child in the house?

"I know what you're thinking," she challenged again.

He shrugged. "You were pretty close last time. What am I thinking?"

"That I'm just using my mother as a receptacle for all my childhood trauma."

He inclined his head in a conciliatory gesture. "Right again."

"But *you're* wrong," she said, leaning her arm up on the seat. Their hands, he noticed, were a mere inch apart, their knees even closer. He remained still while she went on. "Seven months later, she married Daphne's father, a cheerful, wonderful man who was kind and loving to me, and who gave my mother all the paternal security she needed. We moved to a bigger house and Daphne was born. I loved her instantly, and she clung to me because once our mother saw my stepfather adoring the baby, she wouldn't have anything more to do with her."

"He was the police commissioner, right?"

Judy took her coffee off the dash and took a long drink. Then she put it back. "Try to keep up. That was husband number three. Number two was a mob boss."

Rob blinked. "You're kidding."

"I'm not. He was gunned down over lunch in a Chinese restaurant because one of his higher-ups saw him talking to the police Commissioner with whom he'd been friends as a child, and thought he was telling him what he knew and making an immunity deal for himself. I was in college. Daphne was ten."

"God."

"Yeah. My mother admitted that she knew what he did, but he was so good to her, she didn't care. Apparently, it didn't occur to her that she was putting two children into a situation where mistakes are corrected by murder. All she knew was that he was good to *her*."

Rob drew in a breath. He could imagine a college-age Judy, possibly just recovering from the echoes of her father's death, learning that the stepfather she loved had been gunned down.

"We were front-page news again," Judy said, "but mercifully not for long. Simple murder isn't half as exciting as sordid scandal. Then came Gordon Stewart, the police commissioner."

"You mean, your mother finally made a wise choice?"

She reached for her cup again and downed the rest of the coffee. He gathered from the small grimace that it had grown cold. "No," she said. "He was a pillar of the community by day and a child molester by night." She drew a ragged breath, and he knew he'd misunderstood what had prompted the grimace. "I was working in Boston by then, but...he had Daphne. I knew something was wrong, but she didn't say anything, and I thought she was just having difficulty adjusting to life with a new stepfather. He seemed so nice, so concerned about her." Judy's hand on the back of the seat had curled into a fist. Rob wrapped his around it and rubbed his thumb gently over her knuckles, wondering how two little girls could have been burdened with such a fate. He'd changed his mind about Judy's mother.

"Take it easy," he said.

Her fist tightened. He continued to rub.

"I went home for Daphne's sixteenth birthday," she murmured, "and discovered she'd run away several weeks before. I couldn't believe they hadn't told me. My mother said they didn't want to upset me. Gordon said he had officers looking for her, but he never quite met my eyes. So I looked into it myself." She sighed, and something seemed to go out of her. "I discovered that she'd worked on the street in Hollywood, but that she'd moved to Las Vegas."

"So, you went to Las Vegas," he guessed.

She nodded. "But I couldn't find her." Judy gave him a pitiful look. "She told me later that she was hiding from me, that she thought I probably wouldn't love her anymore because of what she'd done to survive. So, I lost her for almost ten years."

"Gordon didn't really have men looking for her?"

"No. I suppose he knew if they found her, she'd end up in the system, then she'd probably tell some counselor what he was doing to her. And he couldn't have that."

"Your mother wasn't suspicious?"

She gave him a weary look. "I'm convinced my mother knew what he'd done to Daphne. And that all she thought was, with Daphne out of the picture, she had him all to herself. Sick. She died two years ago and I couldn't find it in me to grieve."

Rob brought her fist down to his other hand and gently rubbed his palm over it. So that was how a woman grew spiked armor over her emotions.

Judy felt a small circle of peace in the midst of the turbulence of her memories and emotions and followed it in surprise, wondering where it came from. Then she focused on it.

Rob Friedman held her hand in his two—had held it for some time. And the soft pad of his palm was stroking gently over the tight fist she'd made. She felt the anguish it represented begin to soften and dissipate. But beyond the anger, there was nothing to depend on.

She withdrew her hand, tossed back her hair and looked boldly into his dark eyes. "That's me, Friedman," she said. "A bundle of neuroses and bad memories. A reporter ruined my life and drove my father to suicide. And you were that kind of reporter in Chicago, weren't you? I've heard the talk—that you used to be big there but you lost your job because you ran a story about a city councilman driving drunk with the wife of a big advertiser. That you'd been told to kill the story but considered it your—'' she made an heroic gesture with her right hand ''—your civic duty to point out the man's indiscretions.''

He acknowledged the truth of that with an inclination of his head. ''You end up on the police blotter, you get written up—that's been a rule in journalism since the news was written on stone tablets. It doesn't matter who you are.''

''Or whose life is ruined?''

''The life is ruined by the criminal, not the writer who reports the crime.''

Rob sincerely believed that was true, but faced with the victim of just such a heroic job of reporting, it was a little difficult to feel righteous about it.

''But the real question here,'' he reminded her, ''is can you work with me without verbally gut punching me at every opportunity?''

Judy let her eyes wander over an impressive pair of shoulders and good biceps. ''You look built to take it.''

He smiled amiably. ''Oh, I can take it. The question is, would I want to? The answer is no. So, if you intend to help me, you have to lighten up. I am a low-life reporter, but I'm not the one who ruined your life. If you can't deal with that, I'll have to do this without you.''

Her chin came up. It wasn't quite a full bristle, but he enjoyed it anyway. ''Oh, really? And how do you propose to fulfill your promise of keeping an eye on me, while taking off without me?''

''I thought you were willing to absolve me of the promise.''

"I thought you said I couldn't."

He grinned. "You mean you're actually starting to listen to me?"

She expelled an exasperated breath. "No, you just talk so much, some of it gets through. All right, I'll do my best to cooperate, but the first time you try to go around me, or give me any trouble, I'll implement my own plan. Is that clear?"

"I'll be happy to work with you," he agreed, "as long as you're civil."

She raised an eyebrow. "Being civil means I have to agree with you, doesn't it?"

"No," he corrected, "it means you have to extend to me the courtesy you offer everyone else." Then he pretended concern. "You don't treat *everyone* the way you treat me, do you?"

"Everyone," she replied, "didn't ruin my life."

He sighed with forbearance. "Neither did I. In fact, given different circumstances..." He paused, his eyes going over her face feature by feature, lingering for a moment on her lips, parted expectantly as she waited for him to continue. His gaze moved down to her breasts, where it stopped for just an instant before slipping back up to her eyes. He sighed again, but turned in his seat to fit the key in the truck's ignition.

"Given different circumstances, what?" she asked. She expected him to reply with something like "a good reporter could *save* your life."

When his soft, dark eyes went over her again and the look in them became decidedly sexual, she felt a jolt to her midsection.

"I think I could add a lot to it," he said with a smile that was arrogantly suggestive. "Probably teach you a few things you never even imagined. And no doubt, learn a lot myself in the process."

She couldn't believe his audacity. She yanked her seat belt into place. "Well, it's fortunate for both of us that we aren't given different circumstances, because I know one of us would be in for a rude surprise."

He turned the key in the ignition and smiled at her over his shoulder as he shifted. "Trust me, Lowery," he said. "It would be you."

CHAPTER THREE

"I TOLD YOU you could have the afternoon off," Rob said from the pasteup board as the bell over the front door announced K.J.'s arrival.

K.J. placed his camera on his desk in a messy corner of the *Tyler Citizen* office and came to look over Rob's shoulder.

"Emergency-room doctor says I'm fine." He pointed to the four-by-five hole in the columns of type at the top of the front-page pasteup. "Did you get the snow geese picture?"

"Yeah. It's pretty good. It's drying."

"What else do you need?"

Rob pointed to the half-page hole on page seven. "Can you put together the used-cars ad? Stuff's on your desk."

"Sure. We going to have room for a photo of the manicurist?"

"Yeah. We'll put her in business news." He pointed to page three. "You get enough on her to do a small bio?"

"No. I had my nails done instead." K.J. walked the length of the boards, perusing the pasteups, then amended wryly, "Of course I did. You want me to cover city council tonight while you finish up?"

"We're in good shape. I can handle both, if you don't feel up to it."

K.J. rolled his eyes as he walked past him into a cavernous back room that housed the rest room, the darkroom, the coffeepot and refrigerator and the two ratty sofas where they sometimes sacked out the night before deadline. He emerged again, pulling on his darkroom apron.

"You're just trying to stiff me of my overtime," he accused cheerfully. "I'm fine. I'll cover the meeting. I'm going to do my film. You need prints of anything else?"

Rob grinned at him as he pasted up a headline. "Won't the solution ruin your manicure?"

K.J. turned back to the darkroom, calling over his shoulder, "I'll charge you for it if it does."

"Hey!"

K.J. reappeared in the doorway, an eyebrow raised in question.

"About this morning."

"Yeah?"

"Thank you for going to Judy's rescue. That wasn't in your job description."

K.J. frowned. "Not as a reporter, maybe. But as a man it was. I like her, even though she doesn't seem to like you. What's that all about, anyway?"

Rob ran over the headline with a small roller that affixed the hot wax on the back of the strip to the pasteup page. "Her father was involved in a scandal when she was a kid, and when it was all over the papers and the television screen, he couldn't take it and offed himself. She blames reporters."

K.J.'s frown deepened. "Deep stuff. Women are so much more complicated than they look."

Rob thought he detected a personal passion in that observation. "Everything okay with Gina?"

K.J. gave him a look of amused exasperation. "Nothing is ever okay with Gina. There's always a problem somewhere, and if there isn't, she creates one. She likes to talk, to discuss, to... *explore* what we're feeling." He winced as though the notion were painful. "I thought feelings were to be acted on rather than 'explored.'"

"That's 'cause you're an unevolved, one-cell guy." Rob stepped back, hands on his hips, to look over the page for artistic merit. It had it. He moved on to page two, where he noticed a jump line missing on the Ingall's F and M rebuilding update. He took a Continued on Page 5 tag off the board and put it in place at the end of the column.

"Why do women consider themselves higher on the evolutionary ladder than us?"

"I don't know. I guess 'cause they're more... compact, more aesthetically designed."

K.J. looked at himself in the mirror on the wall beside him. "I think I'm kind of buff," he said, as though he'd given the matter impersonal thought.

"I hate to break it to you, Kurtis, buddy, but you're only one vote on that score." Rob shooed him toward the darkroom. "Get to work."

K.J. turned away with an indignant expression. His voice could be heard from somewhere beyond the doorway. "To think I could be doing a brilliant comic strip somewhere!"

"Only if *you* were brilliant!" Rob shouted back.

IT WAS AFTER TEN by the time Rob had all the pasteup holes filled except the city-council story, which would fit at the bottom of the front page. He sat in his desk chair, admiring his work. Then his attention was snagged by the world outside as a police car cruised slowly past.

In the darkness beyond his window, Rob could see the lights of Main Street in one direction, the softer lights of the residences on Gunther in another. The small light in the high northwest corner of his window was the one in Judy's living room. He could picture her hard at work at her computer, her intense blue eyes frowning as she worked on the machinations of a plot.

He remembered the brightness in them when she'd watched the snow geese, the almost ingenuous sparkle that had lit her face. Then she'd told him about her father, and the sparkle had been replaced by anguish and the painful acceptance of a mother who'd been more of a child than Judy or Daphne had been.

It wasn't hard to see how Judy's snarly attitude toward reporters had developed. It was an unfortunate fact of journalism that the pursuit of the truth often trampled innocent victims. But the honest reporter was all that stood between the people and the perpetrators of deception.

Rob supposed it was arguable whether it served any purpose to expose one elected official for indiscretion when many of his colleagues were guilty of the same but managed to hide the fact.

He groaned and leaned back in his chair. He was glad to be in Tyler, where he didn't have to make the kinds of decisions where morality and justice never quite came together.

That wasn't to say his life was without problems. At the moment he had two particularly thorny ones—proving Celeste Huntington guilty of murder and deciding what to do with and about Judy Lowery.

He'd tried to call Dave Heath to see if the P.I. had made any progress on the car search, and had had to leave a message. So that problem remained suspended.

And the time spent with Judy this morning had served primarily to confuse him royally. His concern over her safety when the limo had sped away from him had had nothing to do with his promise to Daphne to keep her safe. He'd been worried for himself. And it had been more than the solicitude of one human being for another. It had felt very personal, and Rob couldn't understand why.

He'd been convinced she hated him despite her insistence that what she felt was strong dislike. But when she'd turned to him that afternoon and questioned him about why he'd taken her to see the snow geese, he'd seen interest in her eyes. Then disappointment when he'd told her that he'd known she would want to see them before the area became crowded with gawkers.

Or had he imagined that? The woman did have the ability to turn his wits inside out and spark anger in him with alarming ease. And he hated that. He prided himself on being a steady, rational man. When he'd worked for the *Sun-Voice,* he'd held his ground in the face of crooked politicians, the dangerous underworld, rioting minorities and frustrated police.

And in each case he'd assessed the situation, judged the importance of the story and done his best to fortify his position—all with calm control.

Then along came a woman, smaller than he was, armed with nothing but an irascible manner, and he found himself having to use superhuman means to hold his temper in check.

He was enough of a reporter to see to the root of the problem. He was attracted to her. He just wasn't sure if the anger was directed at her for being the cause of it or at himself for falling victim to it.

The sudden jangle of the telephone startled him out of his thoughts. He reached for it, hoping it wouldn't involve changing the front page at this late hour.

"Tyler Citizen," he said, leaning back to prop his feet up on the desk.

"Rob, it's Dave Heath," a deep voice responded. "You won't believe it. I think I have good news."

Rob knocked over an empty coffee cup when he straightened in his chair, his heart kicking him in the ribs. "What?"

"I found a car that fits the description of your little Mercedes in a toolie's salvage yard in San Diego County. All the VIN numbers have been ground off, so I can't verify those, but I think it's it. You were right. The dealer stored it in a shed, thinking eventually he'd buy a new door panel, front fender, new parts and restore it for himself rather than crushing it. How does it feel to be so smart?"

"Hell, I'm used to it. You looked for evidence of tampering?"

"Brake line neatly sliced halfway, then ripped apart the rest of the way when the brakes were applied. I told the guy who owns the yard that I might have a buyer for it."

"I'll be there tomorrow night. You're a champ, Dave."

"And aren't you lucky to employ me. Let me know when you're coming in, and I'll pick you up at the airport."

"Thanks. See you."

Rob hung up the phone and let out a whoop of satisfaction. K.J., just returning from the city-council meeting, heard the shout and fell back against the open door with a hand to his heart. "Whoa! It's only me! You're not having deadline meltdown again, are you?"

Rob went to pull him inside, closed the door behind him and locked it, then drew him into the back room. Bare wallboard surrounded them, and garish light shone down on the two tacky sofas—one covered in a yellow-and-gold-flowered fabric, the other in balding avocado green tweed.

"This is it," he said.

"You got a date?" K.J. guessed.

Rob shifted his weight. "You want to hear this?"

"Am I on overtime?"

"You're on *borrowed* time if you don't put a sock in it."

K.J. nodded agreeably. "You have my undivided attention."

"I think we've found Daphne's husband's car. I'm going to San Diego tomorrow. You think you can put this baby to bed tomorrow afternoon and handle the mailing?"

K.J.'s eyes lit up. Rob smiled to himself. The kid thought he wanted to be a cartoonist, but he was an editor through and through. When the tension closed around him, his adrenaline pumped. The worse the situation got, the better he liked it.

"Sure. You got everything done?"

"Yeah. We got a press release from Timberlake Lodge this afternoon. There's a group of clog dancers there this weekend. I promised we'd do a short piece on them. You can replace the subscription coupon with it on the bottom of page four."

"What, please God, are clog dancers?"

"It's in the press release."

K.J. nodded, though he looked vaguely disgruntled. "Why do we do these stories on the conferences at the lodge? The place seems to attract every weirdo group in a hundred-mile radius."

"Because they don't pay us for the ad we run for them every month, they trade us a night's lodging," Rob said, going to the refrigerator to inspect its contents. He still had to finish up his editorial on the rebirth of the F and M after the fire, and he'd need sustenance. "That's where your editor goes for R and R. Oh, and remind me to leave my tape recorder with you. I've got the names in that assault case we heard on the scanner."

"Yeah, okay. But back up. You R and R at the lodge? Whooo," K.J. said, twirling his index finger in the air. "Exotic traveller. R and R should take place more than a couple of miles out of town. Put that back, the pizza's mine."

Rob inspected the dried and puckered contents of a square box and willingly handed it over. "What's this?" He reached for a square storage container with a dark green lid.

"Mrs. Marshack brought it for you this afternoon. Forgot to tell you. You were in the darkroom. She said it was a thank-you for taking Judy to see the snow geese."

Rob stopped in the act of prying off the lid. "How'd she know that?"

K.J., happily chewing two-day-old pizza, hunched a shoulder. "Judy told her? I don't know. You know, if that's your idea of showing a girl a good time, we need to talk."

"Yeah, like your love life's going so well." Rob pried off the lid and exclaimed in pleased surprise, "Lasagna!"

K.J. studied him warily. "We don't have a microwave, and it's almost ten-thirty. You're going to eat that cold?"

"You're eating cold pizza," Rob pointed out.

"I don't have to hop on a plane tomorrow."

He had a point, but Rob ate the cold lasagna anyway. He'd flown with the coast guard on rescues over the Great Lakes and never gotten sick. He'd be fine. He'd look at the car, have it transported to safety somewhere until he could get the police on it, then he'd come home to Tyler and put the case together. Piece of cake.

HE WONDERED LATER why it hadn't occurred to him that nothing ever went that easily for him.

The trouble started when he took his seat in the small commuter plane that flew from Tyler to Chicago, where a connecting flight would take him to L.A. There was a woman seated across the aisle from him in the single seat. It was Judy. She looked pleased with herself.

"What are you doing here?" he demanded. He'd considered telling her Dave Heath had thought he'd found the car, but decided against it. He was afraid if Dave was wrong, she'd be disappointed, and if he wasn't, there was a potential for danger somewhere along the way. Celeste had connections everywhere, particularly in the county that had managed somehow to sidestep all the usual procedures followed after an accident like Trey's.

"I'm doing here," she replied with a look of theatrical innocence, "whatever it is you're doing here, because you've been consigned by my sister to keep an eye on me and that's more easily accomplished if we're in the same state.''

He noticed that she wore a soft, roll-necked white sweater that turned her eyes the color of dusk. It annoyed him that he should notice that when he was angry with her.

''I was going to be gone three days tops,'' he said with strained patience, ''and I asked Jake to keep an eye on you. Now he's going to be in a panic when he can't find you.''

''No, he won't.'' She buckled her seat belt as the light went on. ''He knows where I am. And don't act as though it'd be my fault if he was worried. You're the one who promised me just yesterday morning that we'd work together on this, but then wimped out.''

''I did not wimp out,'' he said sharply under his breath as he snapped the buckle of his own seat belt. ''What if Stumpy followed you?''

''How do you know,'' she asked, ''that he didn't follow you?''

''I know how to lose him.''

She made a scornful sound. ''Sam Spade Friedman! Stumpy did *not* follow me. I think he's been too busy with Marion Clark to remember what he's in Tyler to do.''

Rob had to concentrate to prevent himself from shouting at her as other passengers boarded the plane. ''This could turn out to be dangerous. How did you find out I was leaving, anyway?''

''I was out at a meeting with Britt last night when you called to ask Jake to keep an eye on me. Jake came into the kitchen when we came home and told her about it without realizing I was with her.''

"It's hard to believe you could ever be invisible."

"I was behind the refrigerator door, reaching in for a piece of cheesecake. Britt's on my side. She told Jake he'd have to sleep on the sofa if he called you to tell you I knew the plan."

Rob shook his head over the perfidy of friends.

Then the engines revved and the roar was too pervasive to allow for conversation. He looked across the aisle to find her looking straight ahead, a half smile on her face.

Curiously, under the exasperation and concern, there was a half smile inside him as well.

IT WAS EIGHTY-THREE degrees in Los Angeles. Judy followed Rob and Dave Heath across the acres of parking lot, feeling as though her sweater had become a wool blanket. Perspiration stood out all over her body, and she thought with great despair of the other two sweaters she'd packed in such a hurry late last night. Her only hope was that her wardrobe would act as a steam bath and she'd return to Tyler three pounds lighter.

Heath had taken her suitcase and makeup bag and strode ahead with Rob, who seemed to have forgotten her existence. She wasn't hurt, she told herself. She didn't *want* his attention. It was just that when one discounted all his smart and argumentative remarks, he was usually rather solicitous.

And the airplane food had been unappealing, so she hadn't eaten, and now that she thought about it, the cheesecake last night at Britt's had been the last thing she'd put in her stomach. She glanced at her watch. About twenty-one hours ago, if one added the two-hour time change.

She looked up at the sky, saw wavering sunlight reflected off of automobiles and palm trees against a slightly smoggy sky. They appeared to wobble. So did the earth beneath her feet. Earthquake. They had earthquakes here.

Then Rob, who had just turned to speak to her, was frowning. He quickly dropped his bags and reached for her.

She wondered why, then felt herself sink to the asphalt....

"Which one, Rob? The blue one?"

"No, that's long-sleeved. The T-shirt with Shakespeare on it. She's sweltering."

"This it?"

"Yeah. Thanks. Keep your eyes front, Dave, while I get this sweater off her."

Judy hadn't quite come to; it required too much effort. But she lay still against what felt like soft leather and enjoyed the breeze fanning her face. She listened with only vague interest to the conversation taking place very close by, concentrating instead on the delicious coldness on her hot cheeks.

Then she heard the words *get this sweater off her* spoken in Rob's voice and came to full wakefulness with a mighty jolt of all her body processes.

She caught his wrist and looked into his eyes, her own filled with deadly intent. "Don't . . . touch me." There was a threat implicit in the careful spacing of the words.

Now that her eyes were open, she saw that she lay in the rear seat of a large and probably very expensive car, and that Rob sat beside her on the edge of it. A T-shirt was tossed over one of the headrests, and the back of Dave's head was visible in the front seat. He was whistling with studied nonchalance.

Rob continued to fan her with the airline-ticket envelope in his free hand. "I'm not going to touch you, I'm going to touch the sweater. You fainted."

"The first aid for fainting," she protested, feeling very much as though she might explore the experience all over again, "is not the removal of clothes."

"It is if the faintee happens to be wearing a twelve-pound sweater and the temperature is in the eighties. Now stop being silly. This will only take—"

She slapped a hand against the hem of her sweater as he tried to lift it up. "No. I'm not...wearing a bra." She added the last three words in a whisper.

Dave's whistling became louder and more intricate.

Rob leaned over her to whisper in reply, "And you think your double-A bosom is going to incite me to passions beyond my control?"

She opened her mouth to protest his verbal assault, then closed it again, discovering she was more hurt than insulted. "I happen to be a B," she said.

"Right." Distracted indignation was precisely the reaction he'd been hoping for. He had the sweater off her and the T-shirt on in the time it took him to draw breath between sentences. "Okay, Dave. Find the fast lane so we can generate some breeze back here."

"I want to sit up," she protested, feeling as though a great prickly pressure had been lifted off her.

"In a few minutes." Rob began to fan her again. "You look a little green."

Judy closed her eyes and drew a deep breath. Soon Dave was able to pick up speed, and she felt the cool air bathe her overheated body as they moved into the late afternoon traffic.

The wobbly feeling left her, and she opened her eyes. Rob had stopped fanning now that air was moving in the car, but he looked worried.

"This doesn't mean I'm going to be an encumbrance on this trip," she said firmly.

"Did someone say it did?"

"You're thinking it."

"No, I'm not." He was thinking that she had the most beautifully perfect breasts he'd ever seen, whatever her cup size was. But it seemed wiser not to mention that now. "And it would probably be easier on both of us if you'd ask me what I'm thinking rather than presuming to know."

He knew instantly that had been a stupid thing to say.

She asked the obvious. "Then what *are* you thinking?"

Fortunately, along with reportorial honesty, he'd cultivated the wily investigator's skill at pretense. "I was thinking that you're beginning to get a little color in your cheeks." He grasped her shoulders and pulled her up to a sitting position, tucking her in the corner of the seat.

She looked a little tousled, but her eyes were clearly focused on him.

"You didn't eat anything on the plane," he noted. "You hungry?"

Her stomach growled loudly in response.

He laughed and tapped Dave on the shoulder. "Find us some food, Dave." Then he moved sideways to occupy the opposite corner of the back seat, and pulled her feet up to rest on his thigh.

She tried not to notice, but his hand settled warmly on her ankle, and every thought in her head, ever sensory projector seemed to concentrate there.

But he was talking to Dave about driving on to San Diego County after they'd eaten. Rob seemed oblivious to any suggestion of awareness, much less tension.

That was good, she decided. That would be an unwelcome complication at this juncture.

THEY SAT IN A BOOTH in a big, cheerful coffee shop somewhere off the freeway. Judy gazed out the window in fascination as eight lanes of traffic zoomed past, bumper to bumper, without incident. The sky was darkening to dusk, and lights blossomed everywhere—on cars, beside the freeway, in houses occupying the hillside, in the sky as stars began to appear.

She wondered with a pang of loneliness what the evening was like where Daphne was, and whether her sister was happy that she'd entrusted herself and her child to Vic Estevez.

Daphne and Vic had been arguing when they left Tyler, but the situation had been so urgent, so desperate. Confinement together had either solved their problems or increased them.

Rob and Dave laughed, and Judy's attention was drawn back to her companions. The waitress had cleared away the remnants of their dinner and reappeared to top up their coffee cups.

Rob turned to Judy as he'd done at regular intervals throughout the meal, his eyes going over her features in a kind of diagnostic study.

"Feeling all right?"

"Fine," she assured him. "Are we driving to San Diego tonight?"

"We were just talking about that. It's been a long day. Would you rather stay the night here and carry on in the morning? It'll take us a couple of hours to get there."

"I'm ready to go tonight, if that was the plan."

When Rob continued to study her doubtfully, she turned to Dave. "Don't I look fine to you?" she asked.

He leaned his chin on his hand and sighed dramatically. He had the face and body of a film star, and the flirtatious manner of the kind of man a woman in her right mind steered clear of. He'd be a lot of fun, but he'd never be faithful. "Fine doesn't begin to describe it. Think you could find happiness in sunny California with a romantic private detective?" He pointed to Rob with a disparaging wave of his hand. "He may look like a good time, but actually he's very dull."

She smiled blandly at Rob, feeling suddenly much better. That made the opportunity to tease him more than she could resist. "I know that. I'm just using him. When I'm finished, maybe we can talk."

Dave leaned across the table, an eyebrow quirking with interest. "Using him in what way?"

She patted his hand. "I'm sure you don't want the details. You probably think he wouldn't wear a pirate costume and play walk the plank."

Dave expelled a shout of laughter.

Rob's eyes lit with amusement, but mingled with that was the subtle threat of retribution. "You *are* yourself again. We move on tonight, then."

He leaned against the back of the booth while Dave told him about his discussion with the salvage-yard owner.

Judy listened, hemmed into the corner of the booth by the press of Rob's shoulder and the relaxed spread of his knees. Confinement in tight spots usually filled her with the need to break free, but she felt oddly content being wedged in between Rob and the wall.

He gave her that glance again as Dave talked on, only there was a smile in it this time over the "pirate" taunt. He turned back to Dave again as the P.I. made a point, and Judy struggled against a curious sense of rightness.

Oh, no. This couldn't happen. He was the wrong man.

But her body wasn't listening. A little pocket of warmth settled in the region of her stomach and refused to dissipate, despite her warnings.

CHAPTER FOUR

JUDY OPENED HER EYES to see a cactus blinking on and off. She lifted her head to try to focus, and realized she was looking at a neon sign. The Saguaro Motel, it read in script that remained steady as the green cactus, which resembled a trident, appeared and disappeared against the darkness.

She had dozed off on the drive south, and Dave had apparently pulled into a motel parking lot to secure rooms for the night.

That resolved, Judy suddenly became aware of her surroundings. She'd known immediately that she was in the front seat of the wide, comfortable Cadillac, but she had that weird feeling again that should have felt like confinement, but which her body recognized once more as security.

The hand she'd pushed herself up with still rested against the sturdy object that had given her leverage. She now realized that there was warmth under her palm, and a steady thump. A heartbeat.

She turned slowly and found herself eye-to-eye with Rob. And that was all she could see in the shadows of the car—the gleam of light in his dark eyes. His arm rested along the back of the seat behind her. She'd been asleep against his shoulder.

The steady beat under her hand seemed to slip up her arm and into her body, and tick there like something demanding freedom.

He didn't move. "Sleep well?" he asked softly. His voice reverberated around her in the small space, mingling with the demand for release inside her.

She didn't know why she did it. Later, when she tried to reason it through, she couldn't remember what had prompted her. All she knew was that his lips were only an inch away, and in this unfamiliar state of drowsy security, she wanted more than anything in the whole world to taste them.

She saw his eyes read her intention, reflect first surprise, then the same inexplicable need she felt.

She lifted her mouth to his and he met it without taking the initiative from her. She explored the warm, mobile contours of his lips, sparred with his tongue, kissed the corner of his mouth, then nipped at his bottom lip.

She felt his hand move to the base of her neck, pressing her gently against him. The tips of her breasts came to sensory life against his solid chest, and electricity rayed everywhere. She felt as though her blood had been aerated as it flowed to her fingertips, down her legs, up into her brain.

The interior of the car was suddenly bathed in light as the driver's-side door was yanked open. Dave dangled three keys from his fingers. "Rooms 14, 15 and— ah..." His gaze took in their obvious intimacy and Judy's look of mortification.

"Sorry," he apologized quickly. "I didn't mean...I mean, I didn't know you were...Should I have gotten only two rooms?"

"No," Judy replied calmly as she eased herself back into the middle. "We want three rooms. Please get in so we can find our parking spot. I'm exhausted."

She was pleased that her voice sounded normal, because she was truly horrified. And there was clearly no one to blame but herself. She had initiated the kiss. And what's worse, she had *enjoyed* it. She, who hated reporters and was greatly annoyed by this particular one! She, who was supposed to be on a search for evidence to bring her sister home, was playing kissy-face with the enemy.

As Dave parked the car and quickly climbed out to unlock the trunk, she turned to Rob and said combatively, "I know what you're thinking."

He met her gaze with the direct look of a man who knew more about her than she wanted him to know. "Then you'd better lock yourself in your room while you still can," he said, and pushed the passenger-side door open.

AN AUTO-SALVAGE YARD, Judy discovered, was an otherworldly landscape. There were tire hills, canyons of parts she couldn't identify stacked neatly atop one another to an alarming height, rivers of chrome that did truly appear liquid in the sunlight.

Again she trailed behind Rob and Dave as they prowled around the yard, waiting for the manager in greasy coveralls to finish helping a pair of teenaged boys. Dave carried a camera.

Earlier they'd all had breakfast together, and she and Rob pretended the previous evening's encounter of the curious kind hadn't happened. Judy couldn't explain it, so she preferred not to discuss it. He apparently felt the same.

Dave had looked from one to the other when they'd met outside their motel rooms, and must have understood that not even a lighthearted joke on the subject was permissible. He'd launched right into the business of deciding where to breakfast before visiting the salvage yard.

Across the yard, a noisy machine that looked like a long metal box crushed cars that had been stripped of saleable parts into a neat square package that would fit in the back of a pickup truck.

Judy left the men to their perusal of the door of a '67 Mustang, and went to watch as a giant metal claw operated by a crane dropped a Cadillac with a bashed-in front into the machine. Then the sides began to squeeze together like the trash compacter in one of the *Star Wars* movies.

And that was when she saw the cat face at the rear passenger-side window. She blinked, sure she was mistaken. But there it was again—a big, scruffy head, this time at the driver's window.

Then she saw a long, mangy but supple body appear as it sprang to the back seat, then to the front again, searching for escape from the terrifying noise. She guessed the animal suspected that an unpleasant fate awaited him.

She turned to shout for help, but Rob and Dave were not in sight and the machine's noise drowned out the sound of her voice.

She turned back frantically, looking for something to throw to break a window. She found a rock and threw it with all her might, but in her panic she missed and the rock bounced harmlessly off the side of the metal box.

Panic rose in her. She climbed onto the contraption that supported the device, desperate to do *something*.

Then she noticed the button on the driver's-side door standing up in the unlocked position.

Judy reached out to pull the door open at the same moment that the sides of the box rose, throwing her off balance and making a terrible crunching noise. She was caught and yanked back, spun around and crushed in a protective embrace as the pressure popped the windows and glass splintered and flew. There was the whine of folding metal for what seemed an eternity, then silence.

Judy tried to push her way out of Rob's grasp, but found that she couldn't. He now had her by the shoulders and was giving her a furious shake.

"What in the hell is *wrong* with you?" he shouted at her.

She pulled against his grip, standing on tiptoe to see around him, beyond him. "Did he get out?"

Rob shook her again, holding her on tiptoe. She tottered dangerously but was in no danger of falling—his grasp on her was too tight. "I thought you weren't going to be an encumbrance on this trip!" he reminded her angrily. "Your being crushed would definitely have been—"

"Did he get out?" she screeched.

"Who?" he bellowed.

"The cat!"

"He went that way, Alice." Dave's quiet voice intruded on their dueling screams. He pointed in the direction of a stack of tires. A mangy gray cat sat at the top, a rear leg raised in flagrant gracelessness as he groomed it.

Judy put a hand to her heart in relief.

Rob yanked her around again. "You put yourself in the middle of a car crusher for a cat?!"

It had been a stupid thing to do, but she hadn't been operating on logic, she'd reacted on instinct. She wasn't sure a man—a reporter—could understand that.

"It's a living thing," she said reasonably.

He was beyond being reasonable. "You," he said, leaning down until they were nose-to-nose, "were almost a *dead* thing."

She folded her arms and lifted her chin. "And an encumbrance?"

"If you're going to repeat my words, please do it before you forget to eat and fall in a heap, and before you step under a falling piece of concrete. Not after." He took a firm hold of her upper arm. "I think you'd better stay with me."

The owner of the yard, a rotund man in coveralls and a straw hat, hurried in their direction. Because of the roundness of his stomach and the shortness of his legs, Judy thought he appeared almost to be rolling.

"You two okay?" he asked, mopping his brow with a bandana. "What happened?"

Dave explained about the cat.

The man shook his head at the beast, which had completed his toilette and was now watching them with interest. "Turned up a couple of weeks ago. Lost or left. Feed him when I think about it."

Judging by the scrawny proportions of the cat, Judy bet it wasn't often.

"Didn't get cut, did ya?" the man asked. He pointed to a Danger—Keep Out sign posted near the machine, which Judy had missed. "Can't afford a lawsuit. Tell me now, and I'll take you to the hospital."

Rob, calmer now, looked Judy over. "You okay?"

"Fine," she replied. There was something about the cat, safe and sound and sitting atop the pile of tires, that

made her want to smile. "You?" She brushed minis-
cule pieces of glass off the shoulder of Rob's chambray
shirt.

He studied her a moment as though her behavior
confused him. "We're fine," he replied, then seemed to
have to pull his eyes away from her as Dave introduced
him to the manager of the yard, and they shook hands.
"We'd like to look at the Mercedes you showed Dave
day before yesterday."

"Sure. Come with me."

As they all walked on, Judy turned to Dave, remembering something he'd said earlier. "Why did you call
me Alice?" she asked.

He shook his head and smiled wryly. "Because the
two of you act like Ralph and Alice on the old 'Hon-
eymooners.' Although the crusher incident was almost
Lucy and Desi."

Judy gave him a friendly shove, then had to concentrate to keep up as Rob and John Whitsett picked up the
pace toward a ramshackle shed.

She was a little surprised that the sight of the car disturbed her. In the light of a bare bulb, the place of impact was clearly defined. The driver's-side front corner
was indented with the half-circle impression of a telephone pole. The steering wheel was broken and the
windshield shattered on that side.

As the men discussed the car, and Dave pushed the
sprung hood up even higher so that Rob could look inside, Judy thought about how much her separation
from Daphne all those years ago had cost them.

Her sister had loved someone she, Judy, had never
even known. Then Daphne had lost him and had to
suffer the grief all by herself. As though that weren't

enough, she'd had to run away and hide her baby from her husband's controlling mother.

Judy sank onto an old wooden bench behind her and let her mind wander with thoughts of what their lives would have been like if their mother had been different—if there'd been no Gordon.

They should have lived a block apart in the same town. They should have been in each other's weddings, baby-sat each other's children, run back and forth with cookies, leftovers, hand-me-down clothes.

Instead they'd been separated for ten years, living separate lives, until Daphne had come to her a year ago and spent those precious months in Tyler.

"Judy, come look at this."

Judy focused on Rob, sitting on a tarp on the dusty ground beside the car. He beckoned to her. "Brake line's been cut halfway through so that it would rip apart after the brakes were applied a few times. It's pretty clear."

She sniffed, pushed herself to her feet and went to sit beside him.

He frowned as she approached. "What's the matter? The cat's fine."

"I know the cat's fine." She lay on her back, preparing to push herself under the car. "I was just thinking how unnatural it is that my sister loved and lost a man I never even knew. Where, pray tell, do I find the brake line?"

Rob lay on his back beside her and shimmied under the car. She followed.

He pointed up at the flexible rubber tubing that ran to each front wheel.

Judy saw it amidst all the weird angles of the under-side of a car—the neat slicing of part of the tubing, then the ragged tear on the rest of it.

She lifted a hand, but he caught it and pulled it back down. "I don't know what the procedure's going to be here, but if this ends up in a forensics lab somewhere, we don't want your fingerprints on it."

"Good point." She turned her head toward him, her eyes hopeful in the dark, shallow space. "Do you think this'll be enough to nail Celeste? How do we prove *she* did this?"

He squeezed her hand. "It's enough to open the case. And it's obvious that the sheriff's deputy who appeared on the scene of the accident, or maybe the sheriff himself, was somehow influenced to neglect to notify the state police—my guess would be influenced with money. That leads to Celeste. What we have to do is put any one of her men anywhere near Daphne's car the night before the accident."

"And how do we do that?"

"Please. One hurdle at a time."

Judy suddenly started, then gasped in alarm as she felt the stroke of something furry across her cheek. Then she heard the rumble of a purr and knew it was the gray cat. He walked down to where Rob's hand holding hers made passage impossible, then turned around in the narrow space and leaned down to rub his face against hers again. Finally he lay down beside her and rolled onto his back.

"Oooh," she said, pulling free of Rob's hand to stroke the cat. "He likes me."

"Of course he does," he said, sliding out from under the car. "You saved him from becoming violin strings. Come on.'' He took hold of her ankles and pulled gently until she was out from under the car.

The cat followed her, a spring in his step, convinced he'd found a comrade.

Rob lent her a hand up and dusted off the back of her shirt. ''I'd like to buy this car, Mr. Whitsett,'' he said, ''and have it shipped to...'' He turned to Dave. ''Can you store it for me temporarily?''

Dave nodded. ''Got a two-car garage and only the Caddy.''

''Great. Can you get some pictures of that brake line?''

''Do my best.''

While Dave photographed the car, Rob, Judy and Whitsett moved to a cramped and airless little office, where Judy pulled Rob aside.

''Won't that cost you a fortune?'' she asked in a whisper.

He shook his head. ''The car's totaled, and Dave has arrangements to have the car picked up.''

While business was conducted, Judy looked out the window at the gray cat, who had leapt onto the top of an old Volkswagen seat that leaned against the front of the office. His notched tail swished as he looked back at her, four paws neatly lined up under him.

''You remember who brought this car to you?'' Rob asked Whitsett.

The manager had taken off his hat. He was as bald as a melon. ''Yeah,'' he replied. ''The sheriff's office. They bring totaled cars here all the time. Sheriff Ryder himself brought this one.''

Rob caught Judy's glance. It would have taken the sheriff himself to bypass all the usual procedures—the reports that would have resulted in the state sending an accident reconstructionist, who would have looked at the car and certainly found the cut brake line.

Dave joined them in the office and used the phone to call a friend with a flatbed truck, who agreed to pick up the Mercedes the following morning.

Rob shook Whitsett's hand. "We'll be back tomorrow to watch it loaded. Thanks."

He turned to the door and tried to usher Judy out before him, but she resisted.

"About the gray cat, Mr. Whitsett," she said, pointing to the feline now perched on the outside windowsill. She deliberately avoided Rob's gaze. "I take it you're not particularly attached to him?"

He cast the cat a disparaging glance. "Not at all. He's a cussed so and so. Won't come to ya, hisses and spits. Why?"

She braced herself for battle. "I'd like to take him home with me, if that's all right with you."

"All right?" Whitsett laughed. "I'll thank ya in my prayers. Take him. He's yours."

That had been easy, but then that wasn't where she'd expected the battle to come from.

She turned to Dave, skipping over Rob again. "Do you mind having a cat in your car?"

He shook his head. "But how're you going to get him back to Wisconsin?"

"As baggage on the plane," she replied. "It's done all the time."

Rob had been waiting for her to finally look at him. He knew she was avoiding him not because she thought he had enough clout as the male in their traveling party to keep her from taking the cat home, but because she didn't want to be argued out of it—and she'd found herself acceding to his decision on several occasions.

"You're wondering," she said, "what I'm going to do with him in the motel room tonight."

"No," he said amiably. "I expect you'll ask Mr. Whitsett for a cardboard box with holes in it, take it into the room under your jacket and keep the cat in the bathroom."

Her eyebrows went up. He'd surprised her. He liked that.

"I am wondering," he said, "if you've considered that a cat traveling as baggage has to have proof of vaccinations."

Her brows drew together in a stricken expression. "How do you know?"

"Remember the dog show at the lodge? It came up when I did the story on them."

She turned to the window, where the ugly cat was looking in at her. Her usually guarded features softened, and he saw vulnerability in her eyes. And Rob simply couldn't stomp on it.

She wanted the cat. He wanted...well, what he wanted was too inexplicable to explore. He just knew that he wanted her to have what *she* wanted.

"Is there a vet around here?" he asked Whitsett.

The man pointed. "Right on the road. In the strip mall with the supermarket, the book store and the Chinese restaurant."

Rob turned to Judy. She smiled at him. That pleased him a lot more than it should.

"We've got all afternoon," he said briskly. "We'll get him his shots. Think you can catch him?"

"I don't have to catch him," she said, her smile lingering on Rob a moment longer. "He's mine."

"You're sure of that?"

"When our eyes met through the car window," she said, pulling the office door open, "he became mine. Watch."

The men followed her out of the office.

She went to the windowsill and scratched the cat between the ears. He closed his eyes and purred like a Rolls engine. She ran her hand down his humped back in two gentle strokes. He thumped his head against the inside of her arm and leaned into her, the purr becoming deafening.

She put a hand under his front paws and the other under his tail and lifted him into her arms. He hung there, comatose with adoration.

Whitsett put his hat on. "I'd better get a box."

The cat may have loved Judy, but he didn't like the box. They had to tie it closed with heavy twine. He protested at full volume.

"What are you going to name him?" Dave asked, looking for Judy in the rearview mirror. She sat in the back seat, petting the cat through one of the holes in the box.

Rob looked over his shoulder, waiting for her answer. She was grinning. This was going to be good.

"Considering how Rob and I got here," she replied, "and where we found him, I think 'Caddy' would be appropriate."

Dave groaned. Rob turned around and shook his head. He thought it was a great name, but if he looked at her happy face another moment he was going to lose his mind entirely.

They bought cat food, a plastic bowl and a cat carrier at the supermarket, then took Caddy to the vet's office.

By dinnertime, the cat was an accepted member of their entourage. Dave, still weary from an all-night surveillance just before he'd picked them up at the airport, chose to forego dinner and turn in early.

"Want to go for Chinese?" Rob asked Judy.

She pointed to the cat curled in a tight ball at the foot of her bed. "I'd love to, but if he meows while I'm gone, the motel owner might hear him. Could you just bring me back something?"

"I'll get takeout," he suggested. "What do you like?"

Judy took the situation with equanimity when he spread a newspaper in the middle of her bed, placed their Chinese feast on it, then sat beside her, propped up against the pillows. In true male fashion, he took the remote control and channel-surfed until he found the evening news.

Caddy raised his head to sniff the air, but the comfort of food, shelter and attention seemed to have worn him out, and he lowered his head and slept on.

After the news, Rob and Judy watched "Entertainment Tonight" while companionably passing cartons of food back and forth. One of the segments featured the current heartthrob on a nighttime drama dealing with an ensemble cast of friends in a theater company.

Judy stopped eating to watch a clip of one of his love scenes. "Stage Right" was a show she watched every Monday night, curled up in a corner of the sofa with a cup of tea.

When the segment was over, Rob pointed an egg roll at her accusingly. "You growled over him," he said in disbelief.

Only then did she realize that she had her arms wrapped around her bent knees, her chin resting on them as she gazed longingly at the television.

"I did not," she declared, straightening her legs and turning to fuss with her pillow.

"You did. I heard you."

"I didn't growl, I sighed. He happens to be gorgeous."

"He has no chest hair."

"It's fashionable to wax it."

He snapped the last fried wonton in half and handed her a piece. "I can't believe you'd get moony-eyed over a man who'll be dictated to by fashion trends."

"I'm not moony-eyed."

He caught her chin between his thumb and forefinger when she tried to turn away, and looked into her eyes. "Yes," he insisted, "you are."

It was the extra moment he held her that pushed everything off-kilter. An instant before, she'd felt comfortable with him sitting in the middle of her bed. Now it seemed as though lightning had invaded the room. She felt a ripple of sensation under her skin and along her scalp, and there was a sizzle in the air.

She caught his wrist and tried to pull his hand away. But it was warm and strong against her palm, and she could feel his pulse beating against her fingertips. She seemed to forget that her intention had been to remove his hand.

Instead she remembered the night before, when she had awakened beside him in the car and felt his heartbeat in the darkness. The moment had been so rich, so electric—just like this one. And she continued to hold his wrist, ensnared by the turbulent interest in his dark gaze.

"Beautiful moony eyes," he whispered, and closed the small space between them and kissed her.

With him initiating the contact, it had less hesitancy than last night's kiss. His arms came around her tightly, one hand slipping into her hair. He cornered her in the crook of his arm and teased her tongue to life, drew from her the response that had been just below the surface, waiting for that jolt of power.

Then they fell back to the pillows, sexual sparks flying, emotional smoke billowing.

Rob could not remember any woman ever making him feel like this—fascinated, eager, out of control. Among his peers, kissing had gone out of fashion. Couples exchanged witty repartee, then went to bed. The man-woman dynamic had lost all subtlety and mystery.

But here it was, all wrapped up in Judy Lowery, who hated him on principle, but gave him melting looks and simmering kisses.

Rob had no idea what it meant, and he didn't want to analyze it. He just wanted to follow where it led.

Judy felt as though she were equal parts of passion and confusion. Where had this desperate need for Rob Friedman come from? What did it mean? Where would it lead?

A corner of her mind not consumed with her body's wild reaction to the path of his lips along her throat tried to work out the problem. Solving mysteries was her business. It shouldn't be that hard.

Where did it come from? She was confusing a need for him emotionally with her actual need of him to deal with Celeste Huntington and bring Daphne home. Yes, that must be it. But it didn't feel like it.

What did it mean? That she was repressed? That long years of working too hard had made her vulnerable to the first man brave enough to take her in his arms? That was possible, she supposed.

Where would it lead? At the moment, with every pulse in her body ticking out of control, she was afraid she knew. It would lead where passion always led. It didn't matter how honest the emotions, how pure the intentions, how desperate the need. Passion would supercede reason, and the result would be beyond her control. But she'd made that long-ago rule.

He pushed up her T-shirt, and was planting kisses in the concavity of her waist. She gasped softly against the onslaught of sensation, the boneless feeling that invaded her lower body.

But she made herself say his name with firm insistence. "Rob!"

Attuned to the responsive rhythm of her body, he was surprised by the forlorn quality of her voice. He raised his head and leaned over her on an elbow, his body unpleasantly disturbed by the interruption.

He read her intention before she even voiced it. "No more," she said quietly. "Please."

He saw also that it was not a choice she'd made willingly. That struck him as strange in the woman who liked to have things her way.

He fell onto the bed beside her, leaving a small distance between them, and flung an arm over his eyes while he breathed out his complete frustration and disappointment.

"I'm sorry." Her soft voice invaded his slow recovery.

"No need," he replied.

He felt her turn her head toward him. "Aren't *you* sorry?"

He could only be honest. "Profoundly."

Her sigh was gusty. "I'd explain if I could."

"Again," he said, "no need. I understand. But I think you're wrong."

He heard her prop herself up on an elbow. He lowered his arm and was confronted with the surprised bright blue of her eyes. The left side of her straight blond hair slipped from behind her ear and rippled to within inches of his cheek. "About what?"

He folded his hands behind his head and looked her in the eye. "You said it the other day in Brick's office. You think I'm the wrong man."

"You are!" she said with resolute conviction.

He studied her in amusement. "What? Were you unconscious for the last five minutes? And last night in the car?"

"That was..." She made a flat-handed gesture he guessed was intended to express hopelessness in her search for the right word.

"Passion," he supplied for her.

She considered that. "Okay. Passion." She fell back against her pillow and folded her arms. "Passion can flare between any man and woman."

"No. Sorry." He turned toward her and rose on his forearm to argue the point. "*Desire* can flare between any man and woman. Passion suggests feelings that are out of control. And *that* would only happen because *emotions* are involved. That doesn't happen just anywhere or to just anyone. Don't run from it, Judy."

She looked away from him, her hands folded primly at her waist, but he noticed that her thumbs warred with each other. She wasn't calm at all.

"Pardon me for choosing the wrong word," she said. "That was desire, then, and not passion."

"You didn't choose it, I did," he reminded her. "And it stands. You didn't know what to call it. Just like you don't know what to do about it."

She raised herself up on her elbows, temper showing bright pink in her cheeks. He had to sit up to avoid having her collide with his shoulder.

"What do you *want* to do about it? Make love and pick up the pieces tomorrow?" she demanded.

"What *pieces?* Why do you think you'll fall to pieces if you fall in love?"

She sat all the way up and turned away from him. He found himself looking at the graceful line of her back in his baggy T-shirt.

"The women in my family have difficulty with love," she said, her voice flat. "My mother was helpless in its power, and became the slave of whoever offered it to her, even when he used her daughter as well. I like to be in charge of what I'm doing. I don't want to be directed by hormones and urges."

"That," he said flatly, getting to his feet, "is insane. Your mother was your mother, and you are you. Selfishness ruled your mother, not love. I don't think anyone's in danger of confusing the two of you, least of all *you!* But you've got a point with the 'in charge' thing." He came around the bed, hands in his pockets, to look at her. Caddy lifted his head, his eyes half-open. "Lighten up, Judy. Relax your grip on things. Your life isn't going to career out of control if you let yourself go a little. Let yourself feel."

She looked hurt, indignant, anguished. So Rob said what he knew would make her angry, because that at least was an emotion with which she felt familiar. And that would put her back on an even keel. He could argue this out with her another time when it *would* be a good idea for them to make love. Now, he accepted grudgingly, wasn't.

"That was just what was wrong with your book," he said. "You write a very good yarn, but you don't spark that emotional involvement that makes the reader really care. The truth is that you can't write it if you don't know how to do it."

She sprang to her feet in full bristle. So did Caddy. "Get out," Judy said, her voice and her eyes lethal.

Rob walked to the door. It took great courage to turn his back on her.

"All right," he said, facing her as he pulled the door open, his expression steady. "But you can't run away from this. The problem's inside you."

"The problem," she shrieked, "is you!" A cardboard carton that had held egg rolls glanced off his shoulder as he started out the door.

She was probably right, he thought as he pitched the carton back inside. He was the problem, all right. He was falling in love.

God help him.

CHAPTER FIVE

"WHAT'S OUR NEXT MOVE?" Wedged in the tight space of a passenger seat in a 727 somewhere over Nebraska, Judy tried to break the silence that didn't seem to be bothering Rob at all but was making her crazy.

He'd seen the car loaded on the flatbed truck early that morning, had discussed other details he wanted Dave to check out for him as they rode to the airport, had shook the P.I.'s hand warmly as they said goodbye.

Then Rob had seen to their luggage, arranged to have Caddy shipped, then led Judy to a gift shop, where she bought a *Writer's Digest,* and he bought a *Wooden Boat Magazine.*

In all that time he'd been flawlessly courteous, chivalrously attentive to her comfort, but he hadn't said a word that didn't have to be said. And she couldn't stand it another moment.

When he finally lifted his eyes from the magazine—dark, lazy eyes brightened by the high-altitude sunset beyond the window—she was afraid he hadn't heard her.

"Our next move," she repeated. "What is it?"

He pursed his lips. Warm, artful lips. She remembered well what they felt like against hers. "I don't know," he said. "A long weekend on the lake to get the starch out of you?"

She backhanded him in the chest.

There was a smile in his eyes that told her he'd only pretended to misunderstand her.

She sighed, disgusted with herself for having risen to the bait.

"I'll tell Brick what we've got," he replied, putting the magazine down in his lap. "I have the film Dave took. I'm pretty sure Brick can put the legal wheels in motion with it. So, again—I'm afraid we wait."

She leaned her head back against the padded rest and groaned. "I'm tired of waiting. I'll bet Daphne is, too."

"I know," he conceded, "but we've got to put this together so that Celeste doesn't have a way out. Otherwise, it'll serve no purpose. We want Daphne and Jenny to be free of her forever."

She rolled her head against the upholstery to look into his eyes. "Do you really want that?"

He arched an eyebrow. "No," he replied after a moment. "That's why I hired a detective, traveled two thousand miles and put up with you. Of course I want to see them free of her. I like Daphne, Jenny's a doll and Vic's a stand-up guy. I'd like to see them happy. And home." He picked up his magazine again.

She believed him. She'd seen him with K.J. and Dave, and she'd been the object of his support in the matter of Caddy. He cared about his friends.

"And I want it," he said, with a quick, grave glance at her, "because you want it."

She studied him, lips parted, her expression just a little stricken.

He shook his head at her before he looked down at his magazine again. "Don't think about it too hard. We don't want you going to pieces at thirty-seven thousand feet."

THE OFFICE WAS IN CHAOS. The moment Rob walked in the door of the *Tyler Citizen* the following morning, he was assailed by what looked like a lynch mob cast by Hollywood. The men wore plaid shirts, bandanas and Western hats. The ladies wore pastel dresses over yards of petticoat.

Oh, God, he thought. *The plane hit a time warp over Kansas and we landed in Dodge City, circa 1865.*

Then K.J. appeared in a sweatshirt, Lee jeans, and a pair of Adidas, shooting down that theory.

"God, am I glad to see you!" he said, indicating the angry mob dispersed throughout the office. "I can't believe them." K.J. lowered his voice as he followed Rob to his desk. "Clog dancing must dull your sense of humor."

Of course. The clog dancers. Rob gave them a quick smile as they closed in around his desk. "Did you forget to do the story on them?" he asked K.J. calmly.

"No," K.J. assured him hurriedly, opening the paper on Rob's desk and pointing to the two-column story right where Rob had suggested he put it. Timberlake Clogged with Dancers, the headline read.

Rob groaned to himself, but looked up at the group with a courteous smile and guessed what their problem was. "You're upset about the headline?"

"No." A man stepped out of the crowd of plaid shirts and reached over Rob's shoulder to turn the newspaper on his desk to the following page. "We're used to that kind of simpleminded play on words, but the cartoon took it a little far."

"Cartoon?"

The man jabbed an index finger at the box at the bottom of the page. An expertly drawn man and woman peered over a kitchen sink into the cutaway of a clogged pipe. 'Shall we call a plumber,' the caption read, 'or the Western Wisconsin Clog Dancers?' Off-stage, a team of clog dancers waited, wrenches in hand.

This time Rob had to make a special effort not to groan aloud. Again, he smiled at the assembly.

K.J. shifted his weight, obviously prepared to defend his harmless if ill-conceived cartoon.

"We want a retraction," the clog dancers' spokesman said.

"You can't retract a cartoon," Rob said reasonably. "Mr . . . ?"

"Morton. Well, an apology, then." Morton was courteous but firm. "Clog dancing is a uniquely American art form. It was born in the Appalachians and combines English, Irish, Scottish and African dance styles. In the old days, the stomping was used in funeral processions to scare away any restless spirits wanting to steal the dead person's soul on its way to the grave." He fixed K.J. with a bland smile. "A service we'll be happy to provide for *you,* unless we get some satisfaction here." He turned back to Rob. "Clog dancing requires skill and stamina, and we're tired of being the butt of everyone's jokes because of the name."

Rob held back a smile at K.J.'s sudden pallor. "I understand you're going to be in town for the Harvest Potluck and Sing-along next week."

Morton frowned. "Yes."

"Well, the *Citizen* comes out again the night before. How about if we give you a free ad for your demonstration dance, do a bigger story with more information on the history of clog dancing and include a photo?"

The man remained unappeased for a moment, but a murmur of approval went around the crowd. Morton turned to his friends, who nodded. He finally nodded himself and agreed to return the following day for an interview with K.J.

The moment the door closed behind the dancers, Rob fell into his chair, his head beginning to thump. K.J. came to sit on the edge of his desk, looking both repentant and indignant.

"Thanks. I was beginning to feel a rope burn on my neck when you walked in."

Rob fixed him with an even look. "You never play with somebody's name, K.J. Yes, I know you see it done, but it isn't cool. And it isn't journalism. Funny joke, but not a suitable cartoon for the *Citizen*."

K.J. nodded. "Okay. I'm sorry. I'm not fired?"

"Don't be stupid," Rob replied, turning the paper over to look through it from page one. "Who'd go for pastries when it's raining?" He turned serious suddenly. "Did Vic check in while I was gone?"

"Nope. Not a word. Saw Stumpy at Marge's last night. Seems to have a lady friend. I can't decide if he's trying to fool us into thinking he's blending into Tyler, or if he really is. Wouldn't that be a hoot?"

Rob dismissed the matter of Stumpy and frowned worriedly over Vic. It had been almost a week since he'd last heard from the detective, and up to this point, he'd been in touch every few days. Rob was beginning to wonder if something was wrong.

"So, YOU TAKE STUPID chances, hare off across the country without regard for personal safety, common sense or the peace of mind of the people who care about you, and you're surprised that I'm upset?" Britt Marshack placed a square, shallow bakery box in the middle of Judy's kitchen table, then faced her, hands on the hips of an ankle-skimming green wool coat.

Judy blinked at her friend's tirade and smiled in an attempt to defuse it. "Britt, you helped me convince Jake not to tell Rob I knew where he was going and intended to follow."

Britt squared her shoulders and shook a finger in Judy's face. "And got in a lot of trouble for taking your side over good sense." Then her anger slipped and she grinned fractionally. "So tell me what happened. And if anything at all of a romantic nature happened between you and Rob, I want to know that, too."

She pulled off her coat and opened the box to reveal what looked like pumpkin pie, but not exactly.

"Pumpkin cheesecake," Britt said in response to Judy's questioning look. "Get a knife and a couple of forks, and tell me everything."

Judy went to the cupboard for plates and utensils, thinking that she couldn't possibly tell her *any*thing, much less everything. She didn't understand it herself, so how could she possibly talk about it? It had been just a kiss. Well, two kisses. And they'd disturbed something deep inside her because she hadn't been quite the same since. And she hadn't heard from him since they'd gotten back last night.

Of course, she hadn't called him, either.

Britt looked across the table as she settled in the opposite chair. Judy tried to appear innocent, but she should have known better. Britt had five children. She was a veteran in battles of evasion and deception.

Britt's eyes widened. "Don't tell me," she said, a smile brightening her face. "You..." She gestured with the knife in her hands. "You . . . did?"

Judy pushed a plate toward her and tried to look severe. "I don't even want that defined further. And no, I did not."

Britt ignored the plate and continued to study her face. "You did *something*. You look different. Just a little...softer."

Judy rolled her eyes, leaned over the table to take the knife from her friend and cut the cheesecake herself. "He kissed me, okay? Twice, if you're into detail. Actually, I kissed him once and he kissed me once. There. You happy?"

She carried a cut slice on the blade of the knife to Britt's plate and dropped it there.

Britt's smile grew even wider. "Enormously. And what else?"

"And that's it." Judy cut her own slice and sat down again with an air of finality. "I don't have time for that sort of thing right now. We're supposed to be trying to get Daphne, Jenny and Vic back, not fooling around."

"I beg to differ with you," Britt said, picking up her fork, "but there's always time for that. You're just such a pushy, bossy thing that you're afraid you might have to relinquish a little power."

Judy made a scornful sound. "Power over what?"

Britt waved her fork in the air. "Your feelings. Your needs. I have you analyzed. Want to hear it?"

"No."

"Fine." Britt pulled the bakery box toward her. "I'll take the rest of this home with me."

As with everything Judy tasted from Britt's kitchen, it was ambrosia. She pulled the box back toward her. "Do you want to see me turn into a rottweiler? I don't need analysis. I understand myself. This tough exterior is a reaction to my needy, pushover mother, and guilt over what happened to Daphne because I wasn't sharp enough to see it."

Britt chewed and swallowed a bite of cheesecake and studied her in surprise. "I missed the guilt part over Daphne. That's unnecessary, isn't it? You weren't even home to know what was going on."

Judy didn't like to think about it, but it had been on her mind a lot in the month her sister had been in hiding. "I *knew* something was wrong with her when I came home for Christmas just before she ran away. Her smile was phoney, she wouldn't meet my eye and she had developed a few nervous habits. But I was busy with my work in Boston, and my relationship with a senior editor had fallen apart. My brain was in turmoil so I took the easy way out. I put it down to her having difficulty adjusting to a stepfather." She expelled a sigh that hurt as it rose out of her. "I just had no idea how much difficulty. If I'd taken the time to think it through . . . I might have figured it out."

Britt reached across the table to cover her hand. "Judy, you're assuming guilt that isn't yours. Your mother was *there*. She's the one who should have figured it out."

Judy met her gaze evenly. "I'm sure she did. That's why she didn't insist Gordon look for Daphne when she ran away. It eliminated the competition."

"Judy." Britt sighed, her eyes filled with sympathy. "I'm sure that's an ugly thing to live with." Then she patted her hand and went on cheerfully, "What you're forgetting is that Daphne has Vic now. She's able to put all that behind her. Well, it'll all be behind her when Celeste's in the slammer and you can be a family again."

Judy turned her hand to take Britt's and squeeze it. She drew back to rest her chin on her palm. "I'm beginning to wonder if that'll ever happen. Every time that poor girl thinks she's put her problems behind her, something else crops up." She straightened and grimaced ruefully. "And I'm her big sister. I can't be happy until I know she's happy."

"All right. I love my family, too. I know how hard it is to be happy when one of them has a problem, but there's no reason you have to isolate yourself in the meantime." Britt dipped her head to try to meet Judy's eye when she tried to ignore her by paying special attention to her plate. "Are you listening? I know unbounded hilarity is out of the question, but there'd be no harm in turning to Rob for support and comfort."

Judy contemplated her last bite of cheesecake. "He's annoyed with me."

"Someone's always annoyed with you. You're very annoying." Britt polished off her cake and pushed the plate aside. She met Judy's censorious glare with a bland smile. "Next excuse?"

Judy dropped her now empty fork with a clatter and folded her arms. "It's complicated."

"You mean it's scary," Britt challenged. "And you've decided you have to be fearless. Well, let me tell you something I learned when I was all alone with four kids, bills that were multiplying faster than rabbits and no more dreams."

Judy waited, resigned. Britt was the bravest woman she knew, and the best friend she'd ever had. She wanted to run from the object lesson, but respect made her stay.

"I could have saved the farm by myself," Britt said, moving to take the chair at a right angle to Judy so that they were closer, "and I could have managed the kids, but I was lonely and afraid. Then Jake appeared, forced himself into my life when I thought he'd just be a complication, and you know what?"

Judy cooperated by asking, "What?"

"I still had all the same problems, but here was someone willing to share them with me." Britt smiled like a schoolgirl. "Someone with hands twice the size of mine who was willing to work with me, with big shoulders I could lean on, and strong arms willing to shelter me whenever I needed to rest." She leaned toward Judy, serious again. "I can't tell you how freeing it is to let yourself believe in somebody else."

Out of arguments, Judy fell back on an old one. "You know how I feel about reporters."

Britt gave her a reprimanding glance as she gathered their plates. "That's a flimsy old excuse, and you know it. He raced to your rescue the day Celeste came to town, and he kissed you twice."

"One of those times I kissed him."

Britt narrowed her gaze. "That fortifies my point. Something's building between you two, and I think you should just relax and let it hap—aahh! What's that?" She jumped as a ratty ball of gray fur leapt into her lap.

Judy reached out to stroke Caddy's head. "Cadillac. I brought him back from L.A." She told Britt briefly about the crusher.

Britt, plastered against the back of her chair, displayed even deeper horror. "You twit! You could have been killed."

At that moment Judy's mind replayed the scene in slow motion as Rob yanked her into his arms, offering his back to the sudden explosion of windows as the concrete slab crunched down on top of the car. While she pictured that image, she heard Britt's words, *with big shoulders I could lean on, and strong arms willing to shelter me...*

Judy felt a little flushed, a little giddy and very confused. When she refocused, Britt was petting Caddy and telling him he was beautiful, even if he did have a reckless and bullheaded mistress.

"Well." Britt finally stood and handed the cat to Judy. "I have to pick Jacob up at day care, then we're meeting Jake for lunch. Enjoy the cheesecake." As Judy walked her to the door, Britt looked over her shoulder and suggested coyly, "Maybe Rob would like a piece."

Judy opened the door for her. "Then maybe you should take him one."

"You," she said, "have the only pumpkin cheesecake in captivity at the moment. It would be nice if you shared."

Judy hugged her, ignoring the suggestion. "Thanks for coming. Say hi to Jake and the kids."

Britt ran down the porch steps and turned to add with a grin as she waved, "I will. You say hi to Rob."

ROB DOWNED THREE ASPIRIN with a sip of tepid coffee and studied the run sheet for the next edition. There was enough advertising to carry it, but less than one quarter of the ads were camera-ready. All the rest had to be designed, passed by the advertiser for approval, probably changed at least once and carried back before they could be pasted up. In a two-man office, that was always a burden—a tolerable one because it meant money, but a burden all the same.

K.J. emerged from the back room, pulling on his jacket. "How late are you staying?" he asked Rob.

"Not much longer," Rob replied. "You have the cornucopia coloring contest results to get from the school tomorrow?"

"Yep. I'll be there first thing. That means you have to pick up doughnuts."

"Done. And let's do a cartoon on parking meters now that Christmas shoppers are starting to come out."

"I don't get the town's stand on that." K.J. zipped his jacket. "With malls springing up all over the place, you'd think they'd take the meters down to keep downtown shopping alive. But, no. Got to have their revenue."

Rob grinned and waved him off. "That's the spirit. But let me look at it first."

K.J. turned up his collar and left the office.

It was dark beyond the windows, and Rob watched for a moment as his readership dotted the streets and sidewalks of Tyler as they headed home for dinner. He thought of his quiet apartment and wondered if it was time he bought a house.

Things wouldn't change much. There still wouldn't be anyone waiting for him when he got home, but it would mean stability, permanence. And he was beginning to think about that.

When he'd first come to Tyler, he'd thought of the move as a stopgap measure while he decided what to do with the rest of his life. He hadn't been bitter over being fired for defying the *Sun-Voice*'s decision to kill the story; he'd taken his stand with full knowledge of what would result. But he'd been anxious to leave Chicago at that point, and all the crafty political manipulations, big and small, that went on there.

So he'd bought the *Tyler Citizen,* but he'd thought he would run it for only two or three years. Weeklies and biweeklies were famous for wearing out their publishers, and he'd never considered himself a small-town kind of guy. The plan was to build up circulation, sell at a profit and find another job on a big metropolitan paper.

He was beginning, however, to make an interesting discovery. He liked it here. His readers were now his friends—a luxury not often afforded a writer on a big-city paper.

Here his readers sat beside him in church, played on his team in ball games, shopped in the same supermarket and went to the same dentist. He liked living beside the people who were his news.

He was beginning to think of Tyler as home.

But home brought to mind the thoughts programmed into a man hitting forty. They weren't politically correct, but he chose not to edit them—he'd been editing all day and he was tired of it.

He saw two children in footed pajamas on the floor in front of a fireplace—a little boy playing with a shaggy dog and a little girl feeding imaginary tea to a well-worn rag doll.

He sat in a recliner reading the paper, and from his chair he could see the kitchen, where a woman puttered in a crisp apron. A blond woman. Judy.

He laughed aloud and put a hand back to rub at the kinks in his neck. Right. Judy in his kitchen in an apron. He'd obviously sniffed too much fixative.

The bell rang over the door, and he looked up to see Judy standing there in a brown wool blazer over a blue turtleneck and jeans, a plastic-wrapped plate balanced on the flat of her hand.

He pushed himself to his feet, set a little off balance by the scene's similarity to his thoughts.

"Hi," he said. He walked around the desk toward her and she met him halfway. She held the plate out to him.

He eyed her warily. "What's this?"

"Don't look so worried," she said with a laugh. "You're afraid I baked it, aren't you?"

He folded his arms. He could be in trouble here if he wasn't careful. And she was smiling; he didn't want to do anything to change that.

"No," he said finally, "but you were a little hostile when we parted company at the airport last night. I can't decide if this means you want to make peace or eliminate me."

She thrust the plate at him with an amused twist of her mouth. "I know poison is supposed to be a woman's weapon, but I'd use other means."

"A tire iron?" he teased. "A baseball bat?"

She gave him that look again, but there was amusement in it. "No, I'd keep you around so I could make you suffer."

The pain in his neck wandered down to his shoulder and he rubbed there unconsciously. "Now there's an interesting idea to contemplate." He peered through the wrap.

"Britt's pumpkin cheesecake," she said, "and I promise you it's to die for. But not at my hands. Do you have coffee to go with it, or shall I run to Marge's Diner for you?"

He was flabbergasted, though he tried to remain cool. He put a hand to her head. "You don't feel yourself failing, do you? Like you're running down a tunnel toward a bright light?"

She acknowledged the jibe with a grin and slapped his hand away. "Very funny. I just...got to thinking about the trip, and realized that I haven't told you that I appreciate what you're doing for Daphne and Jenny."

He couldn't help but stare for a minute. "Well... you're welcome," he said. "And I do have coffee. Want to have a cup and share this with me?"

She looked for a moment as though she would have liked to, then she put a hand to her slim waist and shook her head. "Already had one earlier. And I've got to get back to my book before my publisher demands the advance back."

Disappointment irritated his shoulder and he pulled at it again as he set the plate on his desk.

"Tension headache?" she asked abruptly, putting her purse down on K.J.'s desk.

He felt a glimmer of hope and ran with it. "I'm fine," he said heroically, wincing deliberately as he rubbed at the spot again. "Just a lot to do because I was gone for a few days." That was good. Casually spoken, but with a forlorn note in his voice.

She pushed him toward his chair and tugged on his arm until he sat down. He decided he liked her pushing his body around. She put her hands to his shoulders. Sensation rayed in every direction. He sat still with difficulty.

"Right here?" she asked, tapping a fingertip at the right side of his neck where he'd been rubbing.

He dropped his head forward. "Yeah, that's it."

She began to massage him, her nimble fingers starting at the base of his skull and rubbing in firm little circles until she reached his shoulders. There he felt the nip of her thumb and fingertips from the nape of his neck to his upper arm, then back again, after which she paid special attention to the sore spot.

"I can feel the knot," she said, working it over. Her breath puffed against his temple, and he felt the bump of her breast against the back of his head. His entire body turned to spaghetti.

She pushed his head forward and began the procedure again with grave concentration.

The ministrations she intended to use to relax him were now beginning to charge him with an energy he fought manfully to contain.

Then she put her fingertips to his shoulders and began to work her thumbs along his spinal column. And his body's sensory network came to life and shot his self-control to pieces.

Heat ran along his limbs, into his fingers, up the back of his neck. Still he caught the shreds of his will and held on.

When her fingers went into his hair to massage his scalp, hope was gone. Rob let her go on with it because it felt delicious, but when she stopped and gave his chair a turn toward her to ask clinically, "Feel better?" he caught her waist in his hands and pulled her into his lap. Flames licked everywhere she'd touched.

"Oh, yes," he said, looking into her startled eyes. "Much better. You?"

She did. He could see it in her dark blue eyes. She might even have been hoping for just this result. But he was beginning to know her pretty well. She never let anything be that easy.

"What're you doing?" Her voice had a catch in it, and her eyes had sparks.

"You came to thank me," he said softly, settling her comfortably in the crook of his shoulder. "Now I want to thank you for the massage. But I can't offer pumpkin cheesecake."

Her arm came around his neck. "That's not . . . necessary."

He shook his head at her and whispered, "Oh, yes it is."

It occurred to him that he was becoming addicted to the taste of her mouth. And that it was paradoxical how a mouth used primarily to harass him could be so delicious.

She seemed to enjoy the taste of him, too. Her fingers tightened in his hair. He felt all the old comforts he'd thought he could never have because he was devoted to his job rise up with the drawing power of her lips. He found himself wanting things he'd crossed off the list early in his career.

He wanted her. And even caught in the throes of it, he knew this was passion and not simple desire. He guessed by the little sound of distress she made without moving her lips from his that she understood it, too.

The bell over the office door alerted him to the presence of a visitor. But nothing was going to make him pull away from Judy.

She pulled away from him, scrambling off his lap as though she'd suddenly discovered he was radioactive. She turned to the woman standing at the counter that separated the front of the room from the desks and pasteup table, and sputtered an apology. She was totally flustered. Rob found that amusing and eminently interesting.

"Reverend," she said, her voice thready. "I'm . . . sorry. We were . . ."

The Reverend Sarah Kenton, in a dark wool coat bulging over her advanced pregnancy, raised a hand to stop her. She was smiling, her eyes going from Judy to Rob, then back again. "It was pretty clear what you were doing, and I can't imagine why you'd want to apologize for it. This is the season to give thanks for our blessings—and the man-woman dynamic is one of our greatest gifts.'' She lifted her shoulders in a gesture that exuded happiness.

Sarah was married to Michael Kenton, a drifter who'd come to Tyler a year ago with a secret that had upset the Baron family. In his business, Rob never listened to rumor, and so far he hadn't been privy to the real facts. All he knew was that Michael had made Reverend Sarah a very happy woman. ''That's not just pulpit stuff, you know.'' She patted her bulging tummy. ''It's a personal discovery.''

Rob stood and went to the counter to shake her hand. ''How nice to have you visit the *Citizen*. What can we do for you?''

She handed him a folder. ''The food bank needs contributions for Thanksgiving baskets, and able bodies to help us put them together, then deliver them. I was hoping you could run my plea until Thanksgiving. The press release includes all the drop-off spots, and the bank has opened an account for us for financial donations.''

''I'll give you bottom front page next edition,'' he said. ''Is your committee getting together in the next few days so we can get a picture of empty baskets or something?''

''Tomorrow afternoon?'' she asked. ''The bare shelves of the food bank should make a significant statement.''

Rob took several paces back to his desk to flip the page of his calendar. ''I have an appointment at the high school at two o'clock. After that?''

"Perfect. I'll get my group together." She smiled and patted the counter with a gesture of finality. "See you tomorrow, then. Meanwhile..." She smiled at them over her shoulder as she pulled the door open. "I hope you remember where you were before I interrupted. Bye."

The moment the door closed behind Sarah, Judy picked up her purse from K.J.'s desk.

Rob turned away from the counter to lean against it and watch her as she made a production of straightening the shoulder strap, dropping it on her shoulder, fussing with it.

She was avoiding looking at him and he knew it. She hated that.

So she drew a breath and made herself meet his knowing dark gaze. "From now on," she said stiffly, "please keep your hands to yourself. We're supposed to be allied in the interest of my sister's safety."

"Who," he asked quietly, "was massaging whom?"

She defended her actions with a reasonably spoken, "That was supposed to be therapeutic."

He grinned. "So was the kiss."

She closed her eyes for a moment. She was trying to hold on to her patience, but she also needed a respite from the look in his eyes. "I don't like you," she said, finally opening her eyes and hoping to unsettle him with the simple truth.

Instead, his grin grew a little wider. "You're making it harder and harder for me to believe that. You've got a thing for me, Judy Lowery. Admit it."

"I do," she said, walking around the counter. "It's called hatred. But I tried magnanimously to put that aside because you have done a lot to help Daphne's cause and I appreciate it. You, however, with your inflated, testosterone-poisoned ego, seem to think every move on my part is sexu—"

She stopped because, in a movement so swift she didn't even suspect it, he closed the distance between them, caught her chin in the fingers of one hand, tipped her head back and kissed her into silence.

She lost track of her tirade. Truth be told, she lost track of everything.

"Oh, shut up," he said softly, when he finally raised his head. "And unless you can do pasteup or darkroom work, you'd better get out of here."

She straightened her blazer huffily and marched to the door. "That's the last time I try to deal civilly with you!" she promised as she yanked the door open.

He didn't appear to believe her. "I still have a couple of hours work," he said, following her, "and I'd really rather not be here all night—particularly if I'm not getting anywhere."

"You will never," she said in a quiet voice strangled with new anger, "get *anywhere* with me!" Even she heard the note of melodrama in her declaration.

She stood just beyond the door on the dark sidewalk, and he leaned a shoulder in the open doorway. "Oh, I've gotten in, all right." He touched the tip of a long index finger just above her left breast. "I think I'm right about there." Then as she looked down where he touched, he brought that finger up and flicked her chin in the old, old joke.

"See you," he said, and closed the door in her face.

CHAPTER SIX

SHE WAS GOING TO kill him. Slowly.

Judy contemplated several methods of getting rid of Rob Friedman while she wandered up and down the aisles of the grocery store. Food shopping always made her feel better about things. It wasn't that she was particularly domestic—in fact, she wasn't really much of a cook—but she always felt better if the freezer was full of microwavable meals and the cupboards full of canned goods and Pop-Tarts. Chocolate-peanut-butter Pop-Tarts had seen her through many plot crises, and even a few personal ones.

But she'd have to buy a Pop-Tart plant to be able to get through this one.

Rob was right: he had gotten to her. And not just under her skin, but exactly where he'd said he had. The swell of her left breast still tingled where he'd touched her sweater through her open blazer.

Now, as she pushed the cart, she freed one hand to secure the two buttons.

And she hadn't remembered to ask him if he'd heard from Vic. That was part of what infuriated her about him—the fact that he knew where her sister was and she didn't, and that he wouldn't tell her where Daphne was because it was safer for her not to know.

She *hated* having that kind of decision made for her. And she hated to have to invest that kind of trust in someone else—particularly a man who represented everything she despised.

The tingle on her left breast mocked her at that final thought, and she remembered how he'd snatched her away from the car crusher, how he'd flown to L.A. on a moment's notice to check out the Mercedes and how he'd helped her arrange to have Caddy shipped home. And she remembered in sharp detail every one of his kisses. Four of them now. She hated that she was counting.

She looked up to find herself in the paper-products aisle, confronted by row upon row of disposable diapers. She sighed dispiritedly. When Daphne had come back into her life, Judy had been ecstatic to have family again. And, certain no life-style could be more satisfying than that of a single woman at the top of the bestseller list, she'd accepted that her niece would satisfy the wistful desire for a child.

But more and more now, as she watched Britt with her children, Judy found herself wishing—and she couldn't quite believe this—that she had her own.

She puffed out a sigh. It was both cleansing and frustrating to admit it to herself. She clung to the thought that this notion had developed because Jenny was gone—had been in hiding with her mother for a month now, and that she, Judy, simply missed her.

But honesty made her admit to herself that that wasn't it. This had nothing to do with Jenny. This was some deep-down longing that she'd suppressed for years because her own life had been too unsettled. But it had surfaced now and was taunting her with a vengeance.

That was Rob's attraction for her, she told herself bracingly as she reached for a roll of paper towels. Her maternal side was seeing him as a source for acquiring a baby.

But her body remembered every place he'd ever touched her, and, since she was torturing herself anyway, she admitted that her preoccupation with Rob had nothing to do with his appeal as a potential sperm donor.

It was him. She was attracted to him. It didn't help that he'd accused her of having a *thing* for him.

Judy couldn't deny it. She'd gotten to the point where her libido ignited if she was within ten yards of him. The knowledge was debilitating. He was a reporter, after all. An arrogant, smart-mouthed reporter.

She shook her head and shuddered as she fell into line at the checkout stand.

Annabelle Scanlon, in line in front of her, noted the gesture and tutted sympathetically. Her blue eyes sparkled and her dark curls bobbed as she put short, plump arms around Judy. Annabelle was the postmistress and knew everything about everyone.

"Catching cold?" she asked. "Weather's taken a turn, all right. Be snow on the ground before you know it." She took a can from her cart and placed it in Judy's on top of the box of Double Stuff Oreos. "You fix that for yourself tonight." She cast a disparaging glance at Judy's jeans and wool blazer. "Got to get yourself warm clear through. You might consider a real coat."

She turned as the salesclerk greeted her and began to load her purchases onto the conveyor belt.

Judy looked down at the can Annabelle had put among her purchases and smiled thinly. She was supposed to recover from her feelings for Rob with chicken soup?

With the back seat of her car filled with groceries, Judy drove home and unloaded her cache. Then she headed to Marge's for chicken fried steak and mashed potatoes and gravy because she felt self-destructive. Afterward, she went on to the department store in Sugar Creek just because she wasn't ready to go home.

She bought gifts for Daphne and Jenny as an act of faith that they would be home in time for Christmas. Judy imagined them in the house Vic had put a deposit on before having to leave Tyler without warning.

Daphne had described it to her in detail, and Judy pictured a tall tree with all the trimmings, gaudily lit against the night. And they would all be there.

Her mind's eye traveled the huge living room, seeing Vic with his Latino good looks, Jenny sitting on his forearm as he held her up to adjust a decoration. Daphne fussed around, looking like an angel in a red dress. Britt and Jake stuffed presents under the tree while their children sang and harassed each other. Rob came around the tree with a cup of punch in one hand. With the other, he tugged a tall, chunky blond in a green wool dress after him. Oh, God. It was her.

Judy made her purchases, put them in the trunk of her car and went home, feeling pursued. She couldn't get away from him, even in her thoughts! She looked at herself in the rearview mirror, prepared to deliver a stern lecture on getting it together.

And that's when she noticed the headlights. She'd seen them behind her when she'd been heading out to Sugar Creek and made the stop at the highway, and she'd seen them behind her when she'd stopped to turn into the department store's parking lot.

And here they were again, though she couldn't distinguish the vehicle, except to guess that it was a truck or a van, judging by the height of the headlights. She knew they were the same lights because the right one was slightly dimmer than the left. What were the odds that the owner of the car would have been headed to the same store, shopped the same amount of time and left right behind her?

Judy accepted with a dry gulp in her throat that she was being followed.

She also accepted that she was frightened. *It's probably just Stumpy,* she told herself bracingly. And after a month of watching his sorry efforts to watch *her,* she found it hard to think of him as a threat, no matter what Brick said.

She checked the rearview mirror again as she stopped at the light at Main Street. The car pulled up right behind her.

This was not Stumpy, who drove a silver Buick. This vehicle, higher and somehow more threatening than Stumpy's car had ever seemed, held a passenger as well as a driver.

The light turned green and she accelerated, practically racing toward the downtown area. She certainly didn't want to be pulled over or forced off the road!

But the driver seemed content to simply follow, staying a car's length behind her, but shadowing her as she turned instinctively onto Gunther.

Judy tried to remain calm. She couldn't go home; that was clear. And the sheriff's office was in the other direction.

Rob came instantly to mind, and she remembered their very recent argument for only a moment before she dismissed it and decided she'd rather put up with his smug superiority than find herself on the edge of town still being followed.

She drove past the *Tyler Citizen* office and swore when she saw that it was dark and the red Escort was gone. She turned onto Second Street and headed for Rob's apartment. She knew he lived somewhere in the modern twelve-plex a block or two beyond Granny Rose's Bed and Breakfast.

She screeched to a stop in front of the building, wondering for a panicky moment if he lived upstairs or down, and if she could get from her car to the building before one of the men caught her.

Then she saw Rob, his figure outlined by an old globed streetlight as he walked toward the apartment building, hands in the pockets of a dark parka.

Her heart leapt with relief. She jumped out of her truck and ran straight at him.

For a moment, Rob thought it was the fantasy he'd entertained for the last few hours come to life. Judy had changed her mind about him. She could admit that she cared about him, after all. And that she wanted him.

But he saw as he opened his arms to her that her eyes were wide with fear and not passion.

"I'm being followed!" she said breathlessly, turning in his arms to point at a dark van that sped past them with a squeal of tires.

Rob pushed her aside and ran into the street to catch a glimpse of the license plate, but the car was too far away to note anything but the distinctive make and color. A Dodge Caravan. Dark blue or black.

He went back to her and put his arm around her. She didn't resist. She *was* frightened. "Did you see a face?" he asked.

She shook her head. She expelled a sigh and her breath puffed out in the cold night air. "No. I noticed them when I came out of the mall at Sugar Creek. He's got a bad light, and I remembered seeing him behind me on my way there. I'm sure it wasn't Stumpy."

"No, it wasn't." Rob pulled her toward the building. "Come on up. We'll call Brick."

Brick was off duty, but another deputy took the report and Rob's description of the car.

"You think Celeste is back already and getting more serious?" Judy asked when he was done. She sat primly on the edge of his sofa, her arms wrapped around herself.

"My guess is it's a scare tactic," he said. He filled the kettle and put it on the stove, then he cranked up the thermostat. "They want you to panic and go running to Daphne to make sure she's safe so they can follow you there."

"Well." Judy boosted herself backward a little stiffly into the corner of the sofa. "I fooled them, didn't I?" She laughed with self-deprecation. "Except for the panic part."

"If you'd panicked," he said, his voice diminishing as he disappeared into a hallway. He was back in a minute with a blanket and continued, "you'd have gone home where you'd have been alone and vulnerable."

"I almost did that," she admitted, raising her arms as he dropped the doubled-over blanket onto her lap. "Then I thought better of it. If I'd really been thinking, I'd have gone to the sheriff's office."

He gave her an amused smile, then went back to the kitchen to take down cups and a tub of instant cocoa mix. "You were thinking," he said. "Just not with your head."

She understood the implication and didn't see, in light of how she'd run straight into his arms, that she could deny that she'd been following her heart and not her head. She'd followed a gut instinct toward safety. And that had led her here.

"I forgot to ask you," she said, choosing to let his statement go unchallenged, "if you've heard from Vic? Did K.J. hear from him while we were gone?"

He brought her a steaming mug of the creamy brown liquid, then sat beside her and put his cup on the coffee table.

"No," he said. She heard the reluctance in his voice, though he tried to cover it with an easy matter-of-factness she didn't buy for a moment. "But any number of things could be causing that. They're a good mile from the nearest phone and the weather could have gone bad."

"Don't give me that," she said. "He has a cell phone. Why would he go a mile...?"

"Cell phones can be monitored," Rob replied calmly. "He didn't take it with him."

She wanted to argue, but that made sense. Still, she felt edgy and anxious. "Well, I can't believe they'd worry us like this if they had another choice."

"I'm not worried," he insisted, reaching for his cup. "And you shouldn't be, either. Even if they were in danger, and we have no reason to believe they are, that's Vic's area of expertise, remember? He survived for three days with an army of drug dealers after him and he not only made it, but he brought them down."

"He didn't have a woman and a child with him," Judy reminded him. She sipped at the cocoa to lubricate her tight throat.

He reached an arm along the back of the sofa and stroked her hair. "That probably only makes him sharper, more determined to come through."

Judy turned to him, wanting more than anything in the world at that moment to throw herself into his arms and sob out her worry for her sister and her family, her own fear and loneliness. But the rule was No Surrender. This alliance with Rob was only temporary, and Judy didn't dare break her rule in the interest of a relationship that would be over when her family was reunited.

She sat forward, beyond the reach of his hand, and sipped at her cocoa, trying to make the movement look casual. "So, where were you coming from at this hour?"

He wasn't fooled. She saw his dark gaze acknowledge her withdrawal without revealing what he thought about it.

"I went to Olsen's Supermarket," he replied. "They're renovating and enlarging the deli and coffee shop, and I promised to go by and have a look."

She glanced at her watch. "At almost eleven?"

He grinned. "A reporter's work is never done. You want to share the bed, or do you want it to yourself?"

She answered that with a speaking glance.

He nodded and stood. "Right. Somehow I knew you'd be narrow about it. I'll find some bedding."

"No, wait." She stood, too, and for the second time that night he thought a fantasy might be realized.

"I can't stay here," she said, picking her purse up off the floor.

"Why not?" He moved between her and the door as she went toward it. "You can't go home."

"I'll have to some time. I have a deadline to meet and I have to be in touch with my editor. And I have to feed my cat." She tried to wave him out of her way. "Thanks for the cocoa, but I have to go home now."

He stood firmly in her way, shaking his head. "That's out of the question. Tomorrow morning I'll take you to pick up your laptop and the cat. You can stay in the back room at the *Citizen* and work until I'm through for the day."

She strove for patience. "Rob, I'm not being deliberately difficult, but this has to be disruptive for you and—"

"You've disrupted my life," he said, "from the moment I met you. I can deal with this. You're the one who's going to find it hard."

She was determined not to let him upset her. "I'm the one," she said, trying to push past him, "who isn't going to do it."

He held a hand to the door as she tried to open it. "I'm afraid you have to. The only way for me to be sure you're safe is to keep you with me."

"I don't *want* to be with you."

"Judy, you came to me."

"Yes, but just looking for—for..."

"Yes?" He raised an eyebrow, pretending simple interest.

"Muscle," she said, knowing that was only half-true. "I wanted them to think I wasn't alone."

He studied her a moment, his expression growing suddenly more serious. "Judy, you aren't alone. They apparently got the message. Did you?"

Judy was suddenly very tired and very confused. What was he talking about? She'd always been alone. Her father had been with her for such a short time, her stepfather had gone out of her life violently, her sister had disappeared and her mother had never really been there.

Sometimes, in the sanctuary of her dreams, there'd been a man who'd held her and loved her and protected her. But when she opened her eyes she was always faced with the sharp reality of her loneliness.

And now, suddenly, this annoying man was like a twin she couldn't shake. Except that he was bigger, stronger, more stubborn than she was. She wasn't sure why she found comfort in that. She just knew he couldn't know she did.

She folded her arms. "All right," she said grudgingly. "If I can be alone in the bed, I'll stay."

"Good. Can you cook?"

"Do you like your Pop-Tarts light or dark?"

"God help us."

JUDY HAD NEVER WORKED in such comfort. She doubted that Caddy had, either. The cat lay in her lap between her stomach and the laptop balanced on her knees.

Judy sat on the flowered sofa in the back room of the *Tyler Citizen* office, her feet crossed on a stack of newspapers. At her elbow were a cup of coffee and a cream-cheese danish.

From the front office came the occasional sounds of laughter and the lively strains of Hootie and the Blowfish.

Rob and K.J. had been going from darkroom to office all morning as photos were developed and ads took shape. Judy marveled at their equanimity as advertisers called with changes and publicity chairmen of social clubs and service organizations brought in last-minute news.

When Judy had witnessed this, having come to the front office to take a call from Britt, she'd pointed to the sign over Rob's desk. "It says News Must Be in by Monday Afternoon to Appear in Thursday's Paper. Why don't you stick to that?"

He'd shrugged, chewing and swallowing a bite of maple bar. "It seems so important to them. And if I can call the shots, I'll do my best to give them what they want."

"If it's that important to them," she said, "they'd have it in on time."

He'd laughed. "I don't know. You ever been in Britt's kitchen when the kids come home from school? I figure any woman who can fit something besides family into her daily schedule deserves my cooperation."

Judy had returned to the back room feeling properly chastised.

In the three days she'd spent living with Rob, traveling back and forth to work with him, she'd learned a lot about the weekly newspaper business, and she'd made a few discoveries about the man.

She liked him. And this was something that went beyond the attraction between them, and their efforts on her sister's behalf that bound them together. This was strictly person to person, man to woman, friend to friend.

But, despite evidence to the contrary in his kisses, she wasn't sure he liked her. He was hospitable and kind and protective—all the things a good host would be. But he wasn't softening toward her in the way she was beginning to feel toward him. Occasionally she would find him studying her, his expression caught somewhere between suspicion and anger.

Her thoughts were suddenly shattered as a man's accusing shouts rang from the front office. "It was a stupid argument between kids!"

Judy moved Caddy onto the sofa and went to the door to listen.

"Your son struck his girlfriend with a closed fist, Mr. Brooks," came Rob's quiet reply. "And he's twenty. That's assault, and that's what we reported."

"I asked you not to!" the man shouted.

K.J. wandered out of the darkroom and joined Judy at the door.

"What's going on?" he whispered.

Judy mimed an expression of uncertainty.

"Yes, you did." Rob's voice again.

"My boy lost his job because of you!"

"Your son lost his job because he proved himself incapable of acting in a civilized manner, not because I reported it."

"I ought to punch *you* all the way to Sugar Creek!"

"You're welcome to try."

Rob guessed that the sudden appearance of Judy and K.J. on either side of him was supposed to be interpreted by his villifier as backup. He tried to ignore them, hoping Brooks's temper wouldn't be doused by their presence.

Rob was spoiling for a fight every bit as much as his angry advertiser was, though for very different reasons. He'd maintained his equanimity for three nights and two days with Judy just feet away from him—just beyond his touch, physically and emotionally.

And he didn't think he could take it another moment. She'd been helpful and compassionate and understanding, though he knew she was worried about Daphne and Jenny, and he found himself wanting to hold her, found himself tortured by the memory of the taste of her mouth.

And the man who stood in front of him was well-known in Tyler as a father who repeatedly bought his son out of trouble and blamed everyone else for the problem.

"Well?" Rob prodded.

Judy and K.J. both turned to him as though he were insane for verbally poking the volatile man.

"I spend three hundred dollars a month with you!" Brooks said, pointing a stubby finger in Rob's face. "But you know what? I'm not spending another dime, I don't care what the damn contract says. How do *you* like being betrayed?"

"*You* know what?" Rob said, pushing K.J. aside to go to the pile of mail on his desk. He extricated a business check, tore it in half and handed it to Brooks. "That's your payment to the *Citizen* for last month's advertising. Take it as a parting gift from me. And get the hell out of my office."

Brooks went purple with rage, then turned and stalked out the door.

Rob stood there with his companions, the three of them momentarily silenced by the backwash of Brooks's unreasoning anger.

Then K.J. cleared his throat and asked gravely, "That wasn't *my* three hundred dollars for this week, was it?"

Rob turned and pushed him toward the darkroom. "It could be if you don't get back to work. And what's with you?" Rob asked, facing Judy, hands on his hips. "I thought you were on a deadline, too. What are you doing out here?"

Judy looked up into his turbulent dark eyes and saw the edge of ill temper. This had nothing to do with Brooks, she realized. Rob was clearly annoyed with her.

Frustrated and confused herself, she replied aggressively, "Well, excuuuse me and K.J. for coming to your defense."

He rolled his eyes. "Thank you, but K.J. gets knocked on his butt in such situations, and I'm not sure how competitive you'd be if there wasn't talking involved."

"Depends on what I'm defending." She looked straight into his eyes and enjoyed upsetting him. "I'm sorry the guy *didn't* punch you, then we'd both know how good I can be."

They stared at each other for a moment, Judy surprised that she was willing to admit that much, Rob clearly shaken that she had.

K.J. hooked an arm around her and pulled her with him toward the back room. "Come on," he said, loud enough for Rob to hear. "Soon as I'm finished, we'll head into the sunset and find a place where we're appreciated. I'll go to work for the *Dallas Times-Herald,* and you can write some hot murder mystery involving oil or something."

"Violence in the Vinaigrette?"

K.J. groaned. "Not that kind of oil, Judy."

SHE KNEW THINGS WOULD GET difficult when she and Rob finally went home together. They were driving her truck because it was more dependable than Daphne's car. It was after eleven, and though Caddy was sound asleep in her arms, Judy wasn't remotely tired. Every nerve ending in her body seemed sharply alert.

Rob was quiet, grim.

The town of Tyler had shut down for the night several hours ago, and it was a short, dark ride home.

"Want a cup of tea before you go to bed?" Judy asked as they walked into the dark apartment and the gray cat jumped down out of her arms.

"No, thanks," Rob said stiffly. "I don't go to bed anyway, I go to sofa."

As he said the words he flipped on the living room light. Caddy was already heading to the middle sofa cushion, where he promptly curled up, purring loudly.

"And that I have to share with a flea-ridden cat," Rob continued, pulling his jacket off and tossing it over a chair. "But, please. Have tea if you want to."

"Why don't we switch tonight?" she suggested amenably. "I'll take the sofa, and you can—"

"No," he said, cutting her off.

"But I don't mind..."

"No."

The tension was palpable. Judy understood it, but didn't know how to deal with it. Because she had this rule.

So making the move to deal with it, she thought with what she considered clear reason, should be up to him. If he conceded first, she might be able to bend the rule.

But all he could do was snarl. Maybe he had his own rule.

He sank into a chair and looked through the mail he'd picked up from the box downstairs.

She stalked into the bedroom, yanked a pillow and the top blanket off the bed, carried them into the living room and dropped them in a corner of the sofa. The edge of the blanket covered Caddy. He didn't move.

Rob looked up at her from his chair, his eyes dark with impatience. "I said..."

She ignored him and walked away, going back into the bedroom to pick up her train case and a change of clothes for the following day. Her arms full, she turned to the door, then stopped abruptly.

Rob stood in the middle of the open doorway, arms folded belligerently.

"I said no," he repeated.

The case in one hand and the clothes over her other arm, she looked up at him, letting the confusion and frustration he made her feel dissolve into simple anger. It was so much easier to cope with.

"And you think that makes it law, I suppose," she challenged.

He nodded. "I do. It's my place."

"You invited me here," she reminded him quietly, though inside her everything was rioting. "I'm your *guest.*"

"Then, as my *guest,* shouldn't you be considerate and grateful and try to cooperate?"

"You're obviously uncomfortable on the sofa." She pointed toward it with the train case. "I, on the other hand, wouldn't mind sleeping on it with my cat, who is not flea-ridden because I powdered him down the day before yesterday. Now, if you'll just step out of..."

She tried to push him aside with the case. He put a hand to the molding, blocking her escape.

"Put your things down," he said quietly, "make your tea and go to bed—in the bed."

They were so close that she could feel the heat from his body. Tension crackled from him.

Her own body felt alive with currents of stress and anticipation. "If you don't let me pass," she said, her voice breathy, "I'll go home. Then if Celeste's men find me, it'll be all your fault."

"No, it'd be your fault," he corrected, still blocking her way, "because you placed your own petty defenses before your sister's and your niece's safety." He fixed her with an accusatory look, then dropped his hand and walked away.

She stared at the empty doorway a moment, then considered running for the front door. But she dismissed the notion instantly. It would be stupid.

She turned to drop her things on the bed and stalked after him into the kitchen. He stood at the sink, filling the kettle.

"Petty defenses?" She repeated his words a decibel louder and a register higher than he'd spoken them, and followed him from sink to stove as he put the kettle on a burner and turned the knob under it.

He reached overhead for a pair of mugs. "You're denying that you're falling in love with me." He put the mugs on the counter. She moved from behind him to his side to look into his face. But all she could see was a set profile.

"How would you have any idea what's going on inside me?" she demanded. "All you've done is snarl at me all day. Why do you suppose that is? Maybe this is a case of it takes one to know one."

She'd hoped to elicit surprise or embarrassment by turning the issue on him, but all he did was shrug a shoulder as he dropped a tea bag into one of the mugs. "I told you that day at the lake that I thought we could have something together." He turned to lean both hands on the counter behind him and look at her directly. "I kissed you."

She remembered that vividly. She wanted it again. But his kisses made her feel boneless and mindless, and she had this rule . . .

She dropped her eyes and folded her arms. "Well, I kissed *you* once."

He laughed lightly. "Right. And scared yourself to death."

"I did not."

He reached into another cupboard for a container of powdered coffee and gave her a skeptical side glance. "Yes, you did. God forbid you should ever break your rule and surrender any part of yourself to someone else. Particularly an emotion. Particularly to me."

"Why should I?" she asked. "You won't let me out of your sight, but all you can do is grump at me because there are no *real* feelings for me on your part. You're just bound by a promise you made Daphne."

He took a step away from the counter and planted his hands loosely on his hips. His eyes darkened even further, and a muscle tightened in his jaw. "That's a very faulty assessment of the situation," he said quietly. "I'll rectify it if you think you can handle the truth."

She, too, took a step away from the counter and dropped her hands to her sides. "You think you can admit the truth?"

He hadn't wanted to do this—not just yet. Because he thought interest between a man and a woman should develop in the right surroundings, not in the middle of a murder investigation.

But feelings for her were growing inside him despite the conditions, and trying to ignore them was making him crazy.

He didn't know what to call it. *Love* was a scary word. And was it the right one anyway to describe this roiling of emotion? This frustration that made him laugh one minute and want to shout at someone the next? Did love make you unrecognizable to yourself? Apparently.

Because all he had to do was look at her now. Her features were carefully schooled to reveal nothing, but her blue eyes were soft despite the forced belligerence, and when they looked into his, he saw honest feeling there. He saw love.

He caught her arms and pulled her gently to him. Something flared in her eyes, but she didn't resist.

He saw her swallow, felt her hands rest lightly at his waist. He threaded his fingers into her hair and shaped her head in his hand.

He felt the tips of her breasts against his chest, her knee between his, the warm puff of her breath against his chin. She was trembling.

"Do you think," he asked softly, "that you'll be able to admit what you feel when I ask you?"

"If you can," she whispered, "I can."

She wasn't giving an inch—at least consciously. And he hadn't intended to, but then he'd never intended to like her, much less love her.

He lowered his head and opened his mouth on hers. Her arms came around his back and he felt her lean slightly against him for balance and better access.

It occurred to him with stunning clarity that he could go through life just this way, with Judy Lowery wrapped around him, leaning on him.

Judy wanted to prove that she could become involved with him without giving up a part of herself. That she could lean into him and hold him, and share these kisses that lived in her memory for days.

But when she felt his fingers tighten in her hair, felt the hand splayed against her back crush her to him, felt the kiss reach deep inside her to spread warmth in every little corner of her being, she felt the change begin to take place.

Hope billowed inside her. The future seemed suddenly a friendlier place. Angry thoughts softened and seemed suddenly less important. She heard laughter and music, smelled flowers, tasted...love.

She pulled away with a start and looked into his eyes, her own big and startled.

"What do you feel?" he asked, catching her hands before she was completely out of reach. "Now. Quick. Without taking time to think."

"Scared," she replied honestly. "Upset." And that didn't begin to describe it. Tears were just a breath away. It wasn't as easy to bend the rule as she'd thought; she'd held fast to it for so long. So she asked too quickly and a touch defensively, "What do *you* feel?"

When he dropped her hands and let his head fall back in exasperation, she folded her arms protectively and looked down at the floor. "You make me feel...warm, hopeful. I'm afraid to feel that. I know harsher realities."

"That was life with your mother," he said. "Someone who never put you and Daphne first. We're talking about life with me."

Life with him? Her eyes widened. "We are?"

He was almost as surprised as she was, but it took him only a moment to consider and reply aggressively, "Yeah. We are. And you want to know what I'm thinking? I'm thinking that I love you. And I also think that if you could let go of that prickly armor and let it happen, you could love me."

She stared at him, and he could see in the depths of her eyes that she wanted to believe him. But she couldn't quite muster the faith. He guessed if he'd grown up the way she had, he might find it difficult, too. Fortunately, the newspaper business had taught him patience.

The kettle screamed in his ear. He reached out to switch it off, and poured the hot water into their cups. When he turned to hand the tea to Judy, she still stood in the same spot, her eyes unfocused. A tear slid down her right cheek.

She came to awareness suddenly, took the tea from him with a glare and exclaimed, "This is all your fault, you know."

He studied her tousled hair and the disconcerted look in her eyes and smiled. "I hope so," he said.

CHAPTER SEVEN

ROB KNEW HE HAD turned the kettle off. So why was it still whistling? He tried to turn over and couldn't. There was a weight on the small of his back.

Then, miraculously, the shrill sound stopped. But in its place came a sharp shove to his shoulder.

"Rob! Rob! Caddy, get off him." There was an ill-tempered whine of displeasure, the weight was removed from his back, then the room was bathed in light. He turned in protest, shading his eyes against the glare, and found Judy standing over him in gray sweats. She was holding the cordless phone.

"It's Dave," she said under her voice. "He sounds upset."

Rob came awake and sat up, snatching the phone from her. "Dave? What is it?"

"It's what isn't," Dave replied.

Rob tried to clear his brain. "Huh?"

"My garage," Dave said. "It is no more. Burned to the ground with the Mercedes in it. Fortunately, I'd left some stuff on the ground I was too lazy to pick up, so I parked my Caddy on the street last night. It's my guess your friend the rich broad has been here."

Rob was suddenly completely awake. "No!" he said.

"Yes," Dave corrected. "But we've got my pictures,

and whoever did this for her dropped the top of a gas can. They're taking it away for fingerprints.''

That was good, but would it tie Celeste to Trey's murder or just incriminate one of her thugs? Rob wasn't sure.

He swore again. "Are you okay? Did your house go up, too?"

"No. Fortunately, the garage is detached, but I had lots of great combustibles in it. I smelled the smoke, but by the time I got to it, the car was engulfed. It's still too hot for me to look, though I'm sure the brake line's melted."

"Dave, I'm sorry."

"Not your fault. Get this lady."

"I will. I promise."

"I'll be in touch about the fingerprints."

"Thanks. Take care of yourself, Dave."

"Yeah. You, too. And take care of Judy. I'm coming for her if she loses interest in you."

Judy didn't know what to make of the ironic glance Rob sent her before he said goodbye to Dave and hung up the phone. The rest of Rob's side of the conversation had sounded so grave.

"What?" she demanded as he leaned against the back of the sofa in the tangle of blankets and ran a hand over his eyes.

"Dave's garage mysteriously caught fire," Rob replied. He glanced up at the clock over the television. It was quarter past two.

"Oh, no." She sank down beside him. "Dave sounded okay."

Rob nodded. "He's fine. But his garage is gone."

She felt relieved that Dave wasn't hurt, but she suspected the worst about their evidence. "The car?"

"Burned to a shell," he said wearily. "Brake line melted. Gone."

Judy leaned an elbow on the back of the sofa and dropped her head on her forearm. She imagined Daphne and Jenny and Vic, marooned in some wilderness cabin somewhere, waiting to come home. And waiting. She closed her eyes.

She felt Rob's hand on her hair, rubbing gently. "We've still got the pictures. Don't lose faith."

"How did they know about the car?" she asked. "Were we followed to California?"

He shook his head, his eyes hardening. "I don't think so. It's my guess Celeste has bought a lot of people along the way. Either she bought Whitsett, too, and he told her we'd been there, or Sheriff Ryder saw the car leave town on the flatbed, drew his own conclusion and called her."

"But how did they know Dave had stored the car?"

"If it was Whitsett, he heard us make the arrangements. If it was Ryder, he might have just followed the flatbed to Dave's. It's only about fifty miles."

Rob stood abruptly, wearing a long-sleeved white thermal shirt and white cotton briefs. He was dialing the phone as he moved.

Judy was about to make a teasing remark about his choice of sleepwear, hoping to cover the flare of desire she felt at the sight of his long, strong legs and tight, cotton-covered backside, when a loud, reverberating crash shocked her out of her thoughts.

Three men in black burst into the room, and she felt her arm nearly torn from its socket as Rob reached for her and yanked her behind him.

The largest of the three closed in on them as the other two remained flanking the door. "No one has to get hurt,'' he said in a high, raspy voice at odds with his large proportions. ''Just give me the pictures.''

Rob was moving backward as the man advanced, and it took Judy just an instant to realize he was pushing her toward the bedroom and, presumably, a door she could close behind her as she ran away or called for help, or whatever course of action she chose.

''What pictures?'' Rob asked.

''Don't be cute,'' the man said.

Rob grinned. ''Can't help it. I just am. Though I can't say it pleases me that *you* think so.''

Judy wanted to hit him, since she couldn't reach the thug advancing on him. How dare he be clever at a time like this.

The thug grabbed a fistful of Rob's T-shirt and pulled him right up against him. ''The pictures,'' he said again in a squeak.

Watching the brute's narrow brown eyes from behind Rob's shoulder, Judy was surprised when a small move on Rob's part made the beady eyes widen to saucer size. The man's mouth took on the same shape, then his complexion went from white to purple and he half fell against Rob.

Rob removed his fist from the man's stomach and let him fall. Then he gave Judy a backward shove into the bedroom and turned to face the other two men, who dove at him.

Judy heard the nasty, flat sound of fists hitting flesh as her eyes scanned the room for a weapon. She was sure her eyes had passed over one in the past three days while not completely registering it as such—and then she spotted it in the corner of the room near the closet. A baseball bat! A corner of her mind removed from panic remembered Rob's suggestion once that her weapon of choice would be a blunt instrument.

When she ran back into the living room, one man had Rob's arms pinned behind him. As the second man advanced on him, Rob raised both feet and kicked at him.

Judy brought the bat down with all her might on the shoulder of the man holding Rob. He cried out in pain, loosened his grip and fell to his knees. Judy hit him again as Rob lunged at the second man. The bat broke in two and Judy's prey went down.

The man with the squeaky voice was on all fours, shaking his head and trying to focus on the action. Judy hit him with what was left of the bat and he fell over onto his back.

She looked up to see Rob standing over the third man, who appeared to be out cold.

Then she blinked as a pair of sheriff's deputies ran into the room. They stopped short just inside the door at the sight of the inert bodies strewn around the floor.

The older of the two officers grinned at Rob as his partner hunched down to assess the health of the body closest to the door. "Why'd you bother calling? Next time I have a B and E, I'll call *you*. Brick's on his way, incidentally. He told us to call him in if anything moved on this."

Rob picked up the cordless phone still on the entertainment center, where he'd placed it when the men broke in. The light was on, indicating an open line.

"I was calling to leave a message for Brick," he said, then put the phone to his ear. "Wanda?" he asked. He smiled. "Yeah, thanks. You were right. We did need help. Here, I'll give you Billings." He handed the phone to the older deputy.

Judy was beginning to feel that same deep-down tremor that had overtaken her after Celeste and Gunnar descended on her home over a week ago. She tried to buoy herself by remembering that she hadn't been afraid when she'd felt Rob needed defending, but it didn't seem to help.

He came to put a hand to her cheek and ask solicitously, "Are you all right?"

She drew a breath to pull herself together and gestured with the hand that still held half a baseball bat. "I'm fine. I hope you're not next in the batting lineup, or anything."

He ran his thumb gently over her cheekbone, as though his attention were centered on something other than the words she'd spoken. Then he replied with a smile, "No. But Hank Aaron signed that bat. I think he'd approve of your swing. It must have hit one too many line drives for it to break like that."

She couldn't even return his smile because under all her concern about Rob's safety and hers was the simple horror that she, who talked big but was at heart a peaceful woman, had struck two men with a baseball bat!

"I'll make some coffee," she said, and handed him the splintered wood. She stepped over the squeaky-voiced man's prone form and went into the kitchen, trying to suppress the tremors, at least until after the deputies were finished.

An hour later, the three men littering the carpet had been removed, and she and Rob, who'd slipped on a pair of jeans, sat together on the sofa, with Brick occupying the hassock in front of the big chair because Caddy occupied the chair itself.

Judy folded her arms and tried to give Brick her report calmly and logically.

Rob thought he knew what was wrong with Judy. Not that whatever it was was visible to Brick. He was taking notes as Judy answered all his questions in a quiet, unimpassioned voice. She sat in the middle of the sofa, still in her gray sweats, her bare feet tucked under her, her face pale but composed.

And that was how Rob knew the attack had upset her. She was never composed. She had two modes that he was aware of—laughing and argumentative. She could be quiet and serious as she was now, but he'd seen that only when they'd talked about Daphne's safety or discussed their own relationship. And this wasn't about that—or was it?

Her voice wavered when she answered Brick's questions about the bat. Rob put an arm around her shoulders, and though she didn't pull away, she did nothing to acknowledge his touch. It was as though that careful insulation that stood between them in their relationship was somehow involved in this. She appeared to be coping and functioning, but he knew she was doing it from a comfortable distance.

"Okay, that's it." Brick flipped his notebook closed, tucked it into the pocket of a battered old football jacket and leaned forward, elbows on his knees, to fix them with a look that was both triumphant and concerned. "Now, I have a few things to tell you."

Judy sat forward. "What?"

"A warrant's been issued for Celeste Huntington's arrest. They couldn't get through to Dave so they called me."

"We just spoke to him before the goons arrived." Rob sat forward and explained about the fire. "They picked her up on the strength of the photographs?"

Judy gasped. "The pictures did it?"

"They'll support the story, but what gives the San Diego P.D. its most powerful evidence is that the sheriff caved."

"You're kidding."

"Nope. Told 'em everything. Seems Daphne had taken a cab to a lunch meeting the afternoon Trey died, but Ryder, aware of the family's prestige and position, tracked Celeste down at her Bel-Air house. After he told her what had happened and assured her that a single car accident meant there'd be an investigation, she burst into tears. She told him that Trey had been despondent over gambling debts and had confided to her that he was considering suicide. She felt sure that he'd deliberately driven into the pole.

"She didn't want his wife to know that and his child to have to live with it. She also didn't want the press to get hold of that information because any further investigation would prove he'd been losing company money as well and making deals with unsavory people to cover the losses.

"She asked him to doctor the report to say skid marks on the road and a dead rabbit suggested he'd tried to avoid the critter and hit the pole. She then offered Ryder a large sum of money to get rid of the car and circumvent the investigation."

Judy frowned. "But wasn't it Daphne's car? Was Celeste entitled to do that?"

Brick nodded. "All the cars belonged to the corporation. Anyway, the bribe allowed the sheriff to send his very bright son to Yale. But when Ryder was approached with the evidence, he told them everything.''

Rob and Judy looked at one another in disbelief.

"Only problem is . . .''

They turned back to him in unison.

"Celeste is nowhere to be found. I figure she knows we're on to her and she's pretty desperate now, so I want the two of you to lay low until we have this handled. Her maid at the Palm Beach house says she packed warm clothes, so she could even be here. I've got roadblocks set up in and out of town, and the state police are on the lookout.''

Rob knew precisely what his next course of action would be. But he wanted to talk to Brick about it alone.

"I've got a newspaper to run,'' he said.

Brick nodded. "Fine. Do that. But I want the two of you to stay in town and stay together. You hear me?''

"Right.''

Brick fixed Judy with a firm stare. "We're going to find the Huntington woman, then we'll bring Vic and Daphne and the baby home. Now it's up to us.''

"Right,'' she said quietly.

The police captain looked from one to the other one more moment, then pushed himself to his feet. "Good. I'll let you know what's happening.''

Rob shook his hand and moved with him toward the apartment entrance. "Thanks, Brick.''

"Sure. Good night.''

Judy heard the men at the door as she rinsed cups and put them in the dishwasher. The tremor inside her threatened to take over.

While she was trying to decide how to react to Brick's news about the sheriff's confession and the arrest warrant for Celeste, her body was doing its own thing. It was panicking.

Judy was ecstatic at the news, because it did mean things were rising to an outcome, but it seemed the danger level had risen considerably, too. No one knew where Celeste was, and she'd packed warm clothes.

The night Vic had taken Daphne and Jenny away, he'd told Daphne to pack warm clothes and hats and gloves, Judy remembered. Did Celeste know where they were? Or had she simply come to Tyler, where it was also hats-and-gloves weather? Judy didn't know. She hated that.

She felt short of breath, but everything else inside her seemed to be operating at top speed. She wanted to scream. But screaming was a sort of surrender, and she had this rule...

"It's four o'clock in the morning," Rob said, coming to take a glass out of her hands and put it aside. "I think that can wait until later."

She picked up the glass again and placed it upside down on a plastic spike in the dishwasher. "I want to do the dishes now."

Rob took her arm, pulled her away from the dishwasher and closed the appliance door. This was not the time he'd have chosen to force a confrontation, but she looked about to fly apart, and if that was going to happen, he wanted it to happen while he was still with her.

"Let's talk about this," he said, trying to draw her toward the living room.

She pulled against him, reaching with her free hand for the sponge on the counter. "I don't want to talk about it."

He took the sponge from her and tossed it into the sink. "Well, I do. And I think you should."

"That's the reporter talking," she said, yanking on her arm again, pulling at his fingers with her other hand. "You have to know every grisly little detail, don't you? Well, I don't want to share it with you!" By the time she'd finished that little speech, she was screaming.

He wondered if that was a sign of deepening distress or of insulation being ripped away. He proceeded blindly.

"Afraid I'll understand and sympathize and you won't be alone anymore? Afraid you might appreciate that in me and find you even welcome it?"

She punched his arm. "No one welcomes nosiness. Now, let me go!"

He turned her away from him to ward off her blows, wrapping his free arm over hers and confining it as he pulled her back into his chest.

"All right," he said gently, "if you don't want to talk, do you want to cry?"

The very question made the tears erupt and stand in her eyes. She sniffed and swallowed, determined not to let them fall. She'd been without comfort a major part of her life, and she could do without it now.

But she realized with horror that she wanted it desperately. They'd been attacked by thugs, she'd hit two men with a bat, her sister and little niece had a madwoman after them, and Judy felt powerless to do anything about it.

"Of course I don't want to cry!" she replied angrily, but as she did, a tear fell down her cheek and onto his hand, and she heard him sigh. He lowered his head to rest his cheek against hers, still holding her tightly.

"It's going to be all right," he said. "I promise you. Vic will keep them safe, and Brick will find Celeste. I know it's hard for you to believe in anyone, but this is Tyler. Things are different here. You can believe in us."

Suddenly whatever it was she held between them was just too hard to sustain. All the energy she'd once had that had helped her maintain her distance now seemed to stall in the face of the energy Rob employed to pull her toward him.

She leaned her head back against him and began to sob.

Rob felt both relief and anguish. He turned her in his arms and held her closely as she poured out her fears in a tearful, anguished jumble of words. He rubbed her back and kissed her temple, talking quietly, countering all her fears with the outcome as he saw it, telling her again and again that everything would be all right.

She quieted after a long time, but continued to cling to him. He let himself enjoy it; her moments of dependence on him were few and far between.

She drew a deep breath. "What do we do now?" she asked into his shoulder.

"Let Brick and the L.A. police do their jobs," he replied. It was easier to lie to her when she wasn't looking at him.

She leaned away from him to gaze into his face. He looked back at her with a studiedly neutral expression.

"But Celeste's maid said she packed warm clothes. What if she knows where Daphne and Jenny are?"

He shook his head. "She can't know. It's November, Judy. It's cold everywhere except Florida and southern California, and she's on the run from those places. Now, come on. Let's go to bed and try to get a few hours sleep."

She dropped her arms from him and said grimly, "You take the bed. I don't think I could sleep."

"Judy..." He caught her hand as she tried to walk away from him.

She turned on him suddenly, her eyes brimming with tears again. "Rob, I hit two men with a baseball bat. Contrary to your opinion of me, I don't do that kind of thing every day. I'm upset."

He pulled her back to him and looped his arms around her waist. "I know. You're not violent by nature. That's a definite plus. But your safety was being threatened."

"No, you had shoved me into the bedroom," she said, caught on the tide of her own self-flagellation. "*Your* life was being threatened, and I was..." She stopped as she realized what she was about to admit. She understood for the first time the real depth of her feelings for Rob as she remembered the moment she'd gone to his defense, no other thought in her mind but that no one would hurt him as long as she drew breath.

Rob saw the sudden wariness in her expression, the aborted flow of honesty. She seemed to subside, to draw back into herself to think.

"You were what?" he asked with a small smile, remembering her swinging to his defense like some wild warrior queen. "Pleased?"

Her eyes were unfocused and she replied absently, "No."

"Panicky?"

She thought a minute and shook her head. "No."

"Eager to see me get it?"

She came out of her thoughts at that and focused on him, a trace of humor visible in her deep blue eyes. "There have been moments. But that wasn't one of them."

He was beginning to think he had her, and it took all his self-control not to shake the truth out of her. "Then what were you thinking?"

Her soft, round breasts rose and fell against him with her intake of breath. The humor in her eyes remained, but was now overlaid with a grudging acceptance, as though she were admitting something to herself as well as to him.

"I was feeling terror," she said, her eyes reflecting it. "Terror that you would be hurt. That I might..." She faltered, finding the admission required more courage than she'd expected.

"Don't make me guess," he pleaded softly.

She put her hands on his forearms and felt the tension there. "I was afraid I might lose you," she said in a whispered rush, "and I didn't know what I was going to do."

She wrapped her arms around him, but he held her away, determined not to be satisfied with anything but the admission in its entirety.

"Why?" he asked.

A quirk of her lips acknowledged his demanding stubbornness. "Because I love you. Because I need you."

Rob took a minute to let the words settle inside him, accepting that she needed him as an added bonus. He hadn't expected that. Then he closed his arms around her and held her tightly against him. "There, now. Was that so hard?"

"Yes." She hugged him with satisfying enthusiasm. "You're a reporter—you're used to digging up the truth. I'm a mystery writer. I'm used to hiding it until the end."

He laughed and kissed her soundly. "It is almost the end. In a few days they'll find Celeste, lock her in the slammer, and we can bring your sister home and do all the things the two of you haven't been able to do all these years you've been apart."

Judy leaned against him and again imagined Christmas at the farmhouse on which Vic had placed a deposit. She wanted to believe that in another five or six weeks they'd all be there, celebrating together.

Rob lifted her in his arms and carried her into the bedroom. "Which side of the bed have you been sleeping on?"

"The middle."

"Figures. Well, tonight you'll have to pick a side or share the middle."

She looked up at him as he held her over the bed. "What side will you be on?" she asked in a whisper.

He put her down on the right side, then sat on the edge of the bed to lean over her and kiss her gently.

"You look exhausted," he said, smoothing the hair back from her face.

She wrapped her arms around his neck and pulled him down to kiss him slowly, seductively. "I am. I'm exhausted from pretending I don't want you. Come to bed."

It occurred to him that it wasn't entirely fair to make love to her one night and leave her without telling her the next, but she began to nip at his ear and the thought fled.

She held the blankets up and he crawled in beside her, moving into her embrace, taking her into his. They sighed in unison, two bodies fitting together as though they'd originally been one.

He pulled the grey sweatshirt off her, and thought her ivory skin looked iridescent in the darkness. She shimmered like a vision, the full globes of her breasts an invitation he'd often been sure he'd be forever denied.

But she rose against him as he lowered his mouth to one dark nipple, then the other, and he felt her little shudder of pleasure, heard the small, ragged gasp.

He planted kisses from her throat to her waist, then pulled the sweat bottoms down and off her and tossed them onto the floor. Her lush contours entranced him, and he studied them with reverence, then touched her with the same adoration. Her hips were round, her thighs long and graceful. He traced them with his lips and felt her stir. Then she turned to push him onto his back.

Judy ran her hands under his thermal shirt to push it up and encountered rippled muscle and nicely molded pecs. It amazed her that tenderness could be cloaked in such impressive proportions.

He raised his arms to accommodate her efforts to remove the shirt, and she took advantage of his temporary blindness as she pushed the shirt over his face to plant kisses down the center of his chest and stomach to the waistband of his briefs.

He groaned and laughed as he cleared himself of the shirt, then used it as a sling to wrap around her shoulders and pull her to him. For a moment he was distracted from his purpose by the touch of the beaded tips of her breasts against his chest.

Their groans mingled as he held her to him with a hand to the back of her head and kissed her until he had no breath left.

She collapsed atop him, gasping and limp. Then she knelt beside him and scooted her way down the bed as she tugged his briefs and jeans down and off him. His attempt to draw another breath failed as her long-fingered hand traced from his chin to his knee, then back up his thigh, skimming his manhood with a fingertip before she stroked over his stomach and up his chest.

A conflagration came to life inside him—instant, out of control.

He pulled her down on top of him and traced the softly molded contours of her back, her hips, her thigh. Her roundness was so right in his hand—the shape of the earth, the sun, eternity.

Judy recognized in his touch everything her life had ever lacked—tenderness, cherishing, steadiness, comfort. Strength. His was the embrace that would protect her, and the open arms that left her free to be.

"Rob," she whispered, all the deep affection and astounding passion she felt for him expressed in the sound of his name.

He pulled her down beside him, in the cradle of his arm, and leaned forward to kiss her because the sound of his name on her lips in the silky darkness left him speechless.

He drew her knee up and stroked a hand down her thigh to the heart of her femininity, covering it possessively.

She pushed against his touch, tightening her hold on his neck, and he dipped a finger gently inside her. She turned her face into his shoulder and sighed.

Judy couldn't move. His intimate touch seemed to have stilled her entire body, yet she felt anything but quiet. It was as though the processes of breath and heartbeat waited for a sign to continue.

And then it came. His gentle, circular stroke brought a little gasp of air to her lips, a little jolt to her heart. Her lungs began to draw and expel, her heart to thrum, both accelerating with the movement of his hand.

Pleasure danced beyond her, teasing her, torturing her, and even in the greedy throes of waiting for it, she surfaced sufficiently to want to be sure he would not be excluded.

Distracted by the press of her against him, by the exquisite tension in her as she waited for what he could bring her, he missed the downward movement of her hand or he would have stopped her.

He wanted the moment to be hers, filled with a generosity he couldn't offer if he found pleasure with her.

But when her hand closed on him, she left him no choice. He pulled her over him and entered her with one swift thrust. Fingers linked, they moved together as pleasure tightened around them, then burst over them in a brilliant, quaking climax that seemed to go on and on. Their eyes met and he saw the stunned look in hers. She saw the startled expression in his.

Judy collapsed against Rob's chest, and he wrapped his arms around her, trying to find normalcy, reality, in the aftermath of an experience that had shaken him to the core of his being.

It upset him for an instant that he couldn't seem to stabilize his emotions, that he still felt everything in extremes—passion, joy, love that consumed him.

Then Judy raised her head from his shoulder to look into his eyes and smile, and he knew why he couldn't find his comfortable reality—his reality had changed.

It no longer belonged to him alone. It included Judy, and had altered from the calm, unimpassioned, professionally removed stability of the career reporter, to a life shot with all the hyperboles he'd once scorned in everyone else.

Now that he understood it, he felt himself relax.

"You're smiling," Judy observed.

Rob pulled the blankets up over her and held her in place when she would have shifted off of him to lay beside him.

"No," he whispered, pressing her head back to his shoulder and kissing her hair. "Don't move. With you in my arms, I'll be smiling for a good, long time."

She made a contented sound and kissed his collarbone. "When we get up, you'll have to repeat that so I can record it and play it back to you those times when you *won't* be smiling."

Rob stroked her hair, glad she couldn't see his face. By this time tomorrow it was she who wouldn't be smiling, and he felt a sharp pang of guilt that he couldn't simply be honest and tell her what he intended.

But he knew her. She'd insist on going along and the fight would be on, and he didn't want that. He wanted her safe in Tyler with Britt and Jake while he did what he had to do.

He closed his eyes as the pang of guilt became a painful stab. He tried to get some sleep.

CHAPTER EIGHT

BRICK HUNCHED HIS shoulders under the old football jacket he wore, and jammed his hands in his pockets as the raw November wind blew around him.

"What's wrong with you?" he demanded of Rob, who walked beside him across the deserted park. The day was cold and damp, the sky leaden, the trees now almost bare of their leaves. "We can't talk in a nice warm restaurant, or my office?"

Rob turned up the collar of his parka. "No. I wanted to talk to you while you were off duty, and I don't want us to be overheard. Why are you being such a wimp? I thought you were this tough football jock before you turned supercop."

Brick grinned. "I was, but that involves steam baths and hot rubs. What's on your mind, Friedman? We still haven't heard about the fingerprints on the gas cap."

"I know. I just wanted to tell you I'm going to check on Vic and Daphne."

Brick stopped in his tracks, his expression combative. "What?" he asked flatly.

"They've been out of touch for more than a week," Rob said. "I'm worried. I've been telling Judy that Vic hasn't called because the weather's been too bad for him to get to the phone, but...I don't know. He's up a creek up there. If he's got a problem, he can't leave Daphne and Jenny alone to deal with it, and he won't want to move them from there on the chance they're spotted."

"You two didn't set up any way for *you* to call *him?*"

"No. With Celeste watching, it was too dangerous."

Brick made a scornful sound. "Stumpy's almost more of a danger to himself than to you. I saw him at Marge's last week, having lunch with Marion Clark and Paul Bullard. He managed to dump his coffee in Bullard's lap and elbow Marion's salad onto hers."

Rob laughed. "You're kidding!"

"Nope. Truth is, I don't think his heart's in larceny anymore. I think Tyler's gotten to him."

Rob nodded grimly. "It got to Vic. It got to me. So I need you to have your roadblock look the other way tonight when I take the Timber Lake Trail to the old highway."

Brick stared at the horizon and started walking again. Rob walked along with him, hoping the police captain wasn't going to prove difficult. "So?" Rob prompted.

Brick leaned down to scoop up a fast-food bag in his path and lobbed it at a mesh trash basket near a picnic table. He scored.

"I hate people," he said thoughtfully, jamming his hands in his pockets again, "who think they can run the world because they have money."

That was a sentiment Rob could agree with, but he wasn't sure where Brick was going with this, so he simply listened.

"And I hate them especially," the cop added, "when they mess with my people."

That sounded good. "So, you're not going to give me any trouble?"

"Not exactly." Brick clapped Rob on the shoulder, grinned widely and picked up the pace. "Come on. Let's go see Stumpy."

"What?"

JUDY STARED AT THE WORDS on the screen of her laptop and had a revelation. No, it was more than that; it might even be an epiphany.

She understood finally what Rob was doing.

She watched him smile at her over the top of the newspaper as he read their horoscopes aloud, the copy read on her monitor, *and she analyzed his gaze. It was gentle, sweet even, and she knew with certainty that it said goodbye.*

However hackneyed it might be, her art was imitating life. All day long Rob had been giving her just the look she'd described in her heroine's husband.

They'd gotten up after ten and he'd kissed her good-morning, a loving softness in his eyes. Then he'd made breakfast while she showered, smiled at her over the oatmeal, made cheerful conversation as they drove to work and kissed her every time he passed her perch on the sofa on his way to the darkroom.

It was guilt, Judy concluded, and it took the compilation of just a few facts to figure out why he was feeling guilty.

He'd spent all afternoon getting ads approved and checking story details—a job he usually left to the day before deadline. He'd pasted up a few pages, and earlier, when she'd gone into the front office to snag a doughnut from the box on K.J.'s desk, she'd walked by Rob's and noticed he was working on an editorial—a very last minute project.

Then he'd asked her if she minded if he used her truck for a late interview with the graveyard-shift watch commander at the sheriff's substation. He'd arranged for Britt to pick her up on her way home from the store so that Judy wouldn't have to be alone while he was busy. "K.J.'s covering a basketball game," he'd said with that sweet smile, "and there'd be no one here with you."

That had been an hour ago. She was appalled that it had taken her this long to come to the conclusion that he was ducking out on her tonight. He was going to wherever Vic, Daphne and Jenny were hidden. Judy was as sure of that as she was that she loved him. The rat.

She waited until he'd run out to call on another advertiser, and went into the bathroom with the cell phone so that K.J. wouldn't hear her call Britt.

"Is Rob intending for you and Jake to baby-sit me while he goes to warn Vic and Daphne that Celeste is on the run?" Judy blurted the question, then added firmly, "Our friendship hinges on this, Brittany Marshack. Yes or no?"

There was an instant's silence. "Don't threaten me," Britt replied after a moment, "or I'll tell everyone my fifteen-year-old daughter checks your spelling."

"Yes," Judy demanded, "or no?"

"Yes," Britt replied, "but he knew you'd make a scene and carry on if you knew he was going and you weren't. You know, like you're doing now."

"Okay." Judy heard the bell over the front door, and K.J.'s "Judy, can you get that?" shouted from the darkroom. "Now listen carefully," she said, "because I only have a minute to get this out. This is what you're going to do." She followed that direction with a short but precise list of commands. Then she added gravely,

"And if you breathe a word to Jake, and this gets back to Rob, I'll never forgive you, I promise. Do you understand me?"

Britt listened in silence, then said with quiet emphasis, "*You* are going to be the one in trouble when all this is over and Daphne's back home again, so you'd better be ready to explain yourself and make a few changes in the way you operate. Do you understand *me?*"

"Yes," Judy replied. "Now, will you do it?"

"Yes. But you're a snot."

"Thank you. See you tonight."

The bell over the office door had signaled the arrival of an older woman in a pink velour jogging suit who wanted to pay her subscription. Judy had prepared several subscriber receipts in the days she'd been coming to work with Rob. She performed the duty now and waved the subscriber off with a smile.

She turned to find K.J. standing in the doorway in his darkroom apron, a cup of coffee in hand. "Everything okay?" he asked.

She nodded. "Just a subscriber. I put the money in the box and wrote her a receipt."

"What time's Britt coming for you?" he asked. His glance moved casually to the clock, but Judy suspected it was a way of avoiding her eyes. He was undoubtedly in on Rob's scheme because someone would have to keep the paper going while Rob was gone.

"Five-thirty. You going to Brick's office tonight for this story, too?" She asked the question casually as she walked past him, back to the sofa.

"Ah . . . no." He cleared his throat. "No, I have too much darkroom work to do. This edition's really photo heavy."

"Brick going to be there?"

She saw a trace of panic in K.J.'s eyes, though his features remained steady. "I don't think so," he replied. "I believe Rob's interviewing a deputy on swing shift."

"I see." So except for the basketball game, they'd coordinated stories. ·

The telephone rang, and K.J. reached for the cordless just as she did. "I'll get it," he said, walking toward the front office with it. "You get back to your book." The panic in his eyes changed to relief.

Judy smiled at his back as the office door closed.

ROB GLANCED AT HIS WATCH as he loped the last block to the office. It was 5:26. Darkness had fallen, and the streets of downtown Tyler were a bit busier than usual as people headed home to dinner.

Britt was coming at 5:30, and he had to see Judy before she left. He was shocked by how urgent the need was, how bereft he felt at the thought of missing her and being unable to say goodbye. Haggling partners at the drugstore couldn't agree on what to feature in their monthly sale, and had kept Rob waiting forty minutes while they argued over corn pads and plasters versus feminine-hygiene supplies. He'd been pretty desperate and very grateful when they'd gone with the corn pads.

As he burst through the door, Judy was slipping into her coat. He felt a rush of love as she smiled at him and flipped her straight silky hair over the high wool collar.

He went to frame her face in his hands and kiss her slowly, lingeringly. It pained him that it would be days before he could do this again—and that he couldn't tell her that.

Instead, he drew away and smiled. "Missed you. Any idea what you guys are having for dinner?"

She shook her head as she buttoned the coat. "No, but nothing bad ever comes out of Britt's kitchen. What about you? You going to get takeout?"

"K.J. and I'll probably order a pizza."

She looped her arms around his neck, determined to prod his guilt with a stick. "We can both have dessert after you pick me up tonight," she whispered. She saw a shadow move across his eyes before she pulled him down to her and kissed him.

"All right. That's enough of that," Britt teased from the open doorway. A blast of cold air rushed in to fill the small space. "This is a place of business."

Judy gave Britt a scornful laugh and Rob another quick kiss. "Wasn't she the woman we saw all over Jake at the Friends of the Library Halloween party?"

"He was Don Juan," Britt said. "I was supposed to be all over him. Come on, I've got Jacob in the car."

Rob followed Judy to the door. She turned back to blow him a kiss. "See you tonight."

He watched them get into the car, wait for an opportunity to slip into traffic, then drive away. Loneliness closed in on him.

It startled him that he should feel this way. He'd made love to her only once, but that was all it had taken to turn him into her slave. Her safety was the only comfort he could take in being without her for the next few days.

"She gone?" K.J. asked from behind him.

Rob realized he was still staring out the window, though Britt's car had disappeared from view. He went to the pasteup board. "Yeah."

"She suspect anything?"

"Not a thing."

"When you're at the sheriff's office tonight, you'd better get yourself a Kevlar vest. I have a feeling you'd better be bulletproof next time you see her."

Rob grinned up at him over the boards. "That's how love is, my boy. One life-threatening episode after the other. Sausage and green pepper on my side of the pizza."

"Right."

ROB LEFT JUST BEFORE midnight. He'd put together all the ads and prepared the news, then left the fillers on K.J.'s desk with a few suggestions. Everything else was pretty routine, and K.J. seemed confident that he could handle it.

Rob tactfully suggested he leave a cartoon out of this edition.

He headed north into the dark winter night, taking a back road that skirted Tyler and led to what was little more than a trail just wide enough for the truck to pass. The trail wound around the back side of Timber Lake and eventually deposited him on a road that paralleled the highway for a good twenty miles. Certain he'd evaded Brick's roadblock, Rob took the next turn to the interstate, which went in a northwesterly direction. He was heading for Minnesota.

He cranked up the heat in the truck and punched the tape deck under the dash, trying to push aside the worries that lay ahead, and those he'd left behind.

He smiled at that thought. If he worried about anyone left behind, it should be Jake and Britt, not Judy. They were the ones who were explaining to her, probably at this very moment, why he hadn't appeared to pick her up and take her home.

He knew Jake would let nothing happen to her. Rob just hoped she didn't do anything too painful to *him*.

Rob didn't know what to think about Daphne's and Vic's situation, why they hadn't been in touch this week. He hoped it was simply bad weather, or some other innocuous reason.

He just knew he had to assess the problem and try to repair it before Judy went wild with worry. And he had to tell them that the warrant had been issued for Celeste's arrest, and that freedom was imminent, thanks to Brick's plan.

A Collin Raye tune about "One Boy, One Girl" filled the cab of the truck, and Rob settled back to watch the road and let his mind play with all the possibilities the song suggested, possibilities that were suddenly open to him.

The night seemed interminable as he drove by one small town after another. Rob sat up straighter and sharpened his attention on the traffic as he drove through the busy interchange at Eau Clair, bypassed that city and headed for Chippewa Falls.

A murky dawn brought daylight but no sun as he pulled up at a rest stop about twenty miles the other side of the falls.

He went to the men's room, then walked around the buildings and picnic tables to circulate life back into his legs. He thought absently that he'd have never made it as a trucker. Or a fiction writer. Too much sitting.

Journalism, fortunately, was ninety percent research and ten percent desk time. And on a small newspaper, he got as much exercise selling advertising as he did doing research and covering meetings.

Thoughts of the newspaper made him imagine Judy sitting in a corner of the ratty flowered sofa, frowning in concentration over her laptop. And that brought thoughts of her astride his hips and driving him to madness.

He strode briskly back to the truck to prevent his body from reacting to that thought. Coffee. He needed coffee.

Leaning in from the driver's side, he took a thermos from the passenger seat and poured a capful of the steaming black brew. It burned his mouth and throat and slid with comforting warmth into his stomach.

He downed the contents of the cup, capped the thermos and then, noting how the front seat was cluttered with his bag, his jacket and a map, dropped it onto the blanket Judy always kept in the jump seat.

There was a loud *thunk* as it landed, followed by what sounded like . . . a gasp?

Rob had one leg already in the truck, but stepped out again. He stared at the blanket for a moment with a horrible sense of foreboding, then gabbed a fistful of it and yanked.

Under it and barely visible was a jeans-clad hip, one arm in red-and-blue plaid flannel, and short, straight blonde hair that could belong to no one but Judy.

She lay on her side, wedged in hiding in the small space. She pushed her hair back out of her face and fixed him with a belligerent glare.

"How stupid do you think I am, Friedman?" she demanded.

An anger so hot and powerful it almost frightened him flashed to life like simultaneous combustion. He literally saw red for an instant, and feared that civility would abandon him completely.

He reached for the driver's seat with a quick, angry gesture, and she uttered a little scream of alarm. But he simply pushed the seat forward and said in a voice barely under control, "Get out of there!"

Judy had known she would have to face this moment eventually, and thought she'd been prepared for it. In fact, just a few moments before, when she'd decided she'd grown cold and stiff enough to pass for a cadaver, she'd even considered forcing it herself. Anything would be better than one more moment on her side cramped into paralysis in the bottom of the small space.

Now she wasn't so sure. She'd never seen Rob's eyes go that dark, or his features without even a trace of the humor that defined him. He waited for her several feet from the truck, looking like a bear in a big oatmeal-colored sweater, his hands on his hips, his expression like thunder.

She was in trouble, big time.

CHAPTER NINE

CLIMBING OUT OF THE truck's jump seat was a feat worthy of an Olympic gymnast. There was barely room to move in the space behind the front seats, and getting out required turning sideways, wriggling feetfirst between the seat and the side of the truck, then finding a spot to place a foot on the edge of the truck body and balancing there while drawing her torso and head out. Then it was an eighteen-inch leap to the ground—backward.

Judy managed the tricky move as far as finding a foothold on the thin rim of the side of the truck while pulling the rest of her body out. Then her balancing leg, which had been the one underneath as she lay on her side for the past five hours, cramped up and gave out from under her. She fell backward out of the truck, suspecting as she gritted her teeth against impact with the asphalt that Rob would simply enjoy the spectacle rather than do anything to help her.

It surprised her when a sturdy grip stopped her midfall, then set her on her feet. The move wasn't necessarily gentle, but she considered herself lucky he'd intervened.

Until he spun her around to face him. "Judy," he said, his voice quiet with suppressed fury, "you are so close to having your next book published posthumously..."

She pulled out of his grip and backed away to a safe distance. "Do you want to hear my side?" she asked coolly.

"Oh, I know your side," he returned, his voice rising a decibel. "Your side is always that you do whatever you damn well please no matter who it places in a difficult situation! Is this where you pass out on me?"

She took his reference to the California trip with an upward tilt of her chin. "That was the result of a lack of food and the sudden heat. And probably a reaction to your nasty disposition. If you'll show a little patience, I'll explain."

He ignored her suggestion. "You just ran out on Britt and Jake?" he asked, spreading his arms in a gesture of abject exasperation. "I know he wouldn't have let you go willingly."

There was nothing Judy could do here but try to remain calm and stand her ground. She drew a breath. "I never went to Britt and Jake's."

He frowned and pointed in the general direction of Tyler. "I saw you get in the car. I watched you drive away."

She shifted her weight. "That was the plan."

He stared at her for one dark moment, then closed the distance between them and repeated ominously, "The *plan?*"

She looked him in the eye and tried to analyze precisely what she felt. She had no doubt it was fear, but it wasn't physical fear, though any woman who hadn't lain in his arms might guess that this towering column of male indignation could mean her harm.

But Rob was so angry that Judy was afraid she'd shattered the fragile relationship that had just begun to show such promise. Still, he had to know that he couldn't simply discount her presence as he'd tried to do, or what they had would never grow.

"I figured out this afternoon what you were planning," she said intrepidly. "And I—"

"How?" he interrupted. "How? I was careful not to say anything you would suspect..."

She took pleasure in giving him a superior smile. "You'd made love to me only hours before," she said quietly. "You didn't just allow me access to your body, you showed me everything you hope and dream as well. Your thoughts. Your plans."

He looked at her as though she'd grown antennae. Then he looked at the sky, at the trees, then back at her. "You're saying you read my mind?"

"I'm saying," she replied serenely, "that you can't reveal all that to a woman, then expect to hide anything from her."

"That's crazy."

"Obviously not. I'm here."

He stared at her for another moment, then he jammed his hands in his pockets, apparently deciding to save that for another time. "Back to your story. You figured out what I was doing and...?"

She firmed her stance. "And I called Britt to ask her if it was true. She said it was."

He made an impatient sound. "But I'd just talked it over with Jake that morning when I picked up the Yes! Yogurt ad. I explained that you'd be safer in Tyler. He agreed to look out for you!"

"*He* agreed," she repeated calmly. "You never spoke to Britt."

His jaw firmed. "My mistake. I thought in the issue of your safety, he could speak for Britt."

"Well, that's where you were wrong." Judy rubbed her arms, the early morning air beginning to chill her. She reached behind the seat for the parka she hadn't needed until now. "She didn't think you had the right to leave me out of this trip any more than I did." That wasn't entirely true, but Judy felt sure once she had time to explain it that Britt would see things her way.

"So." He took a step away from her, then turned back, his eyes turbulent with anger. "Her picking you up at the office was a charade for my benefit? What did she do—drop you off a block away?"

"Two blocks away, actually." Judy shrugged into the coat and ignored the buttons, just wrapping it around her. "When we were one block away, you were still watching us." She ventured a smile, wondering if he was ready for it yet. "Were you missing me already?"

He definitely was not ready for it. He backed her up against the side of the truck cab until she was stuck to it like a loose strip of chrome.

"Don't you *dare* try to charm your way out of this," he warned darkly. "You made love to me one minute, then put on a fake performance for me the next!"

"Isn't that just what you did?" she countered. "You made love to me, then planned to leave me behind while you went to check on *my* sister."

"Out of concern for you!" he bellowed.

"You said we were in this together!"

He put a hand to his eyes for a moment, then dropped it to his side. "If you knew what I was doing," he asked in a quieter voice, "why didn't you just tell me that, and ask to come along?"

"Because I knew you wouldn't let me come," she said frankly. "Or I'm sure you'd have invited me along in the first place, knowing, as you do, that I'm wild with worry." The last she'd intended to add with sarcasm, but the break in her voice blunted its effect.

She turned away from him, feeling as though half her reserves of hope and endurance had been rattled to bits in the bottom of the jump seat and the other half crushed by his narrow-minded view of her presence.

A subtle voice inside her, one almost strangled by her own anger, whispered that she knew his intentions, however high-handed, had been to protect her from harm in a situation filled with unknowns. And she remembered his eyes when he'd kissed her goodbye the night before. He hadn't wanted to leave her, but he'd considered it expedient. Cause for indignation, certainly, but when a woman understood the male mind, not cause for anger.

She turned to him and found that he'd walked a few paces away from her, almost as though he didn't trust himself to remain too close.

"I'll do everything your way for the rest of the trip," she conceded. "I won't argue or even question you about anything. Just please understand..." She was suddenly unbearably weary. "I have to know if they're okay."

He looked at the sky again, as though seeking heavenly supplication, then closed his eyes and shook his head. When he looked at her once more, the anger was banked, but not gone.

"The first time you break that promise," he warned, "you're going home if I have to send you by mail. Get in the truck."

"I have to go to the bathroom."

"God."

ROB FELT HIS EQUANIMITY returning by the time they crossed the corner of Lake Superior on the interstate bridge into Minnesota. He surfaced from his anger to find his way through Duluth and onto Highway 53 going north.

Once out of the tight traffic, he made a conscious effort to relax, figuring he might need his reserves of strength and wit for what lay ahead. And relaxing forced him to remember the guilt he'd felt the night before over leaving Judy in Tyler without telling her what he planned to do. He was guilty of trying to put something past her. If he wanted to be liberal in his thinking, he could admit that in her viewpoint, she had every right to try to thwart him.

But he found it hard to be liberal with her life. It now meant more to him than his own.

He glanced at her, sitting quietly in the passenger seat as she'd promised, staring out the window at the wintery landscape under a gunmetal sky. She hadn't said a word since they'd left the rest stop.

The spire of a church and the column of a grain elevator came into view as they approached a small town. Judy's stomach growled noisily.

"Hungry?" he asked. It was just after noon.

"No," she replied. "I swallowed a grump." She smiled blandly in his direction. "But you're still here, aren't you? Must have been another grump."

A glance in the rearview mirror told him they were alone on the road, and he applied the brake. They slowed to a halt, and he looked at her over the arm he had stretched over the steering wheel. He hated to admit it, but he was glad to see the old combative spirit alive in her eyes. He chose to keep that fact from her.

"You're still on thin ice, you know," he said.

She waved a hand at the landscape outside her window. "That's the nature of this part of the country, isn't it? Especially in winter? Lakes everywhere, and there'll soon be ice on every one of them."

"I'm not talking about the lakes."

"No." She turned to him and smiled again, but this time her expression was conciliatory. "I know. You're talking about me. But you have to agree that you are a grump when you're crossed."

He leveled his gaze on her. "And you're the picture of grace and forgiveness?"

"No, but I don't require obedience from you."

"No, just mind reading, and complete cooperation with your schemes."

She huffed. "I don't have *schemes*. When you're a man and you do something outrageous, it's just a clever plan. If you're a woman, it's a *scheme.*"

"Really. And what do you call stowing away in the jump seat of a truck?"

"You can't 'stow away' in something you own yourself. And if you're still interested in an answer to your original question, yes, I am hungry."

"Pardon me, but do I recall someone making a promise not to argue?"

She drew a deep breath and subsided. "Yes, you do. I apologize—I forgot. It's just that your male rhetoric is so arguable. But the moment my sister is back in Tyler, we're going to take all this up again."

He glanced in the mirror once more and stepped on the accelerator. "You're damned right we are."

"YOU WANT ME TO DRIVE for a while?" They'd polished off sandwiches and coffee, and sat over second cups in an old-fashioned, high-back booth in a cozy little coffee shop. Judy looked into Rob's red-rimmed eyes and knew she had to look as bad. The bottom of the jump seat hadn't been conducive to sleep, but at least she hadn't had to stare at a dark road all night.

He shook his head. "Not necessary."

She made a face at him. "Male bravado talking? You look awful."

He studied her face for a moment, and she braced herself to be told that she looked awful, too. But his eyes roved her features and finally settled on her eyes with a decidedly sexual gleam. "You look wonderful. But that's something else we'll have to deal with later. You ready?"

Unsettled, she followed him to the cashier.

She looped her arm in his as they walked across the parking lot toward the truck. "Don't you need to nap? You've been awake all night."

"I publish a small newspaper," he replied with a light laugh. "I'm always awake all night."

"But what if we encounter trouble? That *is* why you didn't want me along, isn't it?" She took pleasure in teasing him. The dark clouds had parted and a patch of blue sky and sunlight opened overhead. The November breeze, perfumed with the scent of burning leaves, swept around them, lifting the dark hair on his forehead, swirling and disheveling hers. "Will you be sufficiently sharp to defend me against Celeste and her thugs?"

He turned the key in the lock on the passenger door of the truck. "The best defense against Celeste would be to let her have you. You could undermine her whole operation before the day was out."

Rob was surprised when Judy looked genuinely hurt. He sobered instantly and put a hand to her cheek, realizing she was probably far more tired than she appeared.

"I'm your shield for as long as I live," he promised, "You know I wouldn't let anything happen to you."

Her composure crumpled suddenly despite his reassurances. He sat on the edge of the passenger seat and pulled her in between his knees. "Come on." She tried to cover her face, but he pulled her hands down. "All right, I tricked you and tried to leave Tyler without you, but you know I can be trusted to do all in my power to get your family home safely."

She sniffed and dug in her pockets for a tissue. "I know. I just don't want anything to happen to anyone." She produced a crumpled tissue and dabbed at her nose, giving him a grudging glance. "Even you."

"Well, Judy." He tucked her windblown hair behind her ear and held her closer. He rubbed comforting circles between her shoulder blades. "I do believe you're getting serious."

"Yes," she admitted. Then, disliking the satisfied look in his eyes, she added in a detached tone a little hard to maintain with his knees pinching her to him, "I told you I love you."

"Yes." He tucked her hair behind her ear. "But I didn't realize that meant you were thinking about me in the long term."

She looked away. "I wasn't. I can't imagine being tied to you for a lifetime."

"Then why were you upset just a moment ago when it occurred to you that you could end up having to live your life without me?"

The thought still had the ability to cripple her, but he seem to like that notion entirely too much. She pretended to study her fingernails. "Well. There'd be no newspaper carrying Gates's sales ads, no newspaper to donate to the high school's recycling fund-raiser, no newspaper for the bottom of the canary cage.''

''You don't have a canary,'' he said softly, his lips very close to hers.

''Somebody...must.'' She hunched her shoulder against the sensory onslaught of his warm breath in her ear. It was suddenly critical to distract him. She tried to push out of his arms. ''You're sure you don't want me to drive?''

He caught a fistful of her hair and pulled her lips back to his because he was desperate to taste them, and because he had to make it clear she couldn't have it her way all the time. He kissed her until she felt as spineless in his arms as he felt himself, then stood and steadied her on her feet.

''No,'' he replied, helping her into the truck and holding the door open for her. ''Because we're almost there.''

She looked up at him, the seat belt halfway around her. Her eyes ignited. ''We are?''

He smiled, closed her door and walked around to the driver's side. She had a dozen questions, her entire mood raised to high wattage.

He told her the little he knew—that they would be there by late afternoon, that they would have to walk in the last mile and should be at the cabin by dusk.

She passed him a piece of what looked like flat Danish as they continued north on Highway 53.

''Where did that come from?'' he asked.

''I brought my own provisions,'' she said, holding up the small backpack she had tucked in a corner of the jump seat.

He looked away from the road to glance at it doubtfully. "What is it?"

"Half a Pop-Tart," she replied. "Peanut butter-chocolate."

"Don't you have to toast it?"

"No. It's fine cold."

He took a careful bite. It was a little sweet, but palatable. "You mean I just spent money on you for lunch and you'd brought your own supplies?"

"Yes," she replied sweetly, "but I'm sharing them with you, so we're even."

"You had a cup of soup, a BLT, a scoop of potato salad and pie à la mode and we're even?"

She thought a moment. "Of course we are. Chocolate-peanut-butter Pop-Tarts are like gold."

He'd have argued the point, but her smile glowed and that *was* like gold.

GOOSE LAKE CONSISTED of one general store and a rickety lineup of small, squat buildings. Judy looked at them in confusion as Rob pulled up in front of the store.

"Why are there warehouses way out here," she asked, "when there aren't any people?"

"They're not warehouses," he replied, "they're garages. Come on."

It was a general store out of *Little House on the Prairie,* and Judy wandered around it, fascinated, while Rob conducted business with a short, grandfatherly balding man with glasses. He reminded Judy of Wilford Brimley.

There was nothing old-fashioned about the stock, but pots and pans hung from hooks overhead, and there was fruit in apple baskets and pickles in barrels. She wondered if that was for atmosphere or convenience.

On a high shelf near a window lay a black-and-white cat on a folded blanket. Judy reached up on tiptoe to pet him and was rewarded with a purr. But it wasn't as loud as Caddy's, she thought, and wondered how her cat was faring at Britt's.

A little stab of homesickness was countered instantly by the knowledge that in one brief mile, she would see her sister and her niece.

Then Judy came upon a telephone mounted on the back wall. A neatly lettered Out of Order sign had been taped to it. She turned to Rob with a slight inclination of her head.

He followed the gesture as the clerk bent over the preparation of a receipt. Rob smiled and looked as relieved as she felt.

"Garage E," the cuddly clerk said, handing Rob a key. Then he noticed Judy near the phone. "Sorry about that. Been out of order more than a week, but we're kind of in the boonies here, and I'm afraid we're the phone company's last priority." Then he winked. "'Course, you folks being on a honeymoon and all, you probably won't want to be calling anybody."

Judy met Rob at the door, her eyebrow raised at the clerk's comment. "Honeymoon?" she asked quietly the moment they were outside.

"He presumed and I didn't correct him," Rob replied. "And you promised not to argue or question, remember?"

She waved a hand in the air as she followed him to the truck. "Oh, did you think I meant that?"

Rob backed the truck into the garage, then went to the rear to pull out a pack that looked heavy. Judy grabbed the blanket out of the cab, thinking it might be needed at the cabin, and glanced at Rob in time to see him tuck something into the back of his belt, under his jacket.

Her heart thudded uncomfortably. "Was that a gun?" she asked in a shocked voice.

He looked at her impatiently as he hefted the pack. "Did you think we'd hold Celeste off with conversation?"

"Rob, there's a two-year-old at the cabin."

He nodded. "I know. It isn't loaded—I've got the clip in my pocket. Do you have your stuff? We want to get there before dark."

Judy hefted her own pack, then rolled up the blanket and tucked it under her arm. She followed Rob out of the garage and waited while he locked it.

The afternoon was already growing shadowy under dark clouds. Snowflakes began to drift from them with quiet grace.

"Put your hood up," Rob said.

She sighed but complied. He was definitely into SWAT-commander mode. But she'd made a promise not to argue and she'd already broken it several times.

He pulled a woolen hat out of his pocket, jammed it on his head and pulled on gloves. She pulled her gloves out, too, before he could bark another order.

Rob paused before starting up the trail, turning to look behind them and all around.

"What?" she asked quietly.

"Nothing," he replied, turning his gaze up to the sky. Then he lowered it to grin at her. "If you can keep up, we ought to just make it by nightfall."

She rolled her eyes. "Eat my dust, pilgrim," she said, and headed up the trail.

Rob followed, staying a couple of strides behind so he could see around her and watch the pine woods that lined the trail. They were thick and dark, and in some spots made him feel as though they'd slipped into a canyon. The wind whispered in the trees and the snow began to fall in earnest.

Judy slowed to fall into step beside him. She smiled with bland innocence. "Hi," she said.

Apparently the threatening atmosphere had communicated itself to her as well.

He smiled back, mimicking her innocent expression. "Scared?"

"Who?"

"You."

"Yeah," she admitted sheepishly. "This lane was beautiful when we started out, but now it looks menacing, as though something riding a broom could fly out of it. Like Celeste."

He laughed softly and stopped to make a visual survey, as he'd done before they took the trail. "If my calculations are correct," he said, setting off again and pulling Judy with him, "Celeste should be behind us, not ahead of us."

She stopped in her tracks. "What do you mean? I thought we didn't know where she was?"

"Keep going," he said, taking her arm in a gloved hand and urging her forward. "Brick made a deal with Stumpy. Told him that if he contacted her and told her where we were, he could have immunity from prosecution in the attempt to kidnap Jennifer. Angus jumped at the chance."

Judy stared at Rob, openmouthed. He continued to push her forward because she was too distracted to operate on her own. "No! You mean we're . . . bait?"

He smirked. "I knew you'd like this. There's even a wire involved."

She blinked in disbelief. "You're kidding! Do I get to wear it?"

"Sorry. I do."

"Rob, I don't get it." She looked back over her shoulder. "How far behind are they?"

"About twelve hours. Stumpy's setting up Celeste to arrive tomorrow morning. Brick'll be right behind her to grab her when she makes her move. Come on. Keep going."

Judy was growing increasingly befuddled. "But Brick doesn't have jurisdiction up here."

"He's on vacation," Rob explained. "For a week he's not a sheriff, he's just a guy on a fishing trip."

She gasped. "But I don't—"

Before she knew what had happened she was face-down on the carpet of needles and fallen pine cones, Rob on one knee beside her. He'd dropped his pack in front of her head and she heard a metallic slap that meant his gun was now loaded.

Then the stillness became deafening. Snow fell in silent sheets and Judy peered through it, searching for any sign of movement. But there was none. Except, perhaps, the expansion of her chest as her heartbeat thudded out of control.

"Rob?" she whispered.

"Just stay down!" he snapped.

Then she heard the faintest sound behind them and Rob spun on his knee, the gun leveled in both hands.

"Not bad for a newspaperman," a lazy voice said. Judy recognized it instantly and let her head fall to her arm as relief washed over her.

Rob swore as he rose to his feet. "Vic, you no-good so-and-so. You scared the hell out of me."

"You didn't do my nerves much good, either, when I looked out the cabin window and saw movement on the trail." Vic replaced a lethal-looking pistol in a shoulder holster. He was tall and dark and dressed in a black parka, the hood down, his hair collecting snow.

"How are you?" He shook Rob's hand, then reached down to pull Judy up and give her a hug. "Please tell me you're here because Celeste confessed everything and turned on all her goons."

Judy punched his arm. "We're here because we hadn't heard from you and were scared to death!"

He squeezed her shoulders apologetically. "I know. I'm sorry. The phone's broken at the general store. I didn't want to leave Daphne and Jenny to find another one, and I didn't want to take them away from the cabin."

"We saw the Out of Order sign." Judy hugged him. "I'm glad you're all right."

Vic reached down to heft Rob's pack onto his own shoulder. "Daphne'll be thrilled to see you, but I'm sorry you had to make the trip."

"Don't be," Rob replied. "It's part of a plan. How close are we to the cabin?"

"Not far at all. What plan?"

"Lead on. I'll explain once we're there. You okay, Judy?"

She dusted off her parka and gave Rob a scolding glance. "If you discount getting a pine cone up my nose when you shoved me down."

Her hood had fallen off when he'd pushed her to the ground, and he pulled it back up for her with a grin, then reached down to hand her the blanket. He kept her pack to carry himself. "It's too bad you didn't get it in your mouth. Go with Vic. I'll be right behind you."

Judy felt her heartbeat slow to normal as Vic Estevez put an arm around her shoulders and started at a fairly quick pace up the trail.

"Are Daphne and Jenny all right?" she asked anxiously.

"Wonderful. Jenny's happy and thriving, and Daphne's great, but worried about you."

Judy was so relieved she even looped an arm around his waist, below Rob's pack. She and Vic hadn't been the best of friends when he'd first come to Tyler because she'd suspected his motives where her sister was concerned. Then Daphne had learned he'd been hired by Celeste to find her, and Judy credited herself with helping her sister understand that his deception had been because he'd loved her and not because he'd wanted to take her back to Celeste.

When Celeste's men attacked him and Daphne in the parking lot of Timberlake Lodge, Vic had spirited Daphne and Jenny away with him and Judy had spent the last month not knowing where they were. There'd been times when she'd hated him for that.

Now that she did know, and was assured they were safe, she could afford to be generous.

Rob watched Vic and Judy walk on ahead, arm in arm, as he tucked his gun back into his belt. He shouldered Judy's pack and started after them, thinking he would never again complain about slow, dull city council meetings or picky and demanding advertisers. Even they were easier on the nerves than this cloak-and-dagger stuff.

CHAPTER TEN

JUDY FOLLOWED VIC into a good-size cabin dark with early evening shadows and stopped in the middle of an eclectically furnished living room. A fire blazed in a brick fireplace with a sit-down hearth. Setting down the pack, he put a silencing finger to his lips.

He tossed a small pine coffee table aside, kicked a brightly colored, braided rug out of the way and stomped on what appeared to be a door cut out of the floor. She presumed Daphne and Jenny were hidden there.

The action was met with silence.

Judy felt the return of panic. Could someone have gotten to the cabin while Vic was on the trail? "What's the matter?" she demanded. "Where are they?"

He smiled approvingly. "Nothing's the matter. She's just doing what I told—"

His praise of Daphne was suddenly interrupted by the sudden upswing of the trapdoor, the emergence of a platinum blond top-knot and the shrieking question, "Judy? Did I hear Judy?"

Vic looked disapproving as Daphne handed Jenny up to him. The child clutched a bright pink bear almost as big as she was. And on her arm hung a pink patent leather purse.

"I told you not to make a sound until you hear *my* voice," he said as Daphne climbed quickly up the few steps. But she wasn't listening. She and Judy were wrapped in each other's embrace, their voices high-pitched and excited as they both talked at once.

Vic looked at Rob over their heads and made a help-less gesture with his free arm. "The woman is virtually deaf to instructions for her safety."

Rob stretched his tired shoulders. "It seems to be a family trait. For a cup of coffee, I'll explain the plan."

As Vic started to lead the way to a small kitchen, Judy reached for Jenny, careful to cradle the bear, too, and carried her back to Daphne. The women were still looking each other over and giggling like schoolgirls.

Vic frowned grimly. "You're sure you weren't fol-lowed?"

"Not yet," Rob replied. At Vic's raised eyebrow, he pushed him toward the kitchen, where he poured cof-fee from a thermos.

"You were right about Trey's car," Rob said as they sat across from each other at a small table. "Dave Heath found it in a salvage yard south of San Diego, and got pictures of the cut brake line. Good thing, too, because Heath stored it for me until we could get someone to look at it and lost his garage a few nights later in a fire."

"Celeste."

"Right."

"But that leaves us without evidence," Vic mur-mured. "I mean, to a judge, the pictures could be of any car."

"The sheriff who helped her make the car disappear caved under questioning." Rob explained about the lie she'd told and the money she'd offered.

Vic's expression brightened. "So we actually have his confession?"

"Right. And he can tie her to the car, so there's a warrant issued for Celeste's arrest. But guess what?"

"We can't find her."

"Right. So Brick and I put this plan together to get her out of your lives once and for all."

"Brick? Brick can't—"

"He's on vacation." Rob dealt that last bit of information and stared equably into Vic's disbelieving eyes. "You listening?"

Vic considered him, shifted his weight and looked away for a moment, then turned back with a shake of his head. "Yes. Go ahead."

"Remember the hood that got away the night you and Daphne were attacked in the lodge's parking lot?"

Vic nodded.

"Well, he's now an ally."

"What?"

Rob explained about Angus Watson's masquerade in Tyler, how Stumpy had become enamored of the town and Marion Clark particularly, and how Brick decided it was time they took advantage of his situation.

"So, for immunity, he told us all about Celeste, but claims that none of her men knew about her tampering with the car—except probably Gunnar, the chauffeur, who seems to share her confidence and her bed."

Vic winced. "Poor Gunnar. So, Brick had this Stumpy pass on information?"

"Right. Brick had him call her this afternoon and tell her we'd had you stashed in Canada, but that you and Daphne and Jenny and I were meeting here tomorrow morning because we wanted to move you."

Vic checked his watch. "That means she'll be here in the morning."

Rob wondered why verbalizing a plan always made it seem full of holes. But he replied confidently, "Right. And Brick will follow her in. We thought you could wait forever for the authorities to find Celeste, who could hide anywhere in the world, buy anything she needs, pay off anyone she needs.

"This way, if she thinks she can get Jenny, she'll come to you." He sighed and spread his hands. "We'll nab her, and you can come home."

Vic expelled a deep breath. "Good," he said after a moment. Then he reached out to clap Rob on the shoulder. "Good. We'll make it work. But why did you bring Judy?"

Rob sighed. "I didn't. She hid in the jump seat of the truck, and I didn't know she was there for almost four hundred miles."

Vic laughed.

Rob didn't. "I don't think that would have amused you had you been in my place."

"Sorry." Vic tried to look sober as he got to his feet but failed. "It just comforts me to know I'm not the only fallen soldier here."

"Please." Rob stood, too. "No death metaphors."

Vic pushed him toward the fireplace and a brown-and-beige plaid sofa that was in much the same condition as the ones in the back room of the *Citizen* office. But to Rob it felt like the most expensive water bed. He leaned his head against the back and groaned with approval.

"What happened to Daphne and Judy?" he asked, feeling every muscle in his body begin to loosen. He closed his eyes for just a minute. They burned painfully.

"I think they're in the bedroom."

"You ever use a wire?" Rob asked drowsily.

"Yeah. A couple of times."

"Good. Brick gave us one. You're in charge of making sure it works."

Rob could hear Vic building up the fire, then felt a blanket settle over him. And that was all he knew until he was lured awake by the smell of something spicy and the nearby sounds of laughter and happy conversation.

He smiled but didn't open his eyes. The atmosphere was wonderfully pleasant, though somewhere on the edge of his awareness he knew there would be danger out in the darkness, beyond the cozy confines of the cottage and this deliciously comfortable sofa.

But it couldn't intrude until morning, and he was happy to put it out of his mind and try to restore his weary body.

Whatever was cooking smelled marvelous, but investigating it would involve opening his eyes and—God forbid—moving. So he lay quietly, caught in the silky net between sleep and wakefulness, and contemplated how it would taste, whatever it was.

"Rob," a voice whispered in his ear. It belonged to Judy.

He considered the options—ignoring her and letting himself go back to sleep or opening his eyes, looking into hers and seeing one of the myriad of emotions that appeared there when she looked at him—love, confusion, passion, annoyance—if he didn't see the right one, he wasn't sure he wanted to look.

Apparently thinking that waking him was going to require more effort, she climbed astride his lap and sat on him, repeating quietly, "Rob?"

The softness of her bottom atop his thighs was sufficient incentive for him to remain quiet so that she would linger. He kept his eyes closed and relished the moment.

Her lips touched his fleetingly, and he felt her hands on his shoulders. "Rob, wake up. Don't you want to eat something? Vic's made this incendiary chili that's unbelievable."

Rob opened his eyes lazily at that and considered her. Judy was glowing. Her happiness at seeing her sister and her niece had pinked her cheeks and brightened her eyes. Her hair looked like a sheet of gold in the firelight.

And there was love for him in her eyes. He forgot all the difficulty they'd had understanding each other, all the times she'd annoyed him, even the fury he'd felt early that morning when he'd discovered her behind the seats.

He knew only that he loved her, too. And he was anxious for this situation with Celeste to be over so that he could give their future his complete attention.

He rubbed both palms gently up her denim-clad legs from her knees to her hips. "Is it more incendiary than you are?" he asked quietly. He could hear Vic and Daphne puttering in the kitchen, Jenny singing nonsense.

Judy didn't know what to make of the question. She put her hands on his and ran her palms gently up to his shoulders. "Do you mean that I tend to blow up at everything, or that I make you blow up?"

He smiled, his head still resting against the back of the sofa, his eyes lazily perusing her face. They were filled with sexual suggestion. "Both," he replied. "A lot of both." He reached for her waist and pulled her toward him.

She melted onto him and wrapped her arms around his neck. His solidity against her seemed to define the quality of his presence in her life. His steady strength supported her. And though she'd always considered herself a strong woman, she'd had to cultivate a prickly exterior to mask the need left over from her troubled childhood.

Her father and her stepfather had loved her, but not enough to stay when things got difficult, or to give up a life that could only result in pain for those on the fringes of it.

Rob, she knew, would be different. He would stay through thick and thin—and in direct opposition to things as they should have been, that alarmed her. Someone who would actually see things through with her meant she could no longer be alone, holding the world at bay with smart retorts and a cold shoulder.

She would actually have to share her fears, her dreams. She would have to break the rule. She would have to surrender.

She clung to Rob, enjoying the security he offered, but unwilling to let him see in her eyes that she wouldn't know what to do with it for a lifetime. She would have to reinvent Judy Lowery. She wasn't sure she could do that.

But she never surrendered to anything—even her own fear. She made herself look up at him. "I love you," she whispered.

Rob felt the subtle change in her. He saw it in her eyes. Those words should have connected them, but the inflection she lent them tried to wedge the two of them apart. There was a stiffness in her body that denied everything she might have meant.

He looked into her eyes, trying to read them, trying to find something that would give him a clue to what had happened. But the fire was behind her and her features were in shadow.

He decided that whether he understood her sudden shift of mood or not, the truth remained the same. "I love you, too," he said.

IT OCCURRED TO JUDY in the middle of her second bowl of chili that now, at this moment, she had precisely what she'd always wanted. This was the Sunday-afternoon family dinner that she'd dreamed about all those years Daphne was missing. Vic, Daphne and Jenny and Rob and she comprised a warm unit around the too-small, blue-flecked-Formica dinette table.

Vic had explained Rob's and Brick's plan while Rob slept, and though the whole thing terrified Judy, it wouldn't happen until tomorrow.

Right now the cold outdoors was held at bay by the fire in the fireplace, which also kept the coffee hot and the corn bread warm. The delicious dinner had been prepared on a simple butane stove.

She was surprised to discover that, despite her delight at seeing her sister and her niece healthy and happy, the complete coziness of her position was a little frightening.

While everyone else talked and ate, she pretended to concentrate on her food and tried to analyze where all this fear had suddenly come from. What was wrong with her? Fearless Judy Lowery was suddenly afraid of...family? Was that it? And if so, how could that be? That was contrary to all the laws of social behavior.

She could see in Rob's face that he was aware of her sudden confusion; aware that somehow her sister's rescue had turned into some sort of personal crisis for her, Judy.

She must be tired and stressed from the long day on the road, from the argument with Rob that had preceded it and from the long month of waiting for news on Trey's car that had preceded that.

She tried to comfort herself with the thought that a little sleep could change her whole perspective.

Jenny, finished with dinner, had climbed off Daphne's lap and now marched around the table with Bear and her purse, humming "Twinkle Twinkle Little Star" and patting everyone as she passed them.

"We're hoping if we indulge this musical phase," Vic said loudly over the din, "she'll start a rock band and support us while we're still young enough to travel."

He looked and sounded like a doting father, Judy thought. Jenny beamed at him every time she passed his chair, then giggled uproariously and dashed away when he pretended to try to catch her.

Daphne watched it all with an indulgent smile that made Judy think every moment of the past worrisome month had been worth the strain. It would have been obvious to a stranger that Vic and Daphne were soul mates and had made the decision to be life partners.

But to someone who knew Daphne well, it was also apparent that she had shed the past. She'd given up the old life years ago, but when she'd come to Tyler, Judy had seen that the residue of shame and pain still clung to her.

Part of that had been caused by her flight from Celeste, but another part, Judy suspected, by memories of the abusive Gordon and all that had come after him.

Daphne had been suspicious of anyone outside her sister's circle of friends, and though she'd worked for

Britt and helped out at TylerTots, she'd kept to herself
and held everyone else at bay.

Judy dismissed a sudden similarity in her own situation and held on to the thought that now, in what
amounted quite literally to a life-or-death situation,
Daphne seemed deep-down, top-of-the-heap happy. She
laughed readily, as though she'd done it often in the past
month, and her face was aglow with contentment.

Judy turned to the man she knew to be responsible
for the transformation and found him watching her. He
raised an eyebrow and inclined his head in a gesture that
suggested he'd read her mind, and that she owed him
acceptance.

She smiled at him and returned the nod, telling him
silently that he had it.

He went to the fireplace for the coffeepot and topped
up their cups. "We have to talk about tomorrow morning," he said abruptly.

The mood around the table changed as though
someone had flipped a switch. Daphne stopped Jenny's tour around the table and pulled her and the bear
onto her lap, holding her tightly.

Vic, sitting at a right angle to her, smiled encourag-
ingly. "Everything's going to be fine," he said quietly.
"As long as you do what I say."

Judy thought wryly that all men were the same. How
often had Rob given her that very same advice? But she
looked from one square-shouldered man to the other
and decided that if she and Daphne and Jenny were going to be stuck in a life-and-death situation, they may
as well be stuck with two men who were supremely self-
confident in what they were doing.

Daphne turned to Judy, her lips quirked wryly. "I'll lay you odds that you, Jenny and I end up under the floor."

Vic grinned. "You're *so* smart."

Daphne sighed forlornly. "Told you. I feel like a troll down there."

Vic leaned over to pat her arm. "But a safe troll."

Judy fixed him with a concerned frown. "I understand why she has to be under the floor, but why do I?"

"Because he said so," Rob replied for Vic.

Judy turned to him defensively. "I was talking to Vic."

Vic smiled at her as she looked to him for support. "Because I said so," he reiterated, then smiled more widely when she gasped indignantly. "I'm sorry. Do you have years of experience with the DEA?"

She didn't bother answering.

"Then we're doing things my way. And you're going under the floor because you're Daphne and Jenny's last line of defense if anything happens to Rob and me."

Judy rolled her eyes at him. "Please don't try to work me over, particularly if we're facing a lifetime as in-laws. I've seen you and Rob in action, and I doubt that Stallone and Schwarzenegger together could get by you. You want me under the floor because you think I have no street-fighting skills." She folded her arms and fixed Rob with a challenging glare. "Tell him about that night in your apartment. How I saved you with a baseball bat."

Rob sighed soulfully as he nodded at Vic. "She broke my Louisville Slugger on some thug's head. It was autographed by Hank Aaron. Did I mention that?"

Vic shook his head sympathetically. "Hank Aaron. Wow. Really? Can you get it repai—"

Judy leapt out of her chair, pointing with indignation at Rob, who was now laughing, along with everyone else at the table.

"I saved his bacon! There were three guys and I knocked out *two* of them."

Still laughing, Rob caught her wrist and pulled her onto his knees. "Yes, you're a hell of a scrapper, but we don't know exactly what we're going to be up against here." He sobered and said gravely, "You're going under the floor, and the sooner you accept that, the sooner we can finish making plans."

Judy opened her mouth to offer further argument.

"Save your breath, Jude," Daphne said. "This is macho at its most ugly. They don't even hear us."

That seemed to be true as Vic outlined the rest of the plan, which was simple. He and Rob would put up a token resistance, then let Celeste question them about Daphne's and Jenny's whereabouts, and try in the process to make her admit that she had tampered with Daphne's car.

Then Brick would close in for the arrest.

"What if Brick doesn't show?" Judy asked.

Rob didn't consider that a possibility. "He'll be there."

"What if he had car trouble?" she suggested. "What if Celeste's men evaded him? Shouldn't you have a little backup on the chance—"

"He'll be there," Rob repeated. "And this time tomorrow night we'll all be on our way back to Tyler."

Judy looked at her sister and saw that wistful hope in her eyes. Apparently she and Vic had enjoyed their time in the cabin, but Judy knew Daphne was looking forward to real life again, to settling into the gabled farmhouse and being Vic's wife.

Judy wanted that for her, and she wanted to fulfill the rest of the dream for herself—to live nearby with her own family, to share baby-sitting and carpooling and Sunday-afternoon dinners. But could she do it?

Sitting in Rob's lap, she found herself looking down slightly into his eyes. Their dark depths, though quiet, were filled with demands she wasn't sure she could meet.

Everyone cleaned up the kitchen together, then sat by the fire, Daphne and Jenny wrapped in Vic's arms on the sofa, Judy and Rob sitting side-by-side on the floor. They caught up on Tyler gossip for an hour, then Daphne went to the cabin's only bedroom to put Jenny to bed and returned with blankets and pillows.

Vic and Rob went into the kitchen to bring in more wood for the fireplace.

"Will you two be okay on the sofa?" Daphne asked. "It doesn't open out. You'll be scrunched."

Judy was concerned about it, though not for the same reasons Daphne was. "We'll be fine."

Daphne made a face. "I wish I could make you more comfortable. Because I promise you, the hole is not."

Judy shrugged and stood to hug her. "Well, that'll only be for a short time, then we'll be heading home."

Daphne held her for a long moment, and Judy could feel her trembling. "I wish you weren't in danger, too," she whispered.

"Daphne, you're my sister. I'm supposed to face danger with you—it's my job."

Daphne squeezed her, then let go. "Well, you're very good at it. I'll see you in the morning. I wish we had a *Cosmopolitan* or a *Men of the Outback* or something for our time under the floor."

Judy forced a laugh. She really wanted to cry. "We'll just fantasize about Mel Gibson, or something."

The men returned with the wood, then everyone said their good-nights and Vic extinguished the oil lamp that lit the living room. Rob and Judy were left alone in the glow of the firelight.

"You can have the sofa," Rob said quietly. "I'll bunk on the floor."

Judy understood the careful distance he was keeping. Though she hadn't said anything, she'd kept him emotionally at arm's length all evening, and she knew him to be intuitive and astute.

She tried to pretend a control of the situation she didn't feel at all. "You need to rest comfortably," she said in a reasonable tone. "You take the sofa, and I'll take the floor."

"Please." His voice reflected mild impatience. "We went through this at home."

"At home," she said, trying to inject a little lightness into the moody atmosphere of leaping shadows and threats of God-knew-what in the morning, "you *insisted* on having the sofa."

"Now," he said, doubling over the blanket and placing it on the floor, "I'd just like you to be quiet and go to sleep."

She sighed and tossed her pillow on the floor beside his. "You have to make an issue of everything," she accused.

He'd sat in the middle of his blanket to pull off his shoes, and now looked at her in stupefaction. "Me?" he demanded. Hearing the loud sound of his voice, he lowered it to a whisper. "*I* make an issue of everything? You—"

"I just thought that tonight..." she interrupted, emotion rising suddenly and unexpectedly in her. She swallowed, accepting that part of what she felt was the confusing fear, and part was because she knew she'd sabotaged the warmth that had been growing between them. "Tonight, when I could use a little reassurance, we could sleep...together."

"Reassurance." He repeated her word as she placed her blanket beside his and sat to pull off her shoes. He studied her profile against the firelight, trying to assess what had prompted this sudden need to be near him when she'd kept him at bay all evening.

He saw the same strong profile, though there was a slight unsteadiness to her bottom lip, a vulnerability in the line of her neck when her hair slipped forward and exposed the delicate nape. He wondered with sudden insight if she confused herself as much as she confused him.

He stood. "Well, if we're going to sleep together," he proposed, "let's take advantage of the sofa and both blankets." He tossed the pillows to one end of the sofa, then picked up his blanket.

As she stood to comply, he added her blanket to his. He lay on the sofa and pushed himself back as far as possible while covering himself with the blankets. Then he held them open for her.

She came toward him. "You're not going to push me off in your sleep?"

"No," he promised. "And you'll get the warmth from the fire."

Judy climbed in, her back to his chest, and he brought the blankets over her like a protective wing. With his left arm under her and his right wrapped around her, he virtually enveloped her, and she thought she'd never been so comfortable in her entire life.

"Are you comfortable?" she asked quietly.

Oh, sure, he thought. With her soft round bottom pressed against him right where he needed no encouragement, he might as well be on a bed of nails. But they had to get some sleep.

"I'm fine," he replied tersely.

There was silence for a long moment. Firelight flickered and she fidgeted. He tried to move away, but there was nowhere to go.

"Vic and Daphne seem happy," she said.

Nice for them. "Yes, they do."

She sighed. "We'd never be able to find that...degree of comfort with each other," she said, then she was quiet, as though she awaited something. His denial, possibly?

He was tired and cranky. He took pleasure in providing the opposite. "Yeah, you're right."

There was another moment's silence. "What do you mean?" she finally asked.

"What do you mean, what do I mean?" he returned, careful to keep his voice down—and to keep the smile out of it. "I'm just agreeing with you."

"You don't think I could be a wife?" she asked, her tone uncertain. That was a new note for her.

"No," he replied candidly. "At least, not now."

She turned onto her back in the small space. He had to tighten his grip on her waist to avoid losing her over the side. Her elbow was in his stomach, and he had to watch her knee.

"Just because I'm afraid?" she asked, looking up into his eyes, her own reflecting the fire. "Just because it's harder for me to open up? Just because every man in my life who ever meant anything to me bailed out when I needed him most? Just because I find it difficult to take orders blindly because for a long time all I've ever had to depend upon was myself?''

So she did know all that about herself. Maybe there was hope.

He nodded. ''I think you've covered everything. And unless something comes to mean more to you than the possibility of regrets, you're right to stay behind your armor.''

''My father killed himself,'' she whispered, ''because of his regrets.''

And that was the first time, he acknowledged to himself, that she'd admitted that her father's suicide had been his own fault and not that of the press. Maybe she was coming to grips with it.

''That's the decision we all have to make,'' Rob said, pulling the blanket back up over her. ''You stand by your choices because you believe in them. Or you stand up and admit to them if you're proven wrong.''

''I know.'' A tear rolled down her temple and into her hair. ''He just . . . surrendered.''

The word echoed in the quiet shadows of the firelit room. And suddenly, that simple, sadly spoken word explained her to him.

He rubbed his thumb over the streak her tear had left.

''And that's why you have your rule,'' he said, a lot of things clarified for him as he thought about it. ''No Surrender. Only you apply it to life rather than death. If you don't give in to anything, you won't have anything to regret. And you can stay all closed up against pain and disappointment.''

A frown line deepened between her brows. ''Caring about you,'' she admitted, her voice sounding strained, "made me *want* to open up to you. But it also makes me feel as though I owe you all this stuff I'm not sure I have."

She was starting to lose him. "What stuff?"

She shrugged a shoulder, and another tear slipped into her hair. "All that…tenderness Daphne gives Vic, all the—the sweetness that died in me when my father died." She pulled the blanket up to cover her face. "And I *never* cried until I met you. Never. I think we're just not compatible."

Reverse psychology was working for him so far, so he went with it. "No. I think we knew that in the beginning. We just got sidetracked by passion."

"Desire," she corrected, lowering the blanket and sniffling. "Passion involves real feeling, remember? You're the one who said so."

"Desire, then," he amended. "We got confused by the tension of the moment and great sex. But under it all, we're just two people who can't get along."

"Yeah," she said in a small voice. "I used to dream when Daphne was gone and I was alone in Boston that one day she and I would find each other and we'd live nearby and go shopping together and watch each other's kids and get together for Sunday dinner." Judy's voice grew faint and strained.

"Sounds nice," he said. He resisted an impulse to relight the lamp, shake her into sensibility and tell her how it was going to be between them. She had to see it herself or it simply *wouldn't* be.

"But I guess I'll just have to be her kids' maiden aunt," she whispered.

He steeled himself against the sadness in her voice and turned her toward him to make her comfortable against his shoulder. "I guess so," he replied gently,

"But there's no reason you and I can't hold each other this one last time and be comfortable tonight."

Judy felt his arms close around her in the downy cocoon formed by their stacked pillows and his blanket atop hers and thought they certainly didn't *feel* like two people who couldn't get along. But he agreed that they were, and since they couldn't agree on anything but that, it had to be significant.

God, how she wanted it to be different. But she was who she was and he was who he was, and there was no changing either of them. It was the classic stalemate.

"Do you believe in reincarnation?" she asked into his chest.

"No. Why?"

It depressed her that he didn't. "I was just wondering if we'd get another chance. You know. At loving each other."

"I think it's the case of opportunity knocking. If you don't answer, it moves on. Besides, if you and I were reincarnated, we'd probably come back as aliens from different planets, or life forms that couldn't mate or something."

She sighed and punched his chest halfheartedly. "Go to sleep," she said. "You're depressing me."

He smiled to himself, kissed her hair and closed his eyes. Whatever happened tomorrow, he thought, couldn't be any more dangerous than the last five minutes had been.

CHAPTER ELEVEN

THE ROOM WAS STILL in darkness when Judy was awakened by Jenny climbing on top of her and bouncing.

"Auntie Judy!" she exclaimed excitedly. "Bunny hole!"

"What?" Judy asked, trying to surface from a sleep that had been riddled with strange dreams and a melancholy she could still feel as awareness closed around her.

Then she remembered her discussion with Rob last night, and the confrontation with Celeste on today's agenda, and realized the melancholy hadn't arisen out of her dream, it lived in her. It didn't help when she opened her eyes and found herself looking into a bright pink bear face.

"Come on, you sack rat." Daphne scooped Jenny off Judy and shooed her toward the kitchen. "Finish your cereal and your muffin." Daphne slanted a grin at Judy as she handed her a cup of coffee. "Vic told her the space under the floor had been a bunny hole so that she would go into it. Now she thinks it's great fun. She's even willing to be quiet so we don't frighten the bunny."

Judy groaned and took the cup from her, wondering if even coffee would slip down her tight throat. "Where are Vic and Rob?" she asked. "Is there any sign of anybody yet?"

Daphne shook her head. She was trying to look cheerful, but Judy could see the desperation in her eyes. "Vic's bringing wood in and Rob's pumping water, just in case Celeste isn't as smart as we think she is and it takes time for her to arrive." She looked into Judy's eyes and a pleat formed between hers. "Are you okay this morning?"

Judy pretended surprise that she would ask. "I'm fine. We're about to be attacked by a wild woman and her army of thugs. Why wouldn't I be fine?"

Daphne dismissed her reply with a scolding look. "That aside, you look, I don't know... And Rob does, too. What happened?"

She stalled by sipping her coffee, but Daphne waited patiently. Finally, Judy was forced to answer the question. "We just decided last night that it wouldn't work, after all."

"Why not?"

Judy chose the easiest explanation. "He's always trying to push me around."

Daphne blinked. "He's a man. It's in the Y chromosome. And when have you not been delighted at the opportunity to push back?"

Judy felt a large vacancy open inside her. "Since him," she replied, her voice quiet, but high and breathy.

Daphne put a hand to Judy's cheek. "It's all right, sis," she said gently. "Love isn't surrender, it's... acceptance that you need someone."

Judy squeezed Daphne's hand, then freed it and reached down for her shoes. "Yeah, well, some of us have difficulty maintaining our friendships. Are there any more muffins? I'm not going into the bunny hole on an empty stomach."

"Got 'em." Rob appeared with a small plate bearing two muffins, a cup of coffee in his other hand. "Good morning. I put water in the kettle," he told Daphne, "and in the big stockpot."

As he leaned over the small table to set down the plate, Daphne kissed his cheek. "You're a dear. I'm going to like being related to you," she said, then disappeared into the kitchen.

Rob gave Judy a questioning glance as he sat beside her.

"Yes, I told her," she said, "but she doesn't listen. Thank you." She took a muffin from the plate and pulled a small bite from the crusty top.

"You two share a lot of qualities. How do you feel this morning?"

He didn't seem at all self-conscious about the status of their relationship after last night's discussion. Judy found that annoying. She'd slept fitfully and been soothed by his quiet voice and his gentle touch several times during the night. And this morning, with Celeste's attack imminent and no time to ponder the complicated vagaries of her own psyche, she was beginning to think she was crazy.

What *was* so hard about opening up? Sure it was a risk, but Rob had never done anything but treat her thoughts and feelings with care and respect. She had no reason to believe he wasn't capable of doing that for a lifetime.

But when she'd suggested their relationship wouldn't work, he'd agreed. So maybe it wasn't something he *wanted* to do for a lifetime.

She reached for her coffee and decided she really did pick her moments.

She looked at him over the rim of her mug and wondered how he would react to the suggestion that they discuss their relationship again when this was over.

Rob read the look in her eyes as he toasted her with his mug and pretended an amiable indifference. She looked regretful and undecided. He liked that. She must be having second thoughts this morning, but he knew the least pressure applied on his part would turn her in the other direction.

And he didn't want her turning away, he wanted her backed into a corner with no options left but to admit she loved and needed him.

"You know," he said conversationally, "the more I think about it, the more I'm convinced we're right to give up."

She frowned at him. "Give up?"

"Yeah. You know, on us. On the surface it might look cowardly, but when you really examine it, it's very logical. I always thought of myself as a big-city type. I ended up in Tyler because I wanted a small newspaper I could build up and sell at a profit after a few years. I mean, how much of that small-town charm can a body take?"

"You mean . . . you're moving?" She sounded personally affronted by the idea. That was good.

"Yes. Well. You want to be running into me all the time with a new man in your life and remembering that you once made love to me all night long?"

As he said those words, the image of their bodies entwined flashed behind her eyes. She closed them, but the image remained. "No," she said weakly.

He nudged her with his elbow, the gesture holding just the right amount of companionable distance to torture her. He ignored the fact that it tortured him, too. He was on a mission.

"But I'll buy your books," he promised. Then added, "And I'll never see a snow goose without thinking of you." That last was unplanned and dirty pool, but he said it anyway.

Judy looked as though he'd punched her. Then her lips parted as though she had a question, and her hand reached out to him, but never quite connected.

Vic peered around the bedroom door. "Daphne, where's the wire?"

She poked her head out of the kitchen. "You mean the little black box thing on the trunk?"

"Yes, only it's not on the trunk. It's gone."

She shook her head, looking troubled. "I haven't touched it." Then she turned to Jenny. "Sweetie, did you take Daddy's—"

"Ssh!" Vic issued the sharp command at the same moment that Rob heard the sound and sprang to his feet.

A subtle, distant churning disturbed the silence, the sound doubling in volume in a matter of seconds.

Rob and Vic worked in tandem without taking time to discuss it as the sound doubled again, now clearly the rotors of a helicopter approaching swiftly.

Rob lifted the coffee table aside as Vic handed Jenny and Bear to Daphne and kicked the rug away, revealing the trap door. He yanked it up and pushed Daphne toward the narrow stairs.

She stopped to catch the sleeve of his flannel shirt and pull him to her. "Please don't take any chances," she said desperately against his lips. "Promise me."

"I won't. Don't worry. Now go! Come on, Jenny, babe. Into the rabbit hole with Mom."

"Daddy, too!"

"No, next time," he coaxed, catching her little hand and holding it an instant as Daphne lifted her down.

Rob pulled Judy to the stairs. She turned to him, her eyes filled with unspoken messages. She caught the front of his sweatshirt in her fist. "Rob!" she whispered.

The sound overhead had subsided somewhat. The helicopter had landed. He wrenched her hand from him, and because she wouldn't hear anything he said, kissed her quickly and pushed her onto the steps.

Vic dropped the trapdoor, Rob pulled the carpet over it and together they replaced the table.

Rob had just picked up his cup and Vic reached for Judy's muffin when the front door of the cabin burst open.

Huddled together in the darkness, with only a flashlight to illuminate their features, Judy clung to Daphne and Jenny as the crash reverberated over their heads.

There was a moment's silence, and Judy could imagine Celeste walking into the cabin, flanked by her entourage of muscled men. Her voice came clearly through the planked floor.

"Mr. Estevez," she said in the polite and cultured tones Judy remembered from her own encounter with the woman. "We meet again at last."

Vic's voice rumbled through the floorboards. "Yes, I'm sorry, Mrs. Huntington. I'm sure it's no more pleasant for you than it is for me."

"Too true. You've made my life very difficult since you betrayed me."

His reply was polite. "I'm so glad. And I hope my friend has helped as well. Celeste Huntington, this is Rob Friedman with the *Tyler Citizen*."

"We've met," Rob said, also in an impeccably polite tone. "The day she tried to bully Judy into revealing your whereabouts."

Daphne turned to her in openmouthed surprise. Judy shook her head, silently denying that the visit had been a problem, and put a finger to her lips as Celeste spoke.

"Yes. Stubborn young woman. Where is she?"

"Gone with Daphne and Jenny," Vic replied. "I'm afraid you've arrived too late to find them, Mrs. Huntington."

There were footsteps across the floor—light footsteps, as though Celeste had advanced to confront him.

"You must consider me a total fool, Vic, if you think I would believe that for a moment. You wouldn't let her out of your sight. I know that. And Mr. Friedman has had Judy at his side since the day I visited her in Tyler."

"You're welcome to look around," Vic said quietly.

Heavy footsteps moved across the floor in several directions as her men apparently did just that.

"I understand there's a warrant for your arrest," Rob said conversationally.

"My lawyer's dealing with it," she replied.

"Really? The rumor is that you're on the run because you know the evidence is overwhelming."

The sound of her laughter was chilling. "I'm sure you've heard that Mr. Heath had a fire in his garage. I'm afraid the overwhelming evidence is now a pile of melted metal."

"Of which we took photographs before it left the salvage yard."

"My lawyer says that won't matter because you can't prove that the photographs you have were taken of the car that was destroyed."

"Your son's car."

"Was it? I understand all the identifying serial numbers had been removed."

"Interesting that you would know that."

Judy shifted uncomfortably as Rob continued his systematic prodding. She guessed he was trying to coax the woman into admitting details Brick could hear and use against her. Providing Brick was here. Judy felt ill at the thought that he might not be, particularly with the wire missing.

"I've spoken to Mr. Whitsett," Celeste said. "He told me. He also mentioned you'd taken pictures."

Footsteps moved toward her from the direction of the bedroom. "I don't think your daughter-in-law's here, Mrs. Huntington," a raspy voice reported. "We've looked everywhere. There's no attic and no basement."

"She has to be here," Celeste insisted. Her footsteps moved in the direction of the kitchen, then returned hurriedly, the quality of her voice changing from snide courtesy to banked fury. "Look at what I found on the floor in the kitchen."

There was silence. Daphne and Judy looked at each other in puzzlement, then jumped when Celeste's voice exclaimed loudly, "Fruity Angel Flakes, you fools! A children's cereal. They're here somewhere, I tell you. Look again!"

The footsteps dispersed once more, sounding even more urgent this time.

"I'm the one who had the Fruity Angel Flakes," Rob said. "I like the way the milk comes up through the halo."

There was the sound of a slap.

Judy closed her eyes. Daphne squeezed her shoulder.

"I told you to get granola." Vic's voice pretended exasperation. "But, no. You had to have your Angel Flakes. Next time I'm on a fishing trip with you, *I'm* getting the groceries. I put up with the coffee-flavored beer, but if the Fruity Flakes are going to put Dragon Lady, here, in a snit—"

Another slap.

"Fishing trip indeed," Celeste snapped, breathless with anger. "Do you take me for a fool?"

"Yes, ma'am," Vic and Rob answered simultaneously.

Two slaps rang in rapid succession.

Daphne put her lips to Judy's ear and whispered urgently, "Where's Brick?"

Judy raised both hands and shook her head to indicate she didn't know. But this definitely was not going well. She was sure Vic and Rob could handle slaps from Celeste, but she had a nasty feeling Celeste would turn the job over to one of her hoods at any moment.

Her fears were confirmed when the woman shouted, "Gunnar!"

"Yes, Mrs. H?"

"Have you found anything?"

"No."

"All right." There was a loud sigh of resolution. "We'll drop Mr. Friedman headfirst into the lake and see if that refreshes Mr. Estevez's memory."

"Ah . . .'scuse me," Rob said, "but if you want to refresh *his* memory, shouldn't you drop *him* into the lake?"

Judy spread both hands and did a complete turn in exasperation over Rob's taunting responses. Daphne put her free hand over her face.

"Oh, thanks." Vic's voice was sharp with sarcasm. "I let you buy Fruity Flakes and you turn on me. Well—"

"Silence!" Celeste shrieked.

"Mommy!" Jenny whispered loudly. "Why is that lady yelling?"

Daphne put her hand over Jenny's mouth, and she and Judy froze, listening to the silence.

"What was that?" Celeste demanded.

"What?" Gunnar asked.

"That sound."

Judy pushed Daphne and Jenny into the farthest corner and took a fighting stance under the trapdoor, expecting it to open at any moment.

But after another silence, Rob's voice said, "That's probably your conscience, Mrs. Huntington, reminding you that you killed your own son. That's how it starts, you know—a sense of being watched, a feeling of being pursued, things that no one hears but you. Did it sound like your son?"

"Shut up!" she ordered, her voice shrill.

"Do you think he figured out when he lost control of Daphne's car," Vic asked, "that you were responsible? You'd encouraged him to leave her. As he saw himself headed for the telephone pole, do you think he knew *you* were killing him?"

"Gunnar!" she commanded.

Rob saw the blow coming at him and ducked, deciding that something had delayed Brick and he wasn't going to break in, flashing a badge, before those meaty knuckles connected with his face. Vic's fist shot over Rob's head and stunned the big man.

Already doubled over anyway, Rob dove for a pair of legs clad in ski pants that moved to interfere. He brought down a man he thought he remembered from the episode in the Timberlake parking lot six weeks ago. Rob punched him to keep him down.

But a couple of guys piled on top of him, and by the time he was hauled to his feet, Gunnar and another man had Vic pinned to the wall, and Gunnar had a gun to Vic's temple.

"Where are my daughter-in-law and my niece, Mr. Estevez?" Celeste asked. "This is the last time I will ask."

"Safe from you," he replied.

Gunnar cocked the pistol.

Directly under them, Judy knew precisely what the sound meant. And apparently so did Daphne, because she headed directly for the stairs.

Judy yanked her back, covering her protest with a hand over her mouth.

She saw the anguish and desperation in Daphne's eyes and decided it was time she took action.

"Mr. Friedman?" Celeste asked. "Would you like to tell us where they are?"

"Safe from you," Rob repeated.

"Very well," she said. "Dangling over the lake it is. Jorgen, to the helicopter."

Judy turned to Daphne, pointed forcefully to the floor, indicating that she was to stay there, then climbed the steps to just beneath the floorboards. In a state well beyond panic, she wondered what on earth she could do that would save the men and not risk her sister's life.

Then all the footsteps left the cabin and she got the glimmer of an idea.

"GOOD PLAN, Friedman," Vic said under his breath as he and Rob were shoved out of the cabin toward the lakeshore, where the helicopter waited just beyond the trees. "Where the hell is Brick?"

"Something must have held him up," Rob replied, trying to glance surreptitiously over his shoulder in the direction of the trail. He got the barrel of a .45 jammed into his back for his trouble.

"Obviously. Last time I go fishing with you."

"Hey. Muchacho. Have a little faith."

"All right, look. If we're on our own here, let's take 'em when we go through the trees."

"Pardon me, but haven't they already taken *us?*"

Vic cast him a wry glance. "No. We just put up a token resistance on the chance Brick did arrive and we could still get him to overhear Celeste's confession."

Rob couldn't help the grin. "No kidding? Aren't we cool."

"Yes. But I'm not about to be thrown from a helicopter."

"They were going to throw *me.*"

"Yeah, that could be fun. But after you it would be *me,* and it loses its appeal for me there. So, when we get to the trees, grab a branch and let it go, then run like hell to the helicopter. I'll cover you. Idiots didn't even search us for weapons."

"Why? Can you fly a helicopter?"

"Of course."

"What about the girls?"

"Easy. When you take the guy behind you, get his weapon. We'll either mow 'em down or make them run, then I'll put down, you'll get the girls, and we're out of here.''

Rob looked at Vic doubtfully, but the man sounded completely convinced it could be done. Of course he did. Vic had gone to secret-agent school, while he, Rob, had learned to get the who, what, when, where and why in the first paragraph of a story. God.

They were about three yards from the trees when they heard a shout from behind them. ''Hey!''

Rob recognized the voice instantly, and stopped in his tracks. Everyone else did, too. Rob let his head fall back and closed his eyes, thinking that the moment he had Judy alone, he was going to kill her.

He turned with the others to face the woman who marched out of the cabin in jeans and a pale blue sweater.

Celeste turned to Gunnar, who held a gun on Vic. Her eyes were deadly. ''I thought you said you couldn't find anyone.''

''Celeste, she wasn't there,'' he said, shaking his head in confusion as Judy approached. ''She must have been . . . hiding.''

''Well, duh!'' Rob said.

Celeste gave Rob, then Gunnar a revolted look and moved forward to intercept Judy. ''Miss Lowery. I thought you didn't know where your sister was.''

''I don't.'' Judy looked from Rob to Vic, her glance defiant, then turned back to Celeste. ''Vic turned her over to the witness-protection program, and you know how that works. No one knows where they go or who they become.''

Celeste rolled her eyes. ''Your approach to lying is convincing, but I'm afraid the substance of your lies isn't. Diane—or Daphne, as you call her—hasn't been a witness to anything."

"She's going to testify against you," Judy said. She rubbed her arms against the cold air, and the chill that existed inside her as well. It was obvious Brick hadn't arrived, and if this didn't work, Rob and Vic were dead. So, probably, was she.

Daphne and Jenny, at least, were still safe in the hole.

"What could she possibly have against me?"

"Trey told her that you'd encouraged him to leave her. Even hired a lawyer for him."

Celeste dismissed that with a smirk. "Probably millions of mothers do that."

"But I don't think millions of mothers go as far as having a brake line cut to ensure the death of a daughter-in-law."

"There's no proof that I did that."

Judy sighed regretfully. "I'm afraid there's proof that he suspected you'd do something like that, because he got a restraining order against you that day, Celeste."

Celeste stared at her, unmoving. "That isn't true."

"It is. It was in the breast pocket of his suit coat the day he died. The coroner's office gave it to Daphne. You can check courthouse records, if you like."

Celeste paled. "He wouldn't have done that," she said in a small voice. "He loved me." Her eyes were wild and hurt.

Judy pushed her advantage. "He hated you, Celeste. You bullied him all his life, and held the family name and wealth to be more important than anything he wanted. You destroyed every dream he ever had—and then, however accidentally, you destroyed him."

"No," Celeste said, her voice still fragile, her eyes unfocused. Then she sharpened her glance on Judy and screamed, "No!"

Rob made a move toward her, but immediately felt the jab of a gun between his shoulder blades.

Judy glanced his way and pleaded with him with her eyes. He subsided, deciding he would give this one more minute, but if Celeste touched her, he was moving in and taking his chances.

"Easy," Vic cautioned quietly.

"You killed your son," Judy pressed, praying for the right reaction. "You can't blame anyone else for that. You meant to kill Daphne, but you killed Trey instead. You did it."

"Diane did it!" Celeste shrieked, pushing Gunnar away when he tried to caution her to be quiet. "It was her fault! She got between us from the beginning. He used to listen to *me.*" Her face contorted into a mask of bitterness and rage. She looked all of her sixty-eight years for once, and a downward slump of her shoulders made her suddenly appear deflated, empty. "Then he found *her* and had no more use for me. I told him she would be trouble. I told him she would ruin him!"

"*You* killed him, Celeste," Judy said intrepidly.

"But I meant to get *her!*" she shouted, her shoulders shaking as she began to cry. "It was supposed to kill Diane. But he went to that last-minute meeting and..." She spread thin, clawlike hands pathetically, the gumball-size diamond looking incongruous in the setting of snow-topped pine trees. Her voice quieted as she shook her head, her wild eyes spilling tears. "And Trey died instead."

"Celeste!" Gunnar caught her arm and shook her.

She fell against him, sobbing. "We killed my son, Gunnar. We cut the brake line and killed Trey."

Gunnar shook her again. "Celeste, stop it!"

"Yes, Celeste. Stop it right there." Brick came out of the trees, backed by Jake Marshack and a large contingent of local sheriff's deputies.

Judy felt a great rush of relief and let herself sink to her knees.

"I heard everything," Brick said as the deputies began to cuff her men. "I'm arresting you for the murder of Butler Davis Huntington III."

She stared vacantly for another moment, then shook her head. Something imperious and invincible seemed to reassert itself within her. "It's your word against mine, Captain Bauer."

He inclined his head toward Vic and Rob. "My men, here, are wired."

Vic turned a little sheepishly to Rob, obviously wondering how to explain to Brick that he'd somehow lost the wire and compromised the plan.

Rob lifted his ever-present tape recorder from the pocket of his cords and held it up. He pressed a button and Celeste's confession was repeated loud and clear on the cold early morning air.

He grinned at Vic's look of pleased surprise. "A good reporter is always ready to get the quote verbatim."

Brick took the recorder from him and handed it to the deputy in charge as a stunned Celeste was hauled away. "Thanks for the hand, gentlemen," he said. "We'll be right behind you."

Rob went to pull Judy to her feet. Brick and Jake stood by to help as Vic ran into the cabin.

Judy braced herself for loud recriminations. Instead, she heard a gently spoken, "Are you all right?"

She looked into Rob's dark eyes in mild surprise, quickly having to alter her stance from defensive to grateful.

"Yes, thanks." And because she didn't know what else to say to him, she turned to Brick and hugged him. "You were a welcome sight! We'd about given up on you." Then she moved to Jake. "And what are you doing here?"

Brick nodded apologetically. "I was right behind them, but unfortunately, Jake came along to get me lost. When they all climbed into a helicopter, it was harder than hell to keep up in the car. And Jake here, the great trailblazer of downtown Chicago, kept sending me down the wrong road."

Jake listened to the vitriol with a roll of his eyes. "If I hadn't been along, we *still* wouldn't be here."

"One more minute," Rob said in a wounded tone, shaking Brick's hand, "and they were going to drop me into the lake from the helicopter."

"Not to worry," Brick assured him. "We'd have dragged it till we found you."

"Aren't you amusing." He shook hands with Jake. "I'm glad you were along, buddy."

Jake cast Judy a judgmental look. "When Britt finally told me what Judy had done, I suspected it might affect the plan one way or the other, so I called Brick and invited myself along in case he needed backup. She was wild with worry. I promised to call as soon as there was a resolution." He pulled a cell phone out of his pocket and looked around him. "I wonder if the signal can be picked up from here."

"I'm going to check out the helicopter. Come on. I need a witness and you'll have a better chance of finding a signal for the phone beyond the trees. Then we'll all have to go to Lakeview to give our reports."

The two men loped off down the trail between the trees, and Rob turned Judy toward the house. "Come on," he said. "We need jackets. Was that true about the restraining order?"

She made a face. "No, I was just trying to upset her and make her talk."

He laughed lightly. "See, now. Being able to upset people does have its uses."

His tone was amused and pleasant but completely impersonal, Judy noticed—just as though the last frightening half hour hadn't happened. Not that she should be expecting anything else, she told herself. They'd had it out between them. She'd decided she couldn't do it, and he'd decided she was right. It was over, and thirty minutes of terror had nothing to do with it.

Even though seeing Rob minutes from death had jarred her into realizing that however hard it might be for her to love with the openheartedness a permanent commitment required, it would be even harder for her not to have him at all.

She walked with him back to the cabin, memorizing the touch of his hand on her shoulder, remembering when it had held an intimacy that had warmed and renewed her.

They stopped just inside the door because Vic stood there with Jenny in one arm and Daphne wrapped in the other, sobbing against him.

Vic glanced up when they would have retreated and called them back. "Come in. She'll be all right in a minute. It's just been such a long siege for her." He kissed the top of her head.

Judy's throat constricted and tears burned in her own eyes. She knew just a fraction of what her sister had been through, and didn't know how Daphne remained the sweet-natured woman she was.

Judy could only imagine what a relief it was to her to know that the woman who'd been the bane of her existence for two years was going to jail and no longer posed a threat.

Daphne drew away from Vic when she realized Rob and Judy were there and turned to wrap an arm around each of them. "You can't know what it means to me to be free of her." She looked up at Judy, her eyes tear-filled but clear of all the demons that had pursued her.

She held them both tightly, and the action forced them into each other's arms. Judy inhaled the wood-smoke on Rob from their night so close to the fire, felt the gentle rasp of his day's growth of beard against her temple, the taunting, torturous touch of his body against hers even through flannel and denim.

Rob bore it with a friendly smile, but Judy felt it break her heart. She accepted that, rigid as she was, it was her own stupid fault, but that didn't make it hurt any less.

Then Daphne suddenly drew back and swatted Judy's arm, her tearful reaction to the morning's events turning to genuine temper.

"How *dare* you decide that you can take a chance like that, then lock *me* in the bunny hole!" She turned to Rob. "She moved a corner of the sofa onto it after she got out so I couldn't follow her. Do you believe that?" Before Rob could reply, she turned back to Judy. "Vic said you pushed at Celeste until you made her confess everything. With all those men with guns all around you!"

Judy folded her arms defensively. "Somebody had to stay with Jenny," she said calmly, "and that's why I put the sofa over the trapdoor. And as far as confronting Celeste, it was that or have Vic and Rob thrown from the helicopter into the lake. Would you have preferred that?"

"Vic would have thought of something," Daphne said, her head of steam only slightly reduced. "Wouldn't you have, darling?"

"We had a plan, yes," he agreed, pulling Daphne back to him. "But it was flimsy at best, and we hadn't been able to get Celeste to say anything really incriminating. So back off on Judy. You have her to thank for putting Celeste in the slammer."

Daphne eyed her stubbornly for a moment, then smiled grudgingly. "All right," she said, shaking a finger at her, "but don't you ever big-sister me like that again. And *you!*" She turned on Rob.

He took a wary step back.

She hugged him fiercely. "Thanks for being such a friend to us. And thank you for keeping an eye on Judy for me."

He couldn't look at Judy. After being so close to her just a moment before, so close that the side of her breast had been touching his arm, he couldn't pretend the easy amiability he'd been trying since last night to convince her he felt.

Inside he was a raging mass of need and desperate hope, and he couldn't let her see that if his ploy was to succeed.

Daphne took his face in her hands. "I used to dream that I would have a family one day, and that Judy would, too, and we'd live in a duplex and have backyard barbecues in the summer and hay rides in the fall, and our husbands would go fishing together and we'd make cookies and quilts.'' Her voice had risen in excitement as she'd spun out the dream, then she stopped abruptly and laughed. "I don't bake very well, and I don't know how to quilt, but we can still live right next door to each other and I'll have what I always wanted. And you made all that possible." She sighed heavily and hugged him again. "Thank you, Rob. Thank you, thank you."

Rob felt his throat tighten because the sisters who'd spent so much of their lives apart had spent that time spinning dreams that were as close as they should have been.

And now they could have them. Even if it did mean, in the end, that he couldn't share it.

That thought felt like burning coal in the pit of his stomach, but he knew it was an eventuality he had to consider.

When Daphne drew away and turned to her daughter, who was clamoring for her attention, Rob looked up and found Judy looking into his eyes.

CHAPTER TWELVE

"... FOR RICHER, for poorer, in sickness and in health, forsaking all others as long as you both shall live?"

Reverend Sarah, rotund in pregnancy under her gold-trimmed white robe, asked the traditional question of Daphne at the altar of the Tyler Fellowship Sanctuary. Daphne wore an ivory dress in a shimmering fabric that made her look ethereal, and a little explosion of gossamer stuff on her hair, which had been all tucked up under it. She looked up at Vic with such love and adoration that Rob felt the question didn't really require an answer.

Rob, serving as Vic's best man, stood beside him in gray slacks, a dark morning coat and striped cravat, and wondered what it would be like to be so adored, so... necessary to the woman you loved.

Jake Marshack, who stood on the other side of him as groom's man, knew what that was like. Britt glowed like a star when he was near.

But he, Rob, had to fall in love with a woman whom fate and fortune had turned into a strong, eminently capable, remarkable being who took great pride in her self-sufficiency. And by personal design, she'd taught herself to protect those qualities against invasion and possible betrayal.

However logical it all seemed when he considered her childhood, it played havoc with his efforts to try to convince her that she needed him.

Now, five days after they'd all returned to Tyler, found the wire Brick had lent them in Jenny's little pink purse and learned that Celeste had been denied bail pending her trial for murder, Rob was beginning to think his efforts in regard to Judy had been for nothing.

She hadn't reacted at all to his friendly acceptance of the end of their relationship. He'd hoped for anguish, tears, even recriminations. But she was acting in the very same way that he was *play*acting—and the horrible thought was beginning to occur to him that maybe *she* meant it. Maybe she truly did consider them finished.

A lot she knew.

Absently, he heard Daphne's response. But all his attention was focused on Judy, standing on the other side of Daphne in a dress that reminded him of autumn maple leaves at the height of their glory.

Her blond hair had been curled for the occasion and lay in soft tendrils about her face. Curls in the back exposed her neck and made it look long and graceful in the off-the-shoulder dress, which hugged her bosom and waist and fell in fluffy, generous folds to just below her knees.

He would probably be damned for entertaining the thoughts he was having in a church, but the expanse of creamy shoulder reminded him of the night they'd shared. It would be a travesty, he thought, if they could never hold each other again.

She suddenly dabbed at her nose with a hanky she'd concealed in her bouquet of ivory roses.

He turned to the altar to see Sarah give the directive, "You may kiss the bride."

Rob closed his eyes against the painfully heartfelt display, then returned his attention to the proceedings when Sarah presented Mr. and Mrs. Vic Estevez to the congregation.

There were cheers, applause and tears, because now everyone in Tyler knew much of Daphne's story. They now understood that she'd come to Tyler as a fugitive from a life that had brought her much grief, and from a woman who had tried to steal her child.

Sarah Kenton and Alyssa Wocheck had led a delegation of women to Judy's home, where Daphne and Jenny were staying until the wedding. They'd brought shower gifts and promises of friendship.

And now they cheered her courage, her resolution to begin again and her choice to do it in Tyler. And because Vic cut such a heroic figure as the man who'd protected her and Jenny from Celeste and her thugs, they forgave him his deception and cheered him, too.

Vic lifted Jenny into his arms, and he and Daphne began the procession down the aisle.

Rob met Judy as they fell into step behind them. She took his arm and flashed the empty smile she'd been giving him for the past five days.

They stood side-by-side for an hour or more in the reception line, posed for photographs for another interminable period, then mingled with the gregarious guests.

K.J. met Rob at the punch fountain and clapped him on the shoulder. He was looking dapper in a suit and tie.

"You know, you do look like someone the *Dallas Herald* might be interested in," Rob said, handing him a filled glass.

K.J. grimaced. "Thank you. Really? I thought I looked like one of the Smith Brothers." He ran a finger under the neckline of his white shirt.

"Banded collar," Rob noted. "Very fashionable."

K.J. put a hand to his heart in theatrical repentance. "Oh, God. Now I've embarrassed the *Citizen,* haven't I? We're not supposed to be fashionable. We're supposed to be too...sincere to be concerned with style. Gina made me buy it."

Rob held his own glass under the spout and collected punch. "The scruffy newspaperman is tradition, but I don't see why you shouldn't be a trendsetter. Incidentally, I thought your cartoon on the parking-meter issue, with a ticket on Rudolph's ear, was inspired."

K.J. leaned beside him. "Thank you. But I hope you're not going to be leaving me alone again at deadline anytime soon. I thought I was going to stroke out. If it hadn't been for Gina, who kept running back and forth for me when the advertisers changed their minds, I don't know what I'd have done."

Rob tipped his glass against K.J.'s in a toast. "To competent women."

"I was going to toast busty ones, but okay."

Rob elbowed him. "Behave yourself. We've just been to church. So, you and Gina have worked things out?"

K.J. shrugged. "Some things. The rest I guess we'll just work around for now, keep everything loose. Hey. Who's the big guy asking Gina to dance?"

Rob scanned the room, then spotted her in a green wool dress. A tall young man in a dark suit had her complete attention as he gestured widely with his hands, then said something that made her laugh.

"Don't know his name," he replied, "but I think he was part of the crew that rebuilt the F and M. Maybe he liked Tyler so much he decided to stay now that Ingalls's is up and running again."

K.J.'s brows drew together. "Man, what is it? *Every*body's staying in Tyler? Since Stumpy's free of Celeste and got immunity for helping with Daphne's case, he bought the house from Judy and has proposed to Marion Clark. And now this hammer jockey's moving here, too?''

Rob grinned at his bad-tempered vehemence. ''Maybe we're becoming trendy.''

K.J. handed him his glass without removing his glare from the couple across the room. ''Well, he's not moving in on *me*.''

''I thought you were going to keep it loose?'' Rob asked, but K.J. was already stalking away.

''ALL HE DID WAS spend every free moment gathering evidence to build a case against Celeste so he could bring your sister home, saving your hide when Celeste came to Tyler looking for you, keeping you under his wing when things got close with her thugs, then taking his life in his hands to find Vic and Daphne and try to put an end to their exile.''

Britt Marshack, in a long-sleeved red dress and a silly little befeathered hat that somehow looked very chic on her, rolled out the litany in a shameless attempt at persuasion.

She turned her head to check on Jacob, who had found Glenna Nielsen in the crowd and, with the Miller toddler and the Baron twins, now clustered around her, vying for her attention. Britt turned back to the table, speared a stuffed green olive off her paper plate with a sword-shaped plastic toothpick and popped it into her mouth. She chewed and swallowed.

''I think asking him to dance would be a nice gesture,'' she said.

Judy, who was rapidly growing uncomfortable in the tight dress and stockings, was feeling oddly out of tune. Daphne and Jenny didn't need her anymore. Oh, they did, of course, as the sister-aunt backup system most female siblings tried to provide.

But they now had strong, stalwart, devoted Vic to keep them safe, to be their haven.

Judy Lowery, she thought grimly, was out of a job. And that was thanks in part to Rob Friedman.

She played with the empty punch glass in her hand. "If it would be such a nice gesture, why doesn't *he* ask *me* to dance?"

Britt frowned at her. "Because *he* did the favor for *you.* Getting Daphne and Jenny home has consumed you all the time they were away. He's accomplished that for you."

"He knows I'm grateful."

"You think so?" Britt asked with exaggerated innocence. "Gee, I don't know if ignoring a man for five days really sends that message."

"I've been working on my book. Besides, I spoke to him last night."

Britt made a scornful sound. "Yes, you did. You said, 'Would you please pass the parmesan?' last night at the rehearsal dinner. Quite a seductive riposte."

Judy turned on her impatiently. "Britt, we decided it was over at the cabin, okay? It's an old story. He's too demanding."

Britt nodded with every appearance of amiability. "Really. The rat. He's not happy knowing you love him, he'd like to hear it from you. How unreasonable."

Judy drew a breath for patience and resisted the temptation to bean her friend with the fall-flowers centerpiece. "I've told him I love him. I'm just...afraid to *be* in love with him."

Britt's eyes softened a shade. "I know. Been there. It takes courage to let yourself be vulnerable. But there's no other way to get love, Judy."

"Maybe I'll learn to live without it."

"Maybe you're not doing very well at it."

Judy hated that she was that transparent. But it was one thing to be vulnerable to a friend, and quite another to be vulnerable to a man who could take her in his arms and decimate in one night every defense she'd taken over thirty years to build. One deliciously long night.

She spotted him across the room, leaning against a pillar as Jake and Michael Kenton regaled him with a fish story, judging by the wide-apart gesture of Michael's hands. Her heart pushed against her ribs, as though reaching for him.

"I think he's just lost interest," Judy admitted, her own voice surprising her with its high, bereft quality. She sniffed and swallowed and turned to Britt. "Even if I could tell him..." She had to pause for a moment to swallow a sob as she saw him laugh with his friends. It made her remember how he'd often laughed with her and how it had lit her soul. "Even if I could tell him that I need him, he's probably concluded that I'm just too high maintenance if he's hoping for any kind of peace in his life."

"No, he hasn't." That brightly spoken denial came from Gina Santori, who'd apparently taken a chair across from Britt and Judy at the long banquet table while they'd been deep in discussion. Her green dress clung to a neat bosom. Dark hair hung in glossy waves from a filigree clip.

Britt gave Judy a look of smiling superiority and elbowed her, then leaned across the table toward Gina.

"What do you mean?"

Gina shrugged a shoulder as she forked a rose off the top of a huge slice of wedding cake. "I helped at the *Citizen* last week while Rob was gone, and apparently I was pretty good with advertisers, because Rob's asked me to continue to help part-time." She put the tip of the fork daintily into her mouth and closed her eyes to savor the flavor of the frosting.

Britt gave Judy a look of disgust. "You know how long that rose would live on my hips?"

But Gina's eyes were open again, and Judy leaned around Britt to gain the girl's attention. "*And,* Gina?"

"Oh." Gina put her fork down and swallowed. "And I just don't ever remember him being this moody. I mean, I'd go meet K.J. at the office for lunch or something, and Rob was always cheerful and happy. Now he seems continually distracted, and even a little grumpy. And he has a picture of you on his desk."

Judy sat up in her chair. "A picture of me?"

"Yeah. It was taken at the Labor Day celebration at the park. You were sitting on a blanket with Britt. Only he's cut Britt out of it and blown up the part with you."

"Well!" Britt said with feigned indignation.

Gina forked another bite of cake, but left it on her plate for a moment as she frowned thoughtfully at Judy. "Remember that conversation we had on the phone about how K.J. annoyed me because he wouldn't take anything seriously?"

Judy nodded, trying to focus on the question while her mind imagined Rob staring moodily at a photograph of her.

"I finally decided that was stupid," Gina said with a wry twist of her lips. "I saw him put that paper out under pretty tremendous pressure, with me sometimes helping, sometimes hindering, and he always had a joke to keep us going, a smile to encourage me when I wanted to scream. So I got to thinking..." Gina put the piece of cake in her mouth, chewed it and swallowed while staring off into space as she organized the thought.

Judy waited.

Britt tore the fork out of Gina's hand and pushed the cake aside. "You thought what, Gina?"

"I thought..." She waggled her head from side to side. "Why mistrust someone because they're cheerful and happy? I mean, the world gets so serious that sometimes it scares me, and I used to think the only way to protect myself was to be prepared and armed to hold it at bay. But K.J. just seems to wade right in, arms open, and his only weapons are a joke and the determination to enjoy it." She sighed and looked up lovingly as K.J. came to the table with two glasses of punch. "I know that was only a newspaper deadline, but couldn't that work with most things?" She hooked her arm in his as he sat beside her and kissed his cheek.

She looked at Judy, waiting for an answer. Britt waited, too.

Judy felt as though she were caught in a beam of light. Couldn't it work? Couldn't it?

She ignored Gina's and Britt's expectant expressions, stood and took off across the room in Rob's direction. The fishing story apparently over, Jake and Michael had moved on, and Rob now stood alone against the column, surveying the crowd.

HE KNEW IT WAS HER even before he turned in her direction. The band had struck up a string of nostalgic tunes, and couples had begun to dance in the open area in the middle of the hall, so Judy had had to walk around them and approach him from behind.

But in that room filled with the aromas of good food, floral perfumes and herbal aftershaves, her scent floated out to him. He felt her coming, felt all the various receptors in his body recognize and forecast her approach. His flesh heated, his scalp tingled and every nerve ending in his body awoke and waited.

He pretended not to notice. With the blaring music and the loud rumble of conversation, she couldn't expect him to hear her if she called his name. She would have to come closer. She would have to touch him.

Her fingertips were hesitant on his shoulder. She would have to do better than that. He continued to pretend absorption in the music.

Then a delicious shock ran through him as he felt her lips bump against his ear, heard her speak his name in a fairly loud voice that sounded like a whisper in the noisy room.

He turned, being careful not to betray anything except a friendly pleasure in her presence.

She returned the smile in kind, but looked into his eyes with a level of concentration that belied her attempt to appear casual.

"Would you like to dance?" she asked, but he pretended not to hear, taking advantage of the opportunity to lean down to her and make her repeat the question.

Instead she just caught his hand and pulled him after her onto the dance floor. The tune was bluesy and slow, and she turned in his arms somewhere on the edge of the crowd. He wrapped an arm around her waist and reached for her hand, but she had already looped both arms around his neck and leaned her forehead against his chin.

He wrapped the other arm around her and reined in the instinct to carry her off now and institute the plan.

All the signs were there, but she had yet to say anything. He had to bide his time. But that was difficult with his arms filled with her, her silky hair against his cheek, her breasts pressed to the front of his coat.

Then she looked up at him, and what he saw in her eyes dissolved every get-tough thought he'd had since they'd come back from Goose Lake. But if they were going to be happy, he had to hold out.

She put her lips to his ear and he tried not to betray eagerness as he leaned down to listen. "Did you try the coconut shrimp?" she asked.

He was obviously going to have to hold out for some time. He nodded. "They were great."

"The bulgur salad?"

"Also great."

"The blueberry tarts?"

"Not in rented clothes."

She smiled at that, but he couldn't. He wanted to throttle her, but he was trying to stay cool.

She might have read that in his eyes because she looked down suddenly and drew slightly back, though her fingers were still locked behind his neck.

"How've you been?" she asked.

He *was* going to throttle her. He didn't know where his endurance came from. The enormity of the risk, he guessed.

"Busy," he replied. "Stressed. Lonely."

She looked into his eyes again at that. "Me, too." Her voice had quieted and he didn't hear it, but he read the words on her lips.

"Busy?" he asked, being deliberately obtuse.

"Lonely," she corrected. Then she waited. He was supposed to take it from there, he guessed. Well, he wasn't going to.

"Really? With Daphne and Jenny home?"

She stopped swaying to the music and gave him a look of annoyance. He looked back at her innocently.

"Still thinking about moving?" she asked.

"Playing with the idea. 'Course, I need a buyer for the paper first. Why? You consider switching from fiction to journalism?"

She sighed. "Would you come with me, please?" she asked stiffly.

That sounded promising. "Of course," he said.

He was disappointed to see that her destination was simply the backyard of the church, though the fact that it was growing dark inspired hope.

He tried to stop her just beyond the door. "It's freezing out here. Let's get your..."

But she kept moving, and though he could have pulled her back, he was pleased to see determination in her about *some*thing.

She stopped him in the middle of the lot under a frosty moon and caught hold of the sleeves of his coat. "Okay," she said, her voice sounding tight and raspy. Her blond hair and her ivory shoulders and arms were bright in the near-darkness. "Just let me get this all out and...and whatever you want to do about it is up to you."

Judy had known that this would be hard, but she hadn't expected her throat to close and her hands to tremble. She swallowed and drew a breath to compose herself so that she could tell him clearly and logically that she loved him. That she wanted to love him always, if he thought he could put up with her probably bumbling attempts to do so.

Then he pulled off his jacket and wrapped it around her shoulders, and the warmth of it on her chilled skin melted the attempt to remain cool. After that, it all came out in a tangled, incomprehensible mess.

"You know how I feel about my father and—and my stepfather. And what's worse—it isn't that I don't still love them because I do, but when you love someone you have certain expectations and every single time..." She spread her arms to show her helplessness.

She had his full attention, but his eyes narrowed as he apparently tried to make sense of the words.

"I knew it was important not to be bitter," she continued, hoping to clarify her thoughts this time, "because you can't really live that way, and I don't think I am, I'm just—I'm just..." Agitation rose in her as she tried to get the word out and couldn't.

"Scared?" he asked.

"Yes!" she admitted, anguished. "And in the time I've spent with you, I've felt more secure than I've ever felt in my entire life—on one level. I know we talked about this that night in the cabin, but I didn't really get to explain that I said I thought it should be over not because I didn't want to love you, but because I thought if I tried and found that I couldn't, then I'd only be doing to you what my father and my stepfather did to me—promised me love and then left me."

Rob frowned over that information. "You're saying you're afraid for *me* and not for you?"

She shook off the suggestion of nobility. "Well, not entirely. I'm afraid for me, too. I'm not a kid anymore, and even though I want to be loving and gentle and understanding and all the things Daphne and Britt are, I don't know how well I'd do, you know?"

He tried to read between the lines. "You mean, you want to?"

"Yes, I do. The more I think about it, the more I realize that however hard it would be for me to try to be a good wife to you, to listen to your side, and keep my mouth shut sometimes, and understand that a lot of your autocratic attitude is just concern—"

"Wait!" he said, catching her flailing hands and holding them still. "Just say it. Do you want to marry me?"

"I—" she began, but a group of boisterous men composed of Jake, Brick, Michael, K.J. and Paul Bullard, the real estate agent, stormed out into the lot to take hold of Rob and drag him toward the house.

"Sorry, Judy," Brick said with a cheerful wave as he helped push their victim, "time for the bouquet toss and the garter fling. Come on!"

Judy, a mass of nerves and unresolved insecurities, trailed after them into the church. They couldn't have waited another minute for the issue of the rest of her life to be resolved?

Rob had sounded angry when he'd exclaimed, "Just say it! Do you want to marry me?" Had that been in preparation of saying, "Of course I still want to marry you?" or the more likely, "Well, you've got another thought coming, woman. You've confused me so much that I don't know my own name. What makes you think I'd still want to give it to you?"

Barely able to continue a party-mood pretense, even for her sister's sake, Judy hung far back in the crowd of giggling single women vying for the bouquet. Lost in her own thoughts, she missed seeing Gina Santori reach up and inadvertently deflect the bouquet off her fingertips, flipping it toward the back. She missed seeing Christy Hansen leap for it, flail at the dangling ivory bow, then come down again empty-handed.

Judy looked up, startled out of her thoughts by the screams and giggles, just in time for the bouquet of white orchids to hit her in the face.

CHAPTER THIRTEEN

AFTER THE GARTER was flung and, amidst great cheers and guffaws, caught by K.J., Judy and Britt were recruited to help Daphne change, while Jake and Rob put the bridal couple's bags in the Marshack's van.

Dressed casually for a flight to southern California, where Vic's family awaited their new daughter-in-law and granddaughter, Vic, Daphne and Jenny were passed among friends for hugs and good wishes. Then they climbed into the van for the drive to the airport.

Judy felt at once exhilarated and devastated as she chased the vehicle down the street, waving and blowing kisses back to Jenny.

"They'll be happy," Rob said from behind her, his arms wrapping her coat around her. "Come on. I'll take you home."

"Great," she said, and thought that sounded terribly feeble. But their duties during the past half hour of the reception had kept them apart, and the enormous matter of their futures still lay between them unresolved. But Britt had driven the wedding party to the church, so Judy was without a ride home. "Uh, how does it feel to be driving the Cherokee again?"

Rob held the passenger door open for her. "I know I'm going to get where I'm going. A novel experience, considering the past month and a half in Daphne's old Escort."

Judy tried to examine the clues rationally and was forced to accept that they didn't look good. Actually, there was only one clue—the fact that Rob hadn't grabbed her and kissed her and told her he loved her and that he wasn't letting her get away no matter what. He'd simply wrapped her in her coat and offered to take her home.

She had spent the past half hour praying that he'd suggest going back to his apartment to have a cup of coffee and talk things over. But he obviously didn't want her there. He was taking her home.

Well. She'd done her best. She'd made the effort to be open, and she had to consider that for her, that was a step forward. She, like Daphne, could put her broken childhood behind her and start again—without shin guards and a face mask this time. It wouldn't be half as much fun without Rob, but life was full of hard lessons. You had to take the risks and reach for what you wanted when you had the chance, because the world kept turning and the chance moved on to somebody else.

She wondered as he drove in a westerly direction if he'd finally marry some woman he'd known in Chicago, or if he'd stay in Tyler and settle down with a small-town girl. Pain burned inside her at the thought, as though she'd swallowed fire.

"How's the book going?" he asked.

"Very well," she replied, pulling herself together. "My heroine's turned into a scrapper who's fighting tooth and nail for the husband everyone else thinks killed her first husband."

"She knows he didn't do it?"

"She knows she loves him, and it's time she got off her duff, quit grieving and did something to prove his case." The parallel to her own personal struggle wasn't lost on her.

"How?"

"By launching her own investigation, luring the killer out again with the rumor that she found a shirt button at the scene of the crime that the police had missed under a bookcase. Of course, she's in big trouble when the killer isn't who she thinks it is, and they cross paths—not where she intends to lie in wait for him, but earlier, alone in the elevator up to her office."

"Who is the killer?"

"You," she said, "will have to buy the book."

He sent her a grinning side glance. "You mean you're not going to give me one?"

"Of course not," she replied with a little laugh. "You'd only review it in Art Around Town and call it verbose and predictable."

He laughed with her, and she felt suddenly swamped by the comfort of their old adversarial relationship. She was going to miss it as much as she was going to miss his warm, strong arms, his aggravating despotism, his soul-touching kisses.

He made a turn, then brought the utility vehicle to a sudden stop. She peered out the passenger window at the unfamiliar surroundings. She hadn't paid much attention to the direction they'd taken, and now noticed that they'd stopped in a driveway, but it wasn't hers.

A coach lantern in the middle of a broad lawn beside them illuminated a modern brick-and-frame house with a double-door entry flanked by cathedral windows.

"Where are we?" she asked, peering in confusion through the windshield.

"Where did I offer to take you?" he asked, pulling off his seat belt, then opening hers while she dealt with the question.

"You didn't offer, as I recall," she said, the remark made tolerantly rather than critically. "You told me you were taking me...home." She added the last word on a thin note as she tried to piece together what that could mean, and shied from the answer that came to mind. Even in the farthest reaches of her fantasies, it didn't make sense. He lived in an apartment. She lived in an old Victorian in town.

"Rob," she said, needing to establish a foothold in logic. "Neither one of us lives here. And where are we, anyway?"

"Country Meadows Estates," he replied, taking her hands and turning her toward him. "Paul Bullard is putting it up in partnership with Judson and Jeff and a few other people."

She'd heard about that, but the last time she'd been by, this house had been just a wood frame. When had that been? March? April?

"But, I don't—"

He cut her off with a nod and an index finger to her lips. "I know you don't understand, but before we get to that, you never answered my question."

Her heart began to beat hard enough to break her ribs. She put a hand to it.

Rob covered it with his own, his eyes dark and quiet as he lay his other arm over the back of her seat and wrapped her in his tenderness. "What's in there, Judy? I know you love me, but are you willing to do it for a lifetime?"

Emotion choked her, warmed her, raced through every life-sustaining system in her body. "Yes." The word came out clearly despite the tremors she felt. "I do. I have to, I need to, I—"

"But do you *want* to?" he insisted. "I think that's the critical question when everything else goes bad on you and loving each other is all you have left. Love's a lot of trouble.''

Judy looked into his eyes, astonished at the turn things were taking. "Of course, I do. But do you *want* to love me?"

He grinned, and his face was filled with love and amusement and indulgence. "Yes, I do. And fortunately, I'm experienced, because you've always been a lot of trouble.''

She wrapped her arms around his neck and leaned into him, happy laughter bubbling out of her. "And will probably continue to be. But I do love you, Rob. I love you so much.''

He crushed her to him and kissed her neck. "Judy." He said her name with love and relief and promise. "God. I thought I was going to have to kidnap you and cuff you to the pasteup boards until I could get you to see it my way.''

She hugged him fiercely. "I just wasn't thinking straight. I'm so used to losing the men I value." She leaned back to look into his eyes. "I think I forgot that there's a sunny side to life, and that I can have it, too. It's just taken me awhile to get used to it." She frowned suddenly. "What was all that talk about moving, then?''

"Lies," he admitted wryly, "to make you beg me to stay.''

Headlights lit the interior of the Cherokee as a Cadillac pulled into the driveway behind them.

Judy recognized Paul Bullard's car. "He was just at the wedding. What's he doing here?''

Rob turned to push his door open and stepped out of the car, calling to him. Then he reached in for Judy and pulled her out the driver's side.

She gave a little squeal of alarm as he lifted her out and set her on her feet.

"He's going to show us the house. Hi, Paul. Thanks for doing this on short notice."

"All part of the job." The agent bustled past them, holding a big ring of keys up to the coach light on the lawn. He picked one out, then gestured for them to follow. "I think you're going to like this place," he said, turning the key in the lock. "It's the perfect house for a couple of young professionals thinking of starting a family."

Judy blinked at Rob as they followed the Realtor into the house.

"That's just professional patter," Rob whispered, putting a finger to his lips. "Let him talk. Whoa. Oak floors."

Judy wandered from room to room, hand in hand with Rob, lost in a sense of disbelief she couldn't imagine recovering from. This could not be happening to her. Having Rob *and* this house was beyond her wildest concepts of a happy ending—or beginning.

Paul referred to the living room as "the great room." It was painted a warm shade of white and took up both sides of the double entrance. A brick fireplace was shielded with glass doors etched in a floral design.

He turned on the light in the dining room and an eight-globed chandelier sparkled overhead, reflected in a built-in hutch with glass doors etched in the same design as those on the fireplace.

A green-and-white kitchen with every amenity and cupboards also fronted in glass meandered into a nook in the same green and white, but with chintz curtains and booth cushions that gave it a cozy appearance.

The carpet in the master bedroom was the same shade as the walls and had French doors that opened onto a deck with a hot tub. The room was separated from the master bath by a fireplace usable in each room.

Judy put her hand to her heart in a vain attempt to catch her breath. "You know...maybe you don't understand," she said softly as they followed Paul upstairs, "that I haven't made the bestseller list and am probably not likely to in the near future."

He smiled and squeezed her shoulders. "I've been saving for a house for a long time," he replied, "and we're getting it for a steal."

"Rob, you can't trade advertising space for a half-million-dollar house!" But their guide was talking as he led them from bedroom to bedroom, and she had to pay attention.

"Three bedrooms," he said, after they'd been through them, "and a bonus room for an office or for exercise equipment."

He tugged on a strap, and to Judy's amazement a stairway descended from the ceiling. "And a loft for your telescope." He grinned. "Or for throwing water balloons when your guests arrive for dinner. Well. You two take some time to look around. Maybe Judy would like to reinspect the kitchen. I'll be in the car, catching up on some paperwork. Take as long as you need."

Judy stood, her hand in Rob's, in the middle of the empty room. This one was carpeted in silver-gray. Judy put a hand to her spinning head.

"You're sure we can do this?" she asked. "I mean, I love it, and for more than its elegance. It's airy and roomy and..." She winced. "I know it was just salesman's patter, but I can see kids running through here."

Rob wrapped his arms around her. "Me, too. Trains in the living room, cookies spread out on the kitchen counter, a toddler on the trike Jenny's outgrown riding around and around the coffee table. We're getting a real deal on it. Say the word and it's ours."

Judy held tightly to him, her heart swelling with excitement and the very real knowledge that he loved her, and that she loved him. Suddenly all that had once seemed so frightening—promising forever, and keeping the promise—gleamed with all the possibilities of a life of purpose.

She sighed and told him the truth. "I'm so happy." She kissed him deeply, then wrapped her arms around his neck and leaned her head on his shoulder. "Do what you think is best about the house."

If he'd had any doubts about her true feelings, that reply made them vanish. She'd actually withheld an opinion on something and deferred to him.

Rob was arrogant and male enough to think she deserved a reward. He walked her to the room's only window and pointed to a rooster weathervane about a hundred yards away, visible against the moonlit sky. "And look at what you can see from here. Of course, you can see it better in the daylight, but we'll have to make do with moonlight."

Judy stared at the weathervane a moment, then realized what it meant. And everything her life had lacked all those years settled down inside her like something gift wrapped.

That was the weathervane on Vic and Daphne's house. Her sister—the sister she'd loved as a child, missed and longed for so desperately as a young woman, then found and lost and found again—would be just a block away. Just the way Judy had dreamed it would be.

She turned to Rob, put her hands to his face and felt his love stream from him to her, permeate her being and fill it until there was room for nothing but hope and excitement.

Some of it spilled from her eyes, and he pulled her to him. He felt her lean against him and relinquish every hold the past had on her. She was new. He was new. And their love was forever.

concludes with

MISSION: CHILDREN

by Marisa Carroll

Kathleen will do anything to get two orphans out of
their war-torn country, back to the peace of Tyler. A
marriage of convenience to her friend Devon is a small
price to pay. But when they arrive home, they discover
that "their" children aren't orphans, Tyler isn't so
peaceful and their marriage is becoming something
real....

Available in August

Here's a preview!

MISSION: CHILDREN

"DEVON? IS THAT you?" The question was barely more than a whisper. "Is it really you?"

He closed his eyes for a moment against the stirring of desire deep inside him that the sound of her low, slightly husky voice always produced. But he ignored the longing, as he'd learned to do long ago. Letting nothing of what he was feeling show on his face, he reached out and pulled the musty-smelling blanket aside. "It's me, Kath."

"Oh God, Devon. How did you get here?"

The only illumination in the small cubicle came from a guttering candle in a holder on the wall. Its light was minimal; the effect of the small, enclosed space and the dark shadows was disturbingly claustrophobic. Kathleen was sitting on the floor, her back to the wall, looking like the exhausted men he'd just seen in the corridor. He could barely make out her face, but he heard the catch in her voice, caught the sudden gleam of tears in her eyes.

Kathleen, his Kathleen, never cried. Devon stepped through the blanket curtain and hunkered down in front of her. "Kath, are you all right?"

She held a sleeping child in her arms—a little girl. A boy, tall and sturdy, lay beside her, his head cradled on a pillow, his arms wrapped around Kathleen's waist.

"I'm fine." She spoke softly to keep from waking the children, but her breathing had quickened and a thread of hope and excitement wove through her voice. "Did you come with the convoy that brought the medicines?"

"I don't know about any convoy."

"Oh." She made no attempt to hide her disappointment. "I had hoped... Then how did you get here?"

"I walked. At least I walked the last fifteen miles. They wouldn't let me bring the car any closer."

The little girl whimpered in her sleep and snuggled into Kathleen's shoulder. Kathleen bent her head, crooning softly, and Devon had a sudden, almost overpowering urge to reach out and run his fingers through the dark silk of her hair, to assure himself that she was real and alive, unharmed. But he stayed very quiet, the silence wrapping them in deeper shadows and a deceptive illusion of privacy.

Kathleen raised her eyes, eyes the same shade of blue as a twilight autumn sky, the sky of his dreams.

"You shouldn't be here, Devon. It's too dangerous."

"I came to take you home to Tyler, Kath," he said quietly.

Her head came up, then, and a spark of dark fire gleamed in her sapphire eyes. "I'm not leaving, Devon. Not without the children." Her voice was low and steady, filled with urgency and absolute commitment. "But you have to go now. The same way you came. I won't be responsible for what might happen if you stay."

If he hadn't been so damned tired and so damned scared he would have smiled. This was the Kathleen he knew—stubborn, combative, honest to a fault. "Quit playing mother hen, Kath. I can take care of myself."

She smiled, too, just a little, but she was blinking back tears. "Oh Devon, your mother will kill me when she finds out you came after us."

They didn't have time to discuss his mother. "If we don't leave soon we'll all be trapped."

"Then go. I didn't ask you to come." She listened to herself say the words and shook her head. She reached out to touch his cheek, a fleeting caress that was over in a heartbeat. "Go without me."

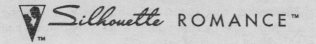

Silhouette ROMANCE™

What's a single dad to do when he needs a wife by next Thursday?

Who's a confirmed bachelor to call when he finds a baby on his doorstep?

How does a plain Jane in love with her gorgeous boss get him to notice her?

From classic love stories to romantic comedies to emotional heart tuggers, **Silhouette Romance** offers six irresistible novels every month by some of your favorite authors!
Such as…beloved bestsellers **Diana Palmer, Annette Broadrick, Suzanne Carey, Elizabeth August** and **Marie Ferrarella**, to name just a few—and some sure to become favorites!

Fabulous Fathers…Bundles of Joy…Miniseries…
Months of blushing brides and convenient weddings…
Holiday celebrations… You'll find all this and much more in **Silhouette Romance**—always emotional, always enjoyable, always about love!

SR-GEN

HARLEQUIN®

A M E R I C A N ◆ R O M A N C E®

LOOK FOR OUR FOUR FABULOUS MEN!

Each month some of today's bestselling authors bring four new fabulous men to Harlequin American Romance. Whether they're rebel ranchers, millionaire power brokers or sexy single dads, they're all gallant princes—and they're all ready to sweep you into lighthearted fantasies and contemporary fairy tales where anything is possible and where all your dreams come true!

You don't even have to make a wish...Harlequin American Romance will grant your every desire!

Look for Harlequin American Romance wherever Harlequin books are sold!

HARLEQUIN®

I N T R I G U E®

THAT'S INTRIGUE—DYNAMIC ROMANCE AT ITS BEST!

Harlequin Intrigue is now bringing you more—more men and mystery, more desire and danger. If you've been looking for thrilling tales of contemporary passion and sensuous love stories with taut, edge-of-the-seat suspense—then you'll *love* Harlequin Intrigue!

Every month, you'll meet four new heroes who are guaranteed to make your spine tingle and your pulse pound. With them you'll enter into the exciting world of Harlequin Intrigue—where your life is on the line and so is your heart!

Harlequin Intrigue—we'll leave you breathless!